HANNAFORD PREP

Make My Move

Also by J Bree

The Mounts Bay Saga

The Butcher Duet
The Butcher of the Bay: Part I
The Butcher of the Bay: Part II

Hannaford Prep
Just Drop Out: Hannaford Prep Year One
Make Your Move: Hannaford Prep Year Two
Play the Game: Hannaford Prep Year Three
To the End: Hannaford Prep Year Four
Make My Move: Alternate POV of Year Two

The Queen Crow Trilogy
All Hail
The Ruthless
Queen Crow

The Unseen MC
Angel Unseen

HANNAFORD PREP

Make My Move

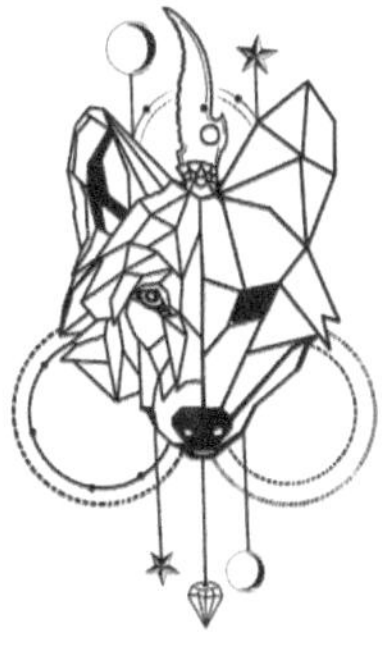

J BREE

To Laura, without whom there would be no book.
Our friendship has always, and will always, be the best thing to ever come from my journey as an author.
Ride or die, Friend.

One

HARLEY

If there's one place I don't want to be on the night before school starts, it's the docks of Mounts Bay.

We're headed to the southern end of them where not a whole lot of actual *boating* happens, but there's plenty of dilapidated warehouses in that area that are now a staple in the party scene of the Bay. I've been to enough of these things to know exactly how fucking bad it is that my dickhead, psycho cousin has run off here for a hit.

Obviously his dealer wouldn't deliver to the hotel.

The longer we drive, the more uncomfortable I become in my own skin. It's like they can all see exactly how fucking shitty my entire existence is once we're looking at the streets I grew up in, and it makes me a fucking dick to be around.

I snap at Avery, "What the fuck is he doing down here? Floss, this is the fucking slums and if he's down here then we'll be scraping him off the fucking sidewalk because there's no way he hasn't run his mouth and been stabbed for it."

"There's nothing I can do about Joey being down here. What do you want me to do, try and reason with the sociopathic asshole? We're lucky Lips found him for us," Avery snaps back from the front seat, and it's like a slap to the face.

My attention is firmly on her because Joey can fucking die for all I care, but what the *fuck* is the Mounty doing down here?

She never goes to parties at Hannaford or shows any interest in drinking, so why the fuck is she at one of the most dangerous fucking places for a girl to be in the entire country?

I'm pissed.

Ash side-eyes me so hard it's like a physical thing, a fist to the side of the head. I ignore it because he's been pissy since I got home from my grandfather's place, ready to argue about any fucking thing, but from the moment we realized Joey was gone he's been savage.

Fuck knows why.

"I'm not leaving my car down here to go get Joey… it'll be gone by the time we get him back," Blaise drawls, still half asleep and driving like a reckless fucking dick.

Avery shrugs as she taps away on her phone. "Lips

says she'll meet us out the front with him so no one has to leave the car."

"And how the fuck do you think she's getting him out of the party, Floss? How can you not see it?" Ash sneers, and I struggle not to roll my eyes at him.

It's obvious to everyone except Ash why exactly he's so fucking focused on her being a danger, but I don't want to think about just how far she's managed to dig herself under the skin of each and every one of us.

Even Morrison is fucking doe-eyed over her.

"Pull up at the gate; he'll let us through," Avery says, pointing exactly where she needs Blaise to drive like he's completely fucking blind.

He doesn't comment, too fucking tired to bother with the inevitable fight, but when he stops in front of the gate and rolls down the window, it's fucking clear that we're not getting in.

"Too late to get in, the party hour is over."

Fuck.

The 'party hour' means it's a very specific type of Bay party, one that the members of the Twelve have put together for a very specific reason, and it makes the entire situation a hundred times worse.

I share a look with Ash but he's just looking fucking livid. Fuck.

How the hell do I fix this?

Avery leans over Blaise to speak to the guy, her voice that icy tone that strikes fear into anyone with half a brain. "We're here to pick someone up. As if we'd want to attend a party in the slums and catch some Mounty disease."

Fuck me.

The guy's lip curls, but Avery already has her phone to her ear. "We're here but the guy at the gate won't let us through."

She pauses for a second and then hands the phone over to the guy. He snarls, "Listen here, kid, we don't let extra in after the open hour. Now you need to tell these little rich fucks to get on out of here—"

His spine snaps straight so fast I think he might've fucking shit himself.

What the fuck?

He fumbles over his words like they're burning him on the way out. "Sorry. I didn't know they were with you. If they had've just said I would've—"

He stops talking abruptly and hands the phone back to Aves, mumbling an apology under his breath and stalking around the car to open the gate. It's fucking weird, his movements are all jerky like he's barely holding his shit together.

"What the fuck is going on?" Ash murmurs to me, as if I'd have a fucking clue, but at this point, it's anyone's guess.

Blaise drives down to the warehouse and we find dozens of gangsters hanging around, all of them staring at the Maserati like they're trying to calculate just how much damage they could do to it.

Thank fuck we didn't come in one of Ash's cars.

Then my eyes land on the Mounty and I might just lose my *fucking* mind.

She's naked… or she may as fucking well be with how little she's wearing. She's standing there in underwear, shimmering as she moves with glitter everywhere and her hair pulled up in a way that makes her look both younger and older at the same time. She's too fucking skinny, the weeks of being back in the Bay have melted away the tiny bit of weight she'd put on by the end of freshman year, and that hits me full force in the gut. Avery has taken care of every last one of my needs from the moment she bailed me outta juvie. I haven't had to worry about where my next meal was coming from or outgrowing my clothes.

Lips has been alone, starving and hanging out at the slums of the Bay.

The guy standing next to her would have to be in his mid twenties and is grinning at her like he's in love with her, and there isn't a fucking chance I'm leaving her here.

Nope.

Fuck that.

I barely register that Joey is passed out and slumped

over some guy's shoulder as he walks him over to Ash, my focus entirely on getting the Mounty in the car and *the fuck* away from here but as I help shove Joey into the car she bounces over to Avery's window with a smirk, murmuring with her like they're besties.

Fuck, I guess they are now.

She finally takes stock of each of us; Blaise watching the gangsters we're surrounded by and Ash struggling to get Joey strapped in the car. When she finally looks up at me, I'm pretty sure she can see just how fucking *pissed* I am.

"What the hell are you doing here?"

I'm not sure what I'm expecting from her but it's definitely not what comes out of her mouth. "Watch your fucking tone, we are not at school."

It's like a slap to the face and my head snaps back. A quick look over my shoulder and sure enough, every last fucking eye is on me. Who the fuck is she hanging around with down here that I need to be sweating over talking to her?

Could tonight get any fucking worse?

I roll my shoulders back and shut the car door, stalking over to where she's still standing there with Avery. I can feel the eyes all following me and my jaw just about snaps, I'm clenching down so hard.

She watches my every move, her body tense, and

Avery curses under her breath at me but I ignore her. I've been on her shit list for months over the Mounty, what's another night of pissing her off if I can find out what the fuck is going on.

"What are you doing here? Dressed like that?" I murmur, and her eyes narrow at me like she's planning my death.

"Do not suggest that I'm a prostitute. I'm here for a job and as soon as I get paid I'm leaving."

Fuck.

What can I say to that with the crowd of thugs behind us ready to slit my throat? Fucking nothing, so I nod at her and wait her out. There's no fucking way I'm leaving her out here, wearing tiny scraps of clothes, with the gangsters of the Bay.

She makes that same little huffing noise that she does when she's pissed and I brace myself for whatever excuse she's gonna throw at me when the lights of another car hit us. I move without really thinking it through, stepping in front of her and trying to crowd her back against the car.

She doesn't take it well.

I grunt as she punches me in the back and snaps, "That would be my payment. You guys need to leave."

Who the fuck is paying her and what could some tiny Mounty orphan do for someone driving a fucking Merc that isn't selling herself?

"We're not leaving without you," I say, crossing my arms as she steps around me.

She gives me a look but the doors of the car are opening and it's clear she doesn't want to be arguing with me in front of the three guys who get out. They're dressed in cheap suits, hair slicked back and guns strapped to their belts but in the wrong position. It's an obvious show of power and intimidation, flashy and so fucking 'Mounty-slum-gangster' that I want to shove Lips in the car and leave.

They look around the empty parking lot and then assess us all one by one. Lips takes their eyes on her body without a flinch but the second they turn that scrutiny onto Avery, she steps in front of her until she is completely obscured from their view. There's something we can agree on.

I really don't want them getting a look at my cousin either.

If they don't hurry the fuck up, Ash is going to realize Avery is in danger here and come out fucking swinging. I let my eyes creep over to the Mounty but she's completely blank... nothing on her face at all even as the car door opens again and another man gets out.

With the sleazy smirk on his face, clearly he's the boss. What the fuck is the sleazeball paying her for if it's not sex?

"Hello, puss."

What.

The.

Fuck.

What the fuck kind of nickname is that? I look him over again and I almost lose my head at the sight of the hard-on he's so fucking nonchalant about. Inside the car Blaise snarls something, having spotted it too, and Avery snaps back at him, but I keep my attention on what the fuck is happening in front of me because if that piece of shit takes a single fucking step toward the Mounty, I'm going to kill him.

Lips isn't as concerned as the rest of us. "Wire my money through and I'll give you the package."

The creep smiles at her and waves a hand. One of his thugs pops the trunk of the car and pulls two bags out.

What the fuck is going on?

"Seriously? I told you I only deal in transfers," Lips snaps at him and *holy fuck*, that's her payment… two giant fucking bags full of cash? What the actual fuck did she do for him? I know she's a fucking genius but there's not all that much I can think of that would demand those sorts of prices.

My brain is still struggling to process when he says, "Sorry, puss. I didn't get the chance to pop this into the bank before they closed. You know how it is. How 'bout you walk that sweet ass of yours over here and get your money?"

The tone he uses with her has my vision going red and

my fists clenching with the need to beat the life outta him. "Like fuck."

The guy takes note of me standing there with her, dragging his eyes over me like I'm a slab of meat for sale. Something stirs in my gut, something bad, because this man is a fucking predator if I ever saw one and I decide here and now that I'm never going to fucking let the Mounty out of my sight in the Bay again.

Whether she likes it or not.

"How about I double the payment and you give me him, puss?" Lips rolls her eyes at him, completely unrepentant as his eyes narrow at her sass.

"How about you get one of your little friends to bring me my money and I'll hand him the package so we can all get out of here, hmm?"

He laughs and waves his guys forward. One of the guys hands me the bags and the stench that comes off of him is fucking putrid. I almost fucking gag and Lips shoves a USB into his hands like she's also trying to shove him away.

The guy walks back over to his boss and hands him the USB. The creep smirks and salutes her with it. "Pleasure doing business with you, puss."

We all hold our breaths until the car is out of the parking lot completely. Once it's out of view, Lips turns and holds her hand out for the bags of cash but I'm not handing them over… not when she'd probably just disappear into the night without us, so instead I head for the trunk of Morrison's car. I tap it gently and Morrison pops it open for me.

Lips is on my ass in a hot second. "What are you doing?"

Once they're secure I give her a look. "I told you. I'm not leaving without you."

She might be a blank slate around the gangsters down here but her emotions are all over her face for me. I try not to crow over that fact, but she gives me so fucking little to work with it's hard not to gloat.

She huffs and snaps, "Fuck. Fine, leave it open. I have the rest of my stuff here too."

I nod and walk over to where the rest of her bags are, where the guy who was flirting with her when we first arrived is still standing and watching us both. As I walk up he takes a step forward, over the bags, and crosses his arms.

I'd love nothing more than to take some of my frustration at this fucking night out on him with my fists. To just smash that longing look he keeps throwing at Lips right off of his fucking face.

So I smirk at him and watch him roll his shoulders back, ready to throw down over some bags and the Mounty.

Fucking *perfect*.

Except then Lips walks over and says, in a voice I've never fucking heard outta her with all its teasing and husky tones, "Luca, it's fine. My feet hurt and I need a bath."

She fucking pouts at him, flirting right back, and he leans down and brushes a kiss against her cheek without breaking eye contact with me.

I'm gonna kill him.

I don't know the where or the how of it, but I'm gonna fucking kill him.

Lips steps around me to grab her bags and then shoves one into my chest with a look.

Doesn't matter.

I've already marked him for death.

As we walk over to the car, the asshole calls out, "I'm going to miss that ass while you're gone, princess."

Lips laughs as I turn back to glare at him, wishing so fucking badly that Avery wasn't down here and there weren't a dozen other gangsters here watching because they're the only things stopping me from taking the asshole down.

"You get more ass than the average Mounty street girl on a Saturday night, Luca. I'm sure you'll survive without mine."

What the fuck is that supposed to mean?

The asshole grabs his chest with another flirty grin and I get the car door open for Lips, ready to shove her in and leave.

I'm gonna spend the rest of the year convincing Avery to get the Mounty to stay with me next summer, as far away from this place as fucking possible.

Lips startles at the sight of the Beaumonts in the backseat and darts around the car to Avery, chuckling when Floss opens the door to her straight away and sliding right in.

The moment I get in the back and shut the door, Morrison takes off, as eager as I am to get the hell out of the slums.

The girls start whispering amongst themselves and I use an arm to help Ash prop Joey up so the cunt doesn't choke on his own tongue.

I wish the fuck he would though.

"Where should I drop you off, Mounty? Feel free to tip me for my services," drawls Morrison. I hear Avery snort at whatever face the Mounty has pulled and for some fucking reason that only pisses me off more.

"She's coming back to the hotel with us," I say.

Ash turns on me with a scathing look and snaps, "Why?"

"Thank you, Lips, for finding my coked-up brother and getting him out of danger before he got himself stabbed by an angry Mounty girl for not keeping his hands to himself," Lips says, the sarcasm dripping from every word.

Ash doesn't know the meaning of backing down.

"Thank you, Mounty, for traipsing around the docks dressed like a slut and tripping over Joey. Do all your clients pay you in large bags of dirty money? Is your *puss* really that good?"

"Ash, *shut your mouth.*" Avery turns in her seat to glare at him.

I ignore Ash's shitty mood completely and lean forward in my seat until I can get half a look at her jammed into the seat with Floss. There's more important shit to know than the fucking money.

I can figure that shit out later and when it comes to the Bay, there's more than a dozen reasons she could be getting paid and each one more dubious than the last.

"Who was the guy with your bags?"

"Luca. He's… he works for the same guy your uncle does. We've known each other forever."

Like I give a fuck about who he works for. "Have you fucked him?"

Her eyes narrow at me. "How is that any of your business?"

Blaise tips his head back and laughs, a total fucking cover-up because I know he's just as fucked for her as I am. "How many of those Mounty guys have you fucked?"

"Why do either of you care?" Avery says in her most dangerously sweet tone and there's absolutely fucking nothing I can say back to that.

Not in this car with the rest of them, and certainly not while Lips still looks at me like I'm the biggest fucking asshole she's ever seen.

This year is going to be a fucking nightmare.

Two

BLAISE

I know before I open my eyes that sophomore year at Hannaford Prep is going to be a fucking nightmare.

The beds are the same, the layout is the same, fuck, even the sounds in the halls outside our room are the same; the problem is that the three guys in this room are completely fucking different than last year.

Ash might kill Harley before we graduate.

He might even kill me and that's not something I ever thought I'd say.

"I don't fucking care what it takes, we need her out and away from Avery."

I would roll my eyes but I'm too busy pretending to be asleep so I don't get dragged into this argument again. I'm so fucking sick of it.

Arbour isn't sick of it though, nope, he's fired up and ready to throw down with his cousin over *his girl.* "For fuck's sake, Ash, use your brain! Do you really think Aves would betray you? Because we both know she's too fucking smart to be lured into a friendship by some Mounty trash. You need to get over yourself and make peace with her."

Ah fuck, now I'm definitely not getting involved.

The room goes quiet, the deadly kind where Ash is working out a full and detailed body disposal plan, and when he finally answers his cousin, his tone is dripping in acid. "You are *blinded* by your own fucking obsession with her, you know as well as I do what happens at the docks in Mounts Bay. Avery isn't going to get caught up in that shit, not when we've spent this long keeping her out of Joey and Senior's way."

There's a pause and then the door slams and Harley sighs. "You can quit pretending to be asleep now, asshole."

I scoff at him, struggling to sit up and stretch out. "Why the hell would I get involved in your bullshit? I don't give a fuck about the Mounty."

Harley's eyes narrow at me, still a little bloodshot from his morning training down at the pool. I swear I'm the only one with a reasonable respect for sleep around here. He stares at me for a second longer, fuck knows what he's looking for, and then he starts packing his bag full of all of his genius-level textbooks.

Fuck that.

I grab a shower and get ready, hating every second of

putting the uniform on. It's like a fucking mask, any little piece of myself that could possibly show through is hidden away behind the rich asshole blazer. I fucking hate it, but that only makes it worse.

Poor little rich kid.

Sad and privileged with Daddy's money but not his love.

I could fucking choke.

When I get out of the bathroom, Harley is waiting and he scoffs at the state of me, mumbling under his breath at the rumpled look I've got. Like I give a fuck about dress codes or what the faculty thinks of me.

We head down to the dining hall together and when I text Ash to meet us there for food, he blows me off, too busy following Avery around and arguing with her. He's going to end up with a fucking stomach ulcer or an embolism at this rate.

I grab a tray, distracted by the sub-par menu for breakfast so I almost miss Harley's obsessive stalker-like action on the Mounty. Fuck, it's full-blown stalker really. He's fucking panting after her and I'm sure it'll only be a matter of time before I'm coming back to our room to find him fucking her on Ash's bed as a giant 'fuck you' to his cousin.

Fuck.

I don't wanna think about that.

What the hell is wrong with me?

"I'm getting to the bottom of some shit, if you're worried about what Ash thinks then now is the time to leave," Harley says, filling his plate up with protein in every form.

I do the same, running on autopilot while I call him out on his shit. "So you're still trying to pretend you're only interested in what's going on with Avery? Right. Totally logical, Arbour, I definitely believe you."

His jaw clenches so hard I think he's going to break his teeth, but at least he doesn't hit me for once.

He's getting fucking jacked.

"In or out, decide now because I'm going," he says, and I shrug at him as I follow him over to where the Mounty is sitting.

No other students are sitting anywhere close to her, wary of both her reputation and her poverty because half of these airheaded rich kids think it's contagious. She looks so different in her uniform, still thinner than last year but she already looks less… wary. Like Avery's friendship has eased something in her and softened her up a bit from the sharp and jumpy Mounty she was last year.

The second she looks up at us both that calmness disappears and she's back to being the same old sharp-tongued Mounty, constantly tearing us down without any fear of what we'll do about it.

No wonder Harley is obsessed.

I ignore the part of me that is also, maybe, just a little bit interested in watching her.

This shit is too messy for me to get involved.

"Seriously. I'm not dealing with either of you this fucking early in the morning unless it's a life or death situation. Is someone bleeding?"

Harley snorts at her and offers her a glass of juice, which she stares at like it's poison and shakes her head. "I'd rather not start my week off with the runs, thanks, asshole."

I glance between them both while Harley roars with laughter, the type he doesn't do around anyone but his family, and if I wasn't so caught up on her words I'd be fucking worried about it, but there's something going on between the two of them. There has to be, what the fuck else would her words mean?

Dammit. Am I jealous of Arbour right now because that's just fucking stupid, getting involved with the Mounty is the worst possible option.

Doesn't stop me from wanting to kill him for the smug grin on his face when he drawls at me, "Don't ask, man. We had a great winter break last year. I like to think that was when we became friends."

She doesn't take that well, pointing a knife at him and snapping, "We are not friends. I'm Avery's friend and you two are firmly Team Ash."

Team Ash?

Since when were there teams? This shit is getting out of hand. The moment I start looking at her, curiously trying to figure out what her deal is, she blushes and starts mumbling at her plate. I shove some food into my mouth but barely taste a thing.

I'm sure Harley sees the blush just as well as I do, the only hint that she was once a fan of my music and can't quite let that shit go, and I refuse to look at the seething jealousy I know is happening in Harley's direction.

He might see just how fucking *smug* I am about it.

I think Harley is about to start a fucking war with me, here and now, over that blush when the doors to the dining hall open and Joey saunters in with his little crowd of simpering assholes to distract us all.

Thank fuck.

"Look, it's only a matter of time before Aves wears Ash down and then we'll all be one big happy fucking family. So stop fighting it. We're friends by association," says Harley.

"Fuck off," the Mounty mumbles with a mouthful of food and though that should be disgusting, it's kind of cute how much she stuffs in. She's not looking at either of us while she does it though, her focus entirely on her plate and it makes me want to poke at her, piss her off a little and see how far I can push her.

"God, are you going to be a grumpy ass like Harley all the time? There's only so much of that shit I can take."

She stiffens at the sound of my voice, like she's startled I'm talking to her, and Harley elbows me with a chuckle, as if he's not pissed at me for daring to speak to her. I laugh back, only because it's that or call him out on it and there's enough drama in our lives with Ash being pissed off.

Harley clears his throat and the moment the Mounty looks up at him he catches her eye, pinning her to her seat with the focused intensity that only he can pull off with her.

She squirms under his gaze and fuck if that isn't distracting, so much that I barely register Harley's words until I realize he really is here to talk business. "Listen, I'm not Ash. Avery can't throw pretty words around and fool me. I know exactly what scratches down a cheek fucking mean. I need you to tell me exactly what happened between her and Rory. I've spent the whole break fucking stewing on it and I need an answer."

Her spine snaps straight like she's been zapped by a couple of thousand volts and she says, her words slow and careful, "If Avery has chosen not to tell you herself then you will never get it out of me. End of story."

Harley's eyes narrow at her, filtering all of her words through his bullshit-meter and deciding if she's legit or just trying to play him.

After a minute he shrugs and says, "Good. I'm glad you're a decent friend to her. She's never had one of those. But I need to know if I need to kill Rory. No, not beat him bloody or start a social campaign against him. I need to know if I need to end his life and fucking bury him somewhere. Because if that piece of shit raped my cousin, if he did that to her, I will end his life. I'm not asking for details, just tell me if he has to die."

Huh.

It's like I can watch the respect she has for him doubling by the second; the more he talks about protecting his cousin in the most violent ways, the more he reels her in.

Maybe it is a Mounty love story for the ages.

I'm absolutely fine with it.

Ecstatic, and I refuse to admit that I'm mostly cool with it because Ash will tear them apart before they even manage to get anywhere and so that makes it safe to be cool with it.

Safe.

Fuck.

"Fine, no details. If I were ten seconds later than what I was, you would be burying that dickhead. But I got there in time."

Right.

Rory has to die.

No way that we can let him walk around here with Avery like he didn't try to fucking rape her. Avery is the closest thing to a sister I'll ever have and the thought of that shit happening to her has me ready to take a baseball bat to Rory's head.

Ash is going to lose his goddamn mind.

Harley side-eyes me but I don't need that to know he's already plotting it all out in his head as well. Fuck, maybe I'll leave it to him just to keep him busy and away… from Ash. Because that's the only thing I need to keep him away from.

I break the awkward silence, the one where we're all vividly imagining the murder of a peer. "Color me impressed. Rory's a linebacker, you're what, five-two? How the hell did you stop him?"

The Mounty snorts at me and drops her silverware onto her plate with the kind of exhaustion that shouldn't be possible for a high school girl. "I'm a Mounty. I'm a foster kid. I was a child of neglect before that. Last year I was the target of a game that had most of the male population of this school following me around bugging me for sex every day. I've had to threaten Harley's psycho cousin with a knife to the dick. You think I don't have experience fighting off rapists? Please. Go back to your privileged, gilded fucking towers and leave me the hell alone."

Well, fuck.

Fuck me.

A baseball bat isn't going to be enough for Joseph Beaumont Jr. but, fuck, I wish I could beat the life out of the psychotic asshole and one glance at Harley is all I need to know he's on board with the killing.

Problem is, the twins aren't on board with it at all. I don't know why, because Joey clearly doesn't feel that same protective energy about his siblings, but it's the way it is.

Doesn't mean we have to like it.

The Mounty glances over at the door before standing abruptly, a grin on her face as she stalks off to Avery who's just arrived, the two of them whispering and looking over at us both.

I've never seen Avery look so happy, relaxed, and *young* as when she and Lips are whispering together.

"Joey has to fucking die. You need to get Ash's head wrapped around that fact because anyone who touches either of them is fucking dead," Harley snarls at me, and for once I completely agree with him.

Whether Ash likes it or not, the Mounty is family now.

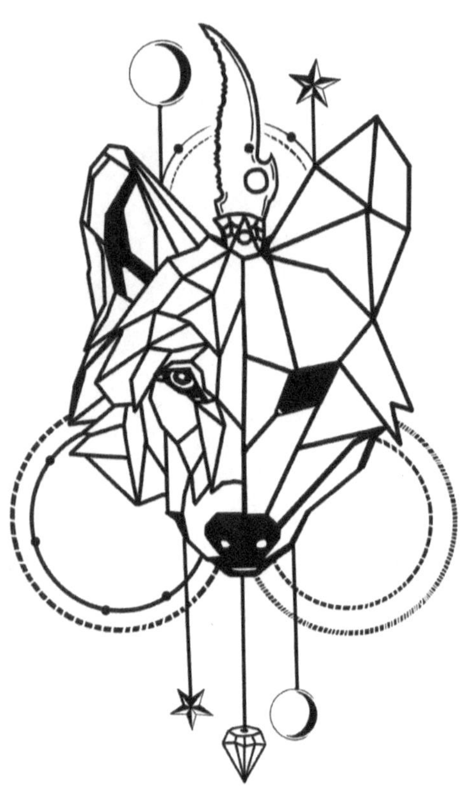

Three

ASH

I've been thinking about how I'm going to kill her.

Every morning starts the same.

My phone buzzes under my pillow where I'm sure Harley and Blaise won't see the message, and it wakes me up with the same amount of dread every time. It's a ticking time-bomb, a guillotine blade teetering over my sister that I'm doing fucking *everything* in my power to keep from hurting her.

Father just sent me a new set of boning knives, maybe I'll try them out on her.

I don't trust the Mounty.

Even with Avery vouching for her, I can't let go of the conviction I have that she's lying to us. Fuck, we all know she's lying, but Avery is so sure that the lies are only about her childhood and the way she grew up in Mounts Bay and not about where her loyalties lie.

The problem is that if my sister is wrong, she could die, and that is completely unacceptable to me. I'm not risking that, not for anyone, and certainly not for a piece of Mounty trash that just keeps luring my family in. Harley is infatuated with her, Avery is sleeping soundly in the same fucking room as her, and even Blaise is watching her more now, especially when he thinks no one is paying attention.

Trusting people is what gets you killed.

Every girl my father and brother have raped and murdered, all of them trusted the wrong person at some point. A family member, a boyfriend, a pimp who promised them a warm meal; every last one of them trusted someone and ended up strapped to a table in Senior's playroom.

I can't trust anyone else, and I'm definitely not trusting some girl from the Bay who's full of secrets and lies. There's no other options here except to keep an eye on her and try to get my family to see some sense.

No matter how much they might fight me on it.

When Blaise announces that he's going to go back to the Mounty for tutoring, he makes the decision for me because there's no way I'm leaving the two of them alone for that long. He's too... curious about her. There's something about her that keeps surprising him and drawing him in, and if he fucking falls for her as well, I'm fucked.

Arguing with Harley is bad enough.

When we both arrive at the library, there's a freshman

already sitting with her, making eyes at her like she hung the fucking moon, and I immediately decide he has to die.

Blaise eyes him up as well, but goes for casual as he takes a seat and says, "Mounty! Lovely to see you again, though I'm a little disappointed you're not in your party clothes. Such a shame."

I barely manage to speak through my clenched teeth at the interloper. "Move. You're in my seat."

The freshman smiles at me like some dopey fucking idiot as he switches seats obediently and Blaise chuckles under his breath at the level of malevolence coming off of me. It's going to be a blood-soaked night in the boys' dorm's fight club.

"Is there a reason you've signed up for another year of pointless tutoring?" the Mounty says with a raised eyebrow at me, but I stare at her until she finally huffs and looks away.

It annoys me that she does. She doesn't back down for anyone else, not the dickhead boys chasing her for the bet or my sociopath brother, but if Harley, Blaise, or I stare her down, she always breaks our eye contact.

It's suspicious as fuck.

The freshman's eyes dart between us both and then he breaks the heated silence.

"I'm Lance. Nice to meet you both."

I immediately forget his name because that is useless

information and the only thing I want from the idiot is his blood on my knuckles and his ass never to perch on this seat with the Mounty again.

Problem is, she just keeps on being nice to the little fuck. "This is Blaise Morrison. Don't insult his music or beat him in choir or he'll get pissy and you'll be miserable for the rest of the year. And this is Ash Beaumont."

He simpers back with a flirty grin, "Ah. A member of the family I should stay away from?"

Blaise smirks between them both, amused at the Mounty's assessment of him.

I don't want to admit that I'm also interested in her take on me.

She sighs and, shuffling Blaise's papers, replies, "Yes. His older brother is insane and his sister would destroy your will to live without breaking a sweat. Ash, here, could beat the life out of you and then run a marathon for shits and giggles. Or just pay someone else to bury you, he's richer than god."

No other student at Hannaford could have come up with a list that good, and I've attended school with most of them since kindergarten.

Suspicious.

We work on all of our homework together, mostly Blaise getting help from the Mounty and the freshman flirting away at her and ignoring her shooting him down politely every time.

Guess he's not any use to her in her plans of fucking us all over.

The moment the hour is up the Mounty starts packing her shit away, eager to get the fuck away from the tension. Blaise is busy frowning at the notes she's given him, looking even more confused than when we first got here, and the freshman pounces on the Mounty like the desperate piece of shit he is.

He jerks his head in Blaise's direction and says, "How do you stay away from them if you're tutoring him?"

I level a glare at him and it catches Blaise's attention as he slings his bag over his shoulder. Good to know we both agree on pulverizing him the moment we can.

The Mounty shrugs, her tone dismissive as she says, "I don't. Avery is my best friend and roommate. I tutor Ash even though he hates me. Joey is hell-bent on murdering me. I'm saying you should stay away from them if you want to survive the year."

"You think you're tougher than me?" He grins at her and, no. Absolutely not. I'm not having him play the macho bullshit card on her.

I might fucking loathe her but she could break him in half with one arm tied behind her back.

I'd also pay to watch that, but for entirely different reasons than Harley would.

"Have you ever broken the bones in a guy's hand in half a second one-handed?" I drawl, and when he frowns at me and shakes his head, I smirk and continue, "Then she's tougher than you."

He blinks at her, utterly dumbstruck at the little brawler Mounty.

"Are you here to study or to try to get into the Mounty girl's panties because you should be warned, she only fucks crime lords," Blaise laughs and she shoves his math workbook into his chest like that will shut him up.

Immediately, the freshman comes to her rescue. "You think you're cool because your daddy bought your shitty punk band a record deal? Write another pathetic song about your feelings, dickhead, and stay out of my business."

The Mounty looks fucking horrified and Blaise stiffens, but I burst out laughing, so loud that the students around us stop and stare. "They're not going to find enough of your corpse left to get an ID by the time we're done with you."

"You didn't want to take my advice at all then?"

The freshman shrugs and murmurs back to her, conspiratorially like they're the best of fucking friends, "Mounties stick together. I don't like the way they talk to you."

And I don't give a fuck what he wants.

The freshman needs to go.

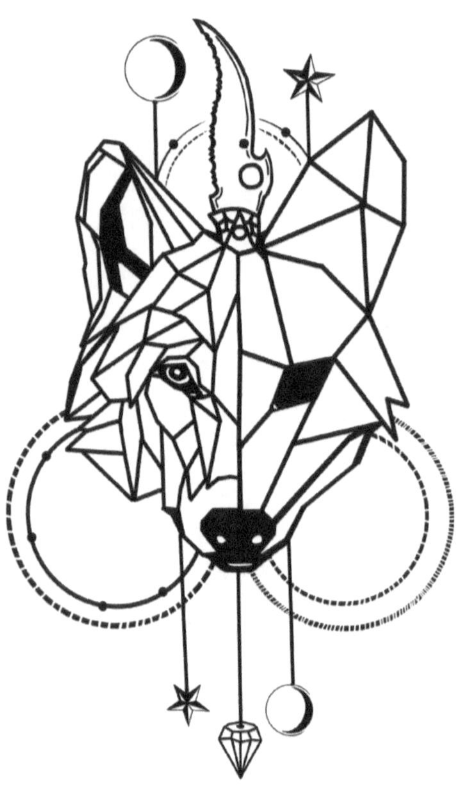

Four

BLAISE

Ash's sour mood about the Mounty only gets worse as the weeks go on.

He comes back to our room from the fight club each night pissed that Lance won't show his face there, and there's nothing on this Earth that Ash hates more than a coward. I think it comes from Joey being a gutless little fuck, hiding behind Senior's money and wielding it against his siblings like the fucking psychopath he is, so the freshman's behavior just won't fly.

It takes Avery's social campaign wreaking havoc on his life before Lance shows up at the fight club and Ash fucking pummels him into the ground. Harley peels him off before there's too much permanent damage, which confuses the fuck out of me until I realize Ash hasn't told him that this whole fucking thing is about the Mounty.

Harley would probably slit Lance's throat in a jealous

fit.

He's getting more and more pathetic over her, chasing her tail around the school grounds, and when Ash brings it up, telling him he stinks of 'pick-me' energy, Harley takes a swing at his cousin for only the second time in his life.

The first time was over his mother's locket and Joey.

Ash loses what little of his mind he has left.

I bounce.

There's absolutely no point in getting between the two of them because this is something they need to get out of their system. Harley needs to let the Mounty go, because I don't see Ash changing his mind about this and we all know that at some point Ash will change Avery's mind about the girl. The twins have never disagreed on something like this.

There's a party held at the groundskeeper cottage at the start of every year and the music is usually decent enough, but it's the copious amount of weed and alcohol that I'm after tonight. Anything to drown out the noise still ringing in my head about the Mounty and everyone fighting over her.

It's fucking boring but it also keeps reminding me about my own tangled mess of feelings for her.

She's too fucking... nice. I mean, she's not nice but she's nice to me without ever asking anything from me in return which is... nice. Fuck. How can I write entire albums about the trauma of my father and hopelessness of the world but I can't fucking unpack what the Mounty is doing to me except to say she's fucking *nice*?

Beers and bongs.

That's what I fucking need.

I've used that shit to run away from my feelings since I was nine; this is the party trick I'm good at and I need it so I head down to the party by myself, dodging the invitations and hands of the girls heading that way as well because that's not what I'm here for tonight. The thought of fucking one of these girls just doesn't sound appealing right now.

I'm not going to think about the whys of it.

I get absolutely fucking trashed in the first hour. There's a table outside and more than enough drugs around that if I wanted to attempt something stronger, then tonight would be the night, but Joey has put me off of any interest in experimenting.

I'm clutching at a bottle of beer and weaving my way onto the dance floor when I spot them.

Avery and the Mounty.

I could ignore them, I *would* ignore them, except they're heading towards the staircase that leads to the sex rooms and no. Nope, absolutely not. Avery goes up there and Ash burns the school to the ground in his rage.

I'm stumbling a little but I manage to get to them before Avery's feet hit the staircase, a hand around her arm to stop her but there's no way to grab the Mounty without tipping Avery over.

My brain feels as though it's working in slow motion, like the sight of the girls talking to each other on the screen on Avery's phone is coming in delayed so by the time I realize they've agreed to split up and the Mounty is still going upstairs, she's already gone and Avery is tugging me over to the dance floor.

Fuck.

Stay with Avery and stop anything that might happen to her, or go up after the Mounty and get her out of the rooms of debauchery. I'm not a prude or against the orgies that happen up there but the thought of her around them has me feeling fucking sick.

Or it's the beer.

Totally the beer, I don't care about the Mounty. Except for her tutoring me better than literally any of the many, many highly paid educators my parents have thrown at me. Or the fact that she has defended me with that sharp tongue and acidic wit of hers. She saved Avery from being raped and beaten even when Avery was tormenting her. I can't think of a single girl in this fucking hellhole who would do the same.

I frown down at Avery, ready to drag her upstairs with me to go after the Mounty so we could drag her back down here where I can keep them both safe, but she smirks at me and holds up the bottle of champagne for me to take.

I'm not proud but after two giant gulps, the pressing need to rescue the Mounty isn't such a big thing anymore. Fuck, she's a big girl. She can take care of herself and getting involved with her while Ash is raging out and Harley is panting after her? Not smart.

We swap the bottle back and forth a few times and when we've polished it off Avery hands me another bottle of whiskey she's found somewhere. By the time it's done I feel fucking invincible and suddenly the Mounty appears, safe and untouched from what I can see.

I feel a hell of a lot more relief than I have any right to, throwing my head back and roaring with the type of drunken laughter that feels just a little hysterical.

Tonight isn't going to end well.

But for right now we just dance and, fuck me, the Mounty can *move*. Avery is all sorts of grace and poise but Lips is… fuck, she's languid and swinging hips and her ass is fucking out of this world. The dance floor is crowded enough that she brushes against me a few times and it's only because of the drunken delay I have going on that I don't do something about it.

Too fucking tempting.

I guess I'm lucky that the drinking finally catches up to me and I have to puke. I stumble outside to puke all over the steps, my stomach cramping like fucking crazy as the girls out there squeal and yell at me for getting it on their shoes. Joke's on them, I couldn't give less of a fuck about any of them.

I barely register anything happening around me until Avery wedges herself under my arm, helping keep me upright as we stumble through the trees toward the school. My feet aren't working right at all and I know I'm leaning too heavily on her but I just can't keep my balance.

Until I can.

The Mounty smells too good, too inviting, too alluring to my completely fucked state and with my eyes shut like this there's nothing else to focus on except the way that she's tucked in tight against me. Thank God my words are all fucked up because no matter how hard I try to tell her that I want her, that I'm sorry for being such a dick to her, and that really I'm the one desperately hoping she picks me, they never come out right.

Just a long stream of mumbling sounds and grumbling.

Neither of them take any notice of me or anything they might be able to decipher from me, though I'm sure Avery will call me out for shit later. She's been around me enough when I'm trashed that she might know what the fuck I'm saying.

Thank God Ash isn't here, he'd read me like an open fucking book.

My eyes stay closed up tight and my legs like jelly

under me; they don't stop fucking wobbling as we walk.

The Mounty smells really fucking good.

She feels good too, tucked up tight under my shoulder, and I decide this is the best type of torture. The type where I know it'll bite me in the ass later but, for now, I don't want it to end.

I almost pitch over when we stop abruptly, the Mounty cursing viciously under her breath and then Avery snaps, "Move, Summers."

Ugh. Annabelle again.

"Give him here. We came together and we'll leave together," she calls out, which is a complete lie but if I open my mouth, I will puke all over Avery's shoes and I like my balls where they are, thanks, so I'll just have to plead my innocence later.

Avery huffs and wriggles until she has a better hold of my waist, my stomach roiling at the movement… wait, no, that's me moving. Fuck. How do I stop the rocking? I can't. Fuck.

I start swallowing, praying I don't puke again, but no one notices. Avery and Lips are too busy trying to get rid of Annabelle.

"He's done for the night. We'll see him back safely," Lips says and I tuck my face into her neck and breathe her in a little more, the scent distracting me from the bile creeping up my throat. I just need to keep it together until we're back up in the dorms; Avery will hate me puking in her bathroom but it'll be better than her shoes.

"You? Fuck no, if he goes home with you he'll be tied to a fucking bed and forced to play out all of your stalker fantasies."

"If he goes home with you, he'll wake up naked and an expectant father. Now fuck off," Avery hisses at her and we start moving again.

I stumble over my feet again, and when Annabelle starts screaming at us, I lift my head away from Lips' neck and yell out to her, my eyes still shut tight, "I told you to leave me the fuck alone, Summers."

Nope.

Gonna puke.

I tuck back into her neck and breathe deeply to ride out the waves of sickness.

I think I pass out for a minute.

I don't remember arriving back to the main building or the stairs at all, only coming aware again when we stop and I sway forward, Avery grunting and cursing at me like a fucking pro which means I'm on her last goddamn nerve before she smothers me in my sleep.

Then the loud sound of the door unlocking, the extra locks the Mounty put on aren't exactly subtle, and they shuffle me inside. I try to open my eyes or thank them or fucking something but then I'm pitching forward without them stopping me until I'm face down on the couch.

Thank fuck it's as soft as a fucking cloud, the blanket that's thrown over me is also one of Avery's cashmere ones, and I'm in fucking heaven.

The last thing I hear before I pass the fuck out is Lips mumbling, "Fucking rich kids," and Avery's laugh.

Ash and I became friends in grade school and I've known all along that Joey was trying to kill him and his beloved twin sister. One look into the older sibling's eyes when he's raging out and you know without a shadow of doubt that he's desperate for blood, destruction, and oblivion.

Boom.

Doesn't matter how fucking drunk I still am, I know exactly what that noise is. There's no one else who'd be showing up to Avery's door in the middle of the night and trying to kick it in, so my brain doesn't even have to come online before I'm moving.

The light comes on in the room and Avery calls out to me but I'm storming toward the door, tearing it open and finding Joey, raving and screaming, with his leg raised to kick out again.

Fuck him.

I dive at him, taking him to the ground with ease because he's nothing but a drugged-up psychopath, and no matter how fucking wasted I am, I can take this asshole out. He bucks and flails wildly to try to flip me off of his body, but I can hold my own in the ring with Harley and Ash so this is fucking *nothing*.

There's nothing more satisfying than beating the fuck out of Joey, just fucking whaling on the asshole until his face is a bloodied mess. Ash never lets it get this far when he's around so I take my chance and fuck him up. The Mounty stalks out behind me and distracts me for a second; the savage look on her face isn't anything new but the fact that she's here ready to back me up is.

Fuck.

I shouldn't have lost my focus, now my stomach is aching and cramping so fucking bad.

Joey's out cold so I move to pin his arms to his body with my legs so he doesn't catch me unaware and then I say, my voice all types of fucked up, "Mounty, I'm gonna fucking puke."

She startles and bolts back into the bedroom for me, thank fuck, and Avery cusses me out with her phone pinned to her ear, reinforcements on the way.

I'm sweating by the time the Mounty shoves a bowl under my nose and finally, *finally*, I empty my guts up. Fuck, when I start puking I just can't fucking stop and I'm feeling miserable until the Mounty runs a wet washcloth over my forehead.

I'm about to say something really fucking stupid, like how much I like her, when Ash and Harley arrive.

Five

HARLEY

Morrison is straddling Joey's limp and bloodied form, dry retching as the Mounty scrubs at his face.

I'm fucking livid.

What the fuck is he doing here and why the hell is Joey showing up here in the middle of the night again? I thought we sorted this shit out with him last year but the psychopath just doesn't learn.

Morrison's only saving grace is the fact that he wasn't so drunk he couldn't help defend the girls, but I'm ready to rip his fucking arms off over the way that Lips is fussing over him.

"What the fuck, Morrison?" I snap, when she starts rubbing his back gently, the sorts of soft touches she gives exactly *no one*. I can hear Avery in the bathroom emptying something in the toilet and gagging, so he must have already been sick.

Fucking pathetic.

He needs to control his drinking before it gets him in shit again.

"This is what death must feel like," he moans and Lips scoffs at him, rolling her eyes because we all know he's gonna start whining over his hangover.

Ash glares at them both as he grabs Morrison under the arms and pulls him off of Joey's unconscious form. Avery appears in the doorframe, her robe tucked tight around her body and looking queasy, and she stalks over to scrub at Blaise's face with a clean washcloth. "If Blaise wasn't here Joey would have gotten in. Lips would have had to stab the asshole."

Lips crosses her arms with a frown, muttering under her breath, "I fucking would've, too."

Fucking Joey.

I don't know how the fuck to get rid of him without having Ash and Avery pitching a fucking fit at me, but we're almost at a breaking point. He needs to be dealt with.

I give Avery a quick hug and then I grab Joey's legs to drag him back to the boys' dorm. I make sure Joey's head slams into every bump and chair leg on the way because I'm almost fucking jealous of Morrison for getting to beat the shit out of him.

I'm also fucking seething with jealousy over all of the soft touches he was getting from Lips but if I start shit with him now, Ash will pitch a fucking fit and make a big deal out of it. Lips is too fucking… jumpy. Every time I think I have a handle on her she throws something new at me and I'm back at square one.

I need to figure out how the hell to get her attention, but the fact I'm even thinking this is pissing me off.

I've never had to work for a girl's attention before. I'm not being an arrogant dick by saying that, there's never been a shortage of girls wanting to chase after me and I've never found one that I wanted enough to go after before so, naturally, I find the most fucking difficult option possible to lose my head over.

Fucking *typical*.

I make it out of the girls' dorm and down the hall toward the junior boys' rooms before Ash catches up to me, seething and spitting in anger.

"We need to get a fucking camera on their door, an alarm, fucking *something*."

I turn another corner and smirk at the loud *thump* noise of Joey's head hitting the stone wall. "Floss will smother you in your sleep if you try to pull that shit on her. They were lucky Morrison was in there."

The sarcasm is dripping from my words and if Ash wasn't so fucking livid about Joey, he'd be giving me shit about it, but the very real danger that Avery is in trumps our petty arguments.

We'd never fucking forgive ourselves if something happened to her again.

"Fuck this, I'm going back there to her. I'll stay there tonight and we can work out a roster so there's always one of us with her."

I give him a look. "She's with the Mounty, who took on a football player to keep her safe, and even fucking wasted Morrison had her back. She's as safe as she'll ever be while Joey is around."

Ash scoffs, "She's a Mounty, not a fucking killer. There's no way she could go up against Joey and survive; if she's as genuine as you think she is, then she's also a naive little girl who's going to get herself fucking butchered."

I'm not going to let that happen.

I already watch Avery's every fucking move, it wasn't that hard to keep Lips on my radar, and this little foiled attack by Joey only makes me more convinced. Lips is not the enemy here.

I just need to get that through Ash's stubborn fucking head.

I'm about to start the same fucking argument we've been having for months when we finally get back to Joey's room only to find half of his dumbass friends waiting there for us.

I fucking hate these poser elitist dickheads and this stupid pretentious fucking hellhole.

Devon looks me up and down and sneers, "He's going to fucking kill you for this. The second he wakes up, you're *fucked*."

I drop Joey's legs to the ground and enjoy the drunken grunt that falls out of him. He still doesn't wake up though. "He knows where to find me, unlike you ass-licking dickheads I'm not afraid of him. Drunk, high, or sober—I can take him."

Ash stares them all down like he's planning their deaths out in the most detailed way and some of the newer flunkies start shaking in their fucking loafers. They might like the infamy of hanging around Joey and having access to his supply of narcotics but one look at the deadly ice in Ash's eyes is enough to have them running.

He is a Beaumont after all.

Devon smirks at us both, staring back at Ash as he replies, "Can Avery take him, though? Can she beat him? Because from where I'm standing, your weakest link has always been the little bitch in the skirt. Fuck, I'm waiting for the day that you all drop the ball and she gets what she deserves."

And that's how Devon finds himself out of school for a month, only returning once there's a metal plate holding his skull together.

He'd be dead if I weren't there to peel Ash off of him and remind him that we're playing the long game.

I finish up my morning swim training late, thanks to my coach pulling me aside to talk about scholarships and colleges again. He's fucking hell-bent on me using my talent to get ahead and it's not a secret that I'm only at Hannaford because my wealthy and connected cousins made it happen.

I don't have the heart to tell him I'll be dead before I graduate.

I haven't let myself believe that maybe Lips is right and she'll be able to get me the hell away from my grandfather. No matter who her friends are down in the Bay, they won't be able to take Liam and Domhnall on. The O'Cronins might have lost the majority of their business to the Twelve but they're still dangerous, plentiful, and fucking crazy. She'd have to have a direct line to someone with a reputation to have half a chance, and what slum lord of the Bay would bother with a kid like her?

We're all just children in their eyes.

My mind always goes back to that diamond she'd handed over to Diarmuid like it was fucking *nothing*. Fuck, she came back from the summer break at least twenty pounds lighter than she'd left, and she didn't have the pounds to lose in the first place.

Is she a thief? Did she make all of these friends of hers

by stealing shit for them?

That might be a theory worth looking into.

Fuck, it's either that or she's fucking a crime lord like Blaise thinks and, stupidly, I refuse to believe that's what's going on with her. She's too… genuine. Her reactions to all of us throwing those insults around at her last year—the indignation was real. She always looks fucking horrified at the thought of fucking any of them which means she's smart enough to know that those girls are disposable.

More disposable than any other Mounty, I mean, which is saying something because no one gives a fuck about the gutter rats in the Bay. I know that for fucking sure because no one gave a fuck about me until Avery and Ash showed up with their fat wallets and unforgiving moral codes.

People here give a shit about the Beaumonts' orphaned cousin. They really, really started to give a fuck about me once they knew I have an inheritance and the unwavering loyalty of my cousins.

Everyone wants a Beaumont, no matter the cost of getting one.

Another reason I came around to Lips, she doesn't give a fuck about their last name… she only started giving a fuck about it once Avery was her friend and she needed to know how to protect her. Fuck, she took up residence as Aves' protective bestie like a fucking pro and it only sealed the deal for me.

My mind is whirling with all of this and more when I almost trip over Lips on the way to our literature class as she stomps out of a fucking storage cupboard like her ass is on fire.

My first thought is she's fucked someone in there, but she's so fucking enraged that I immediately move onto someone attacking her and I'm ready to start fucking swinging.

Then Ash walks out.

Fucking *Ash* because, even though I wasn't expecting it to be him, *of course* he'd be the one going after her. He won't go after Joey, fuck knows why, so instead he'll go after the Mounty.

I frown at her and open my mouth to ask what the fuck is going on between them now, but she cuts me off with a savage snarl, "You need to keep him the fuck away from me until he decides to get his head out of his ass."

Right.

I'm a little bit smug that she's completely immune to him thanks to his shitty attitude.

If only she was the same way with Morrison.

Ash scoffs at her, derisive and arrogant, and calls out over his shoulder as he stalks away, "Stay the fuck away from my friends, Mounty."

I haven't seen Lips this fucking enraged in months.

I keep an eye on her for the rest of the day but she's

so fucking angry that I don't bother trying to talk to her. I need to know exactly what Ash said to her to make her this bloodthirsty, but he's a safer bet to ask later.

When classes end I follow her out to the stairs that lead to the dorms, completely silent because I like my balls where they are and I know that she could tear them off in the mood she's in. I want this girl so fucking bad and this fight with Ash isn't worth me losing what little good standing I've managed to win with her.

Avery is waiting at the bottom with Ash and when he sees the two of us walking together, he turns on Lips with a sneer.

"What the fuck do you not understand about staying away from him?"

Ah, fuck.

Lips steps right up to him and pokes his chest with a finger like she's literally poking the goddamn bear, snarling, "I don't answer to you, asshole. You ever speak to me like this again and I'll bury you."

Avery and I move as one to split them up, and I'm not sure who I'm most worried about. Ash would never raise a hand to a girl but the aftermath if Lips took a swing at him, like I've admired her doing to the other assholes at the school, would be severe. Avery would have fucking kittens over it, and I don't want to have to deal with that shit.

Avery takes Ash, thank fuck, and I grab Lips by the

arm, gently tugging her away from him. She barely lets me touch her, wrenching her arm out of my grip and glaring at me even as he moves back. I ignore her glare and the way that her rejection makes me want to destroy something.

I might kill someone at fight club tonight.

"Ash, you need to calm down and think about this," Avery murmurs, and when he looks at her, he's gutted, betrayed.

"She just said she'd bury me and you're taking her side? Nice, Floss. Proves my point."

Avery flings her arms around his neck and hugs him. "She wouldn't actually do anything to hurt you. She saved me last year. If she hadn't helped me Rory would've raped and beaten me. He might've killed me, Ash. Please just trust me and trust that I know what I'm doing being her friend."

Jesus.

Floss is pulling out the big guns to distract him because the second the word 'rape' comes out of her mouth it's a big game over for her twin.

He can't harass Lips if he's too busy finding Rory and bleeding him out.

His arms slowly rise to hold her and from the corner of my eye I see Lips glance over to me like she can't handle watching them together.

I get it.

It's fucking hard to see two people who live and breathe for each other like that. Ash could've been a fucking psychopathic asshole like his brother but instead he's been nothing but devoted to his twin, protecting her and loving her through everything.

Mounties like Lips don't often get that kind of love.

I had it and lost it.

I don't think she's ever had it so it makes being this close to it even fucking harder, I'm sure.

I glance down at her and whisper, "We need a plan for Rory. I'm done sharing the halls with him."

Her shoulders roll back like she means business. "Agreed."

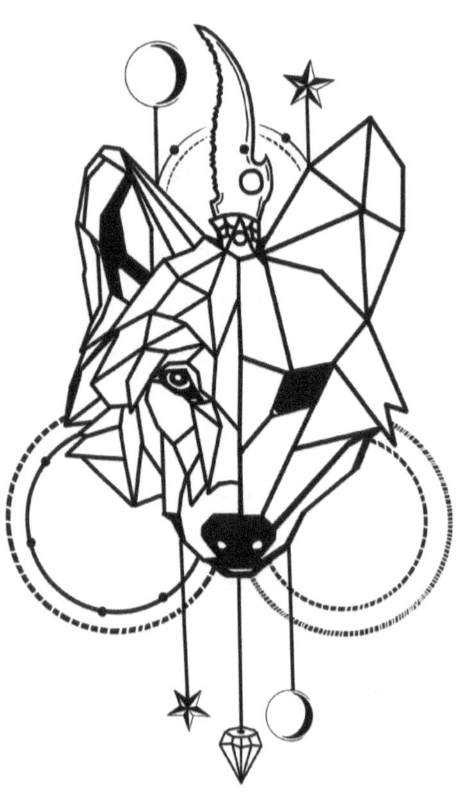

Six

ASH

It's only a matter of time, little brother. Should we carve the Mounty up as well?

I break my phone in half.

It's the third one since school started. Avery will bitch me out for it but the second Joey finds my number and starts up with his bullshit, I lose the ability to regulate my own rage. I fucking hate him, loathe him, and someday I'll find a way to kill him without risking Senior's wrath on Avery.

Until then I'll just keep on snapping phones in a fit and changing numbers.

So I'm already in the worst possible mood when I find Avery and the Mounty sitting together in the dining hall for breakfast. They're laughing and snarking at each other but the moment I sit down they stop, Avery eyeing me warily because even dumb, deaf, and blind she could read my moods with ease.

The Mounty keeps her eyes on her plate of waffles and something about it feels… guilty to me. That's a fucking red flag, and the fact that Avery can't see it fucking enrages me.

I wait until my sister is out of the way before I bring it up; I don't want her jumping to the Mounty's defense and derailing the entire fucking thing before I can get a read on her.

They both have literature classes up first but Avery has dropped down to a slightly lower class this year to focus on her ballet. The Mounty walks her all the way to her class, their arms linked as they whisper together, and even that pisses me off. Why the fuck did Avery have to be friends with her? Why did she have to pick the worst fucking option to finally have as a friend?

I detour to stay ahead of the Mounty, and I find a storage cupboard in the hall that will work because I also don't need Harley tripping over us and interrupting. He's fucking *smitten* with her and it's becoming a problem.

It's easy enough to grab her and tug her into the room with me, shutting the door behind her so we're not disturbed.

I know immediately that the Mounty is pissed off and in fight mode so the moment her fists clench I snap, "Calm down, I just want a word with you."

She whirls around to face me, her eyes narrowed and throwing fire my way. "We just ate together, you didn't have to hurt me to speak to me."

Fuck.

I don't ever hurt girls; I'm *not* my father. She's rubbing at her shoulder, and I try not to lose my goddamn mind about it.

Is she being genuine or does she know that those words are the best way to derail an argument with me? She knows too much about us all for me to be sure, either way I shift away from her a little.

Fuck it.

I need to say my piece. "I didn't think I'd pushed that hard."

She lifts her chin and snaps, "Whatever. What did you want to speak to me about?"

The dismissive tone is like a fucking slap to the face and makes me remember my anger, my shoulders rolling back and my glare once again icy as I snap back, "Stay the fuck away from Blaise and Harley. I don't need you poisoning them with the same shit you've fed Avery. You're a Mounty slut with an agenda and I'm not falling for your little act."

Now she looks as though I've taken a swing at her. "I'm not trying anything with them. I'm actually actively avoiding them both. And don't you ever call me a slut again, I think the *ongoing* bet proves I'm not."

I scoff and cross my arms. "That's why you sit with Harley in every class? And Blaise was in your room last night? You really are working overtime to get them. Just because you're picky about the dick you want doesn't make you any better than any other Mounty."

She huffs and squints up at me like I'm an idiot, which only makes me angrier. "Seating in all of our classes is assigned. He's Arbour, I'm Anderson, we can't change that unless he decides to go back to being an O'Cronin and I think we both know that isn't happening. As for Blaise, I helped your sister carry him back last night. Then I helped him out while he spewed. Should I have handed him over to Annabelle instead? Are you okay with your friends being raped while they sleep by gold-digging tramps? Or is it okay for her to fuck you all, even if you're not conscious and consenting, because her family has money?"

Typical fucking Mounty bullshit, always an answer for everything. This is how she's fooled Avery into believing her, but I'm not fucking falling for it.

She stares at me for a second longer before scoffing and storming out of the storage room right as Harley strides past. He frowns at her and then when I step out after her, he scowls at us both like he's caught me with my dick in her, the jealous asshole. He opens his mouth, no doubt to make an idiot of himself, but the Mounty cuts him off with a snarled, "You need to keep him the fuck away from me until he decides to get his head out of his ass."

I leave them both to make eyes at each other, calling out over my shoulder to her, "Stay the fuck away from my friends, Mounty."

I get through the rest of my day with nothing but my fucking terrible mood to keep me company. When I find Harley still following the Mounty around like a lost puppy and Avery jumps to her defense, there's no stopping me from tearing into her again.

She always fights back, no matter what angle I take, but this time she looks ready to kill me.

Good.

It's only Avery's words that snap me out of it and put a whole new bloodlust into me.

If she hadn't helped me Rory would've raped and beaten me. He might've killed me, Ash.

I will kill that worthless cunt.

When Avery finally coaxes me into leaving her tucked safely in her room, I head straight for the chapel where the fights are being held for the night. I need someone to *bleed* tonight. Whether it's me or some chump I'm beating the shit out of, I don't care. I just need the blood. The moment I arrive, the air disappears from the room, sucked out by the fucking terrible mood I'm in. I strip my blazer off and roll up the sleeves of my shirt in the quiet of the room. No one dares to speak a word, not even when I turn around, ready for a fight.

Everyone here knows what happened to Devon so there aren't any immediate takers.

Fucking pathetic.

I point at Sebastian and watch as he gulps. "Get in the ring."

There's a small reprieve in sadistic messages with my old number cut off but, in the quiet void, the demons that play out in my head get louder.

The good thing about rooming with Blaise and Harley is that neither of them ever say a goddamn word to me about the sleep paralysis, even when Harley has had to shake me out of the grips of them. He barely fucking sleeps, only ever passing out when he's too drunk to remember the nightmares that plague him.

Blaise is morose and probably on his way to becoming an alcoholic, so he's just as fucking bad.

I sleep like the dead, except for when this fucking bullshit happens.

Neither of them look at me when I finally pull myself out of the icy grip of the demon sitting on my chest, wearing my father's face and rummaging around inside me. The worst of these dreams are when he tells me that, under my skin, Avery and I look exactly the same. That he's already pulled her skin back, layer by layer, cracked open her rib cage, and burst her beating heart open in his fist.

I've seen him do that to a girl before.

I'll never fucking forget it either.

I pull a tank top on but I refuse to grab pants for the quick trip over to my sister's room. I'm not going to get another fucking second of sleep without seeing her with my own eyes and knowing that the nightmares are nothing but my own trauma feeding me the worst possible thing that could happen, over and over again.

"You heading to Aves'?" Harley mumbles, his nose in a textbook. Blaise has headphones on with music blaring and one of his lyric books open in front of him. Obviously it's not a good night for any of us.

"I'll sleep there. Make sure Morrison goes to bed sometime soon, he has a pop quiz tomorrow," I murmur back, and Harley nods absently.

Avery is the caregiver, not me, but I've been listening to him freak out about it for fucking days and it'll only get worse if he falls asleep in class... again. Fuck, last year he spent more time asleep on his desk in history class than he did in his bed. With any luck, Harley will get high with him and they'll both get some fucking sleep.

I doubt it, but one can hope.

I grab my new phone, just in case, but I don't even

bother with shoes. Avery will be horrified but I feel antsy, like there's something crawling under my fucking skin, and I just need to get over to her.

There's no one in the halls on the way over there; not a single teacher comes out to see who's walking around, and though I don't attempt to be quiet, my bare feet don't make a sound on the polished oak floors.

It both pisses me off and eases some of the panic in my chest that the Mounty had extra locks installed on the door. I have to knock because Avery won't give me a key now that she has a roommate, something else I'm fucking livid about.

There's never been a locked door between us before. There's never been a need for it, neither of us have ever given a shit about privacy and the only person in our family that I'd gut for walking in on her is Blaise, and he's still fucking freaked about me thinking he's into her.

The idea of either of them being interested in each other is fucking laughable, but I'd never tell him that.

It's too funny watching his panic.

The door opens a fraction and it takes my eyes a second to adjust but when they do, I find the Mounty staring at me like I've shown up on her doorstep dressed like the fucking Devil himself.

"Yes?" Her voice is barely more than a squeak and it irritates me.

Why is she acting like this? Why the fuck is she being

all meek and weird when normally she's nothing but acerbic wit and fire?

"I'm not here for you," I snap and I nudge her out of the way with my shoulder. She grumbles under her breath but doesn't bitch me out for it, just locks up and climbs back into bed.

Avery is alive.

Alive and asleep, completely unaware of my panicked searching for her.

I climb onto her bed and the movement wakes her up. She looks pissed for a second but the moment her head clears and she sees me, she knows. I glare over my shoulder at the Mounty because I don't want her listening in but she slips a ratty set of headphones into her ears and turns her back on us both, the closest to privacy she can give us without leaving altogether.

I want to argue with her and tell her to fuck off for the night, but Avery tugs on my hand until I lie down with her.

"Tell me. Tell me everything and get it out."

I shake my head. "I can't. You don't need to know the details. Just… just let me sleep here."

She nods but her hand stays tucked in mine and even though I can tell she tries to stay awake with me, when I'm calm and quiet she slips back into sleep. I move to the couch a few hours later, when it's clear I'm going to sleep too.

I don't want to hurt her in my sleep if I lash out.

Seven

BLAISE

The problem with Hannaford being one of the most prestigious and exclusive schools in the world is that the faculty has to keep the families of the students updated about behavior and grades at all times.

Avery can keep my records clean about my behavior, but I've never let her touch my grades.

It was tempting, fuck it still is, but there's no point in lying about my grades. I'm not going to college, I'm not taking over Kora, and I'm never going to be the prodigal son that he so desperately wants me to be.

I just need to do well enough that he leaves me alone.

I tell myself that it's desperation that leads me to the Mounty's door, that I'm so fucking behind in all of my classwork because she's the only one who can actually make me understand the inane bullshit we're forced to learn. I think I'll keep telling myself that it's not my fault that she draws me into her, that she keeps showing up in my lyric book, that little pieces of her circle around in my head until I want to write them out.

I keep lying to myself to keep the fragile peace between the only people who have ever loved me for who I really am and not the expectations of what they were hoping I'd become.

I knock before I can chicken out, texting Avery to get to the Mounty would be the coward's way of operating and I'm not that guy.

When Lips opens the door, I smirk at the state of her because it's so goddamn rare for me to see her out of uniform. She grimaces at me like I'm a problem.

I guess that's fair.

Ash has been nothing but a dick to her and I usually only ever show up here with him so it's a safe bet that I'd be here to cause her trouble.

"Avery is in the shower. You're welcome to hang out on the couch until she's out."

I should be nicer to her but instead I go with teasing, maybe even flirty because there's no one here to stop me. "I'm here for you, Mounty."

Her eyes narrow at me for a second and then she drags her eyes over me, slowly taking in every detail of my appearance from head to toe. It's a fucking weird feeling and it takes me a second to realize that it's because she never looks at me. Not really, she glances at me or maintains eye contact when she has to, but even when she's tutoring me she keeps her eyes on the work in front of us.

I can tell she likes what she sees and fuck if that doesn't make me reconsider my plan to just try to forget about this attraction to her.

The grin on my face is so fucking wide and I'm about to do something fucking stupid when she bursts that little bubble.

"No thanks."

What the fuck?

I manage to jam my foot in the doorway right as she tries to slam the fucking thing in my face. "Mounty, for fuck's sake. Hear me out. Please."

She hesitates.

She *fucking* hesitates, but with a sigh she finally steps away and I push the door open again. I straighten myself up and try not to get fucking fidgety now she's looking at me even more like I'm a fucking problem.

Why did I think this would be easy?

"Right," I clear my throat, and just fucking lay it out there, "I've made another deal with my dad. If I graduate senior year with a 3.0 GPA or higher, he's going to let me take a gap year without pitching a fit. I want to fit in a world tour and a new album. I also want to use that time to convince my parents that college isn't for me."

With another sigh, she motions me into the room.

The place is immaculate like always, the shower running so I know where Avery is. Thank fuck she didn't see Lips shut me down, the hell she would give me for it would be a fucking nightmare to endure and if Harley caught wind of it? No fucking thanks. The coffee machine starts beeping and I swear Lips' eyes damn near roll back into her head at the sound.

"You didn't need to come here; I already tutor you. We can go through all of your syllabi and get a plan together on how we're going to make it work," she mumbles as she stalks toward the kitchen.

She fixes us both a coffee, sliding a cup and the fixings over to me, all without looking at me. Now that I've noticed it, I can't stop myself from eyeballing her and wanting to figure her out. Does she ever look at me? It's not like she's fucking shy—did I really put her off of me that badly last year and now we're not ever really going to be friends?

Why does that bother me so much?

I shove that thought away. "Lance is taking up too much of your time. Ash would back off and let you work with me in peace but the little Mounty fuck wouldn't."

The glare she levels at me is fucking savage.

Fuck.

I choose my words carefully, gritting them out because I fucking hate feeling this exposed. "I don't want *Lance* to know how much trouble I have with my classes. He's an arrogant asshole and I'd rather not have to beat the shit out of him if he runs his mouth. If Avery finds out, it'll be the next Mounty hunt."

She startles a little and glances at me before looking away quickly like I've shocked her but, I mean, she knows how fucking useless I am at my classwork.

None of this is news to her.

My skin starts to prickle with hot irritation and I start chewing on my lip to distract myself from it. I fucking hate talking about this shit but before I lash out and say something stupid, she scrubs a hand over her face like she's clearing her head.

She holds up three fingers and, fuck yes, I've won. "Three rules."

I nod.

"One: you'll come to every study session on time and with the agreed work done before. If I'm going to put in the time and effort you will too. I don't care if it's wrong and we have to redo it, you have to give everything a go."

Easy. "Agreed. Next?"

"Rule two: you'll show me respect while we study. We can do it here, Avery has ballet and dance most nights so we can pick a few nights a week and we'll be left to it but I'm not having you get pissy and tearing into me for no reason. Save that for the dining hall or parties or some shit."

Jesus fucking Christ, I can't even argue with her for adding that one in. "Yep. Next?"

"Rule three is simple: don't tell Ash."

What the fuck? "Why? He wouldn't give a shit."

She scoffs at me and heads to the sink to wash out her cup. "He lost his mind over you sleeping here after the party. He cornered me and told me to stay the fuck away from you and Harley. He's practically pissed on your leg to assert his ownership of you."

Fuck me.

I know he's been an ass about her and Avery being friends but I didn't know he'd been that bad about it all. I wonder if Harley knows about this? He'd be fucking pissed if he found out his little Mounty is avoiding us both for Ash's sake. "Alright. But I'm going to have a chat with him about you."

She shakes her head at me. "I don't need your help. He'll figure it out on his own."

I tell myself that I'm not going to try to impress Lips because this isn't about getting to know her or forming a friendship; this is about getting to tour during the summer break without my parents being up my ass about it, and getting the fuck away from my father's special brand of *disappointment* at my inability to do all of the shit he finds easier than breathing.

The problem is that Ash turns up after his tutoring with a shitty attitude over me not showing up and there's fucking nothing I can say about it without breaking one of the rules right off the bat.

I could.

I could probably even convince him not to tell her about it, we've been friends for long enough that he'd leave that detail out of his campaign to get her away from Avery, but something about the way that Lips asked me not to tell him has me shutting my mouth.

Not once has she asked me for anything in return for helping me out. Not even when Ash laid out to her exactly how much she could have charged me for her services, money that wouldn't even register to my bank account but could've probably fed her for months back in the slums she comes from.

"I thought you wanted to actually do well this year? Have you found a new tutor or has Harley decided to stop being an asshole to you to get you away from his little Mounty love?"

The sneering tone is fucking annoying, he never pulls that shit with me and certainly not about this. He knows better than anyone how bad my dad really is and he's gone toe-to-toe with him for me on more than one occasion.

"I've sorted something else out... I didn't want to put

up with that Mounty asshole all fucking year and he's chasing her like she's a bitch in heat."

Ash scoffs and pours himself a drink, just a single glass because he's going down to the dining hall to eat with Avery and walk her to her dance class. It's a decent gauge of his mood; one glass means he needs something to take off the edge but it's not that bad. Two means he's going to beat someone bloody, three is heads-will-roll, and anything more than that is a 'call Avery' situation because if she hears about it from the gossip mills of Hannaford she'll be over here making us regret waking the hell up.

I triple check my bag has all of my homework in it so I'm not breaking the rules right off the bat, and then I sling it over my shoulders as my phone buzzes. Perfect, Avery finally gets back to me about what to grab for dinner and I'm definitely going to make a good impression for our first night studying together.

I'm halfway to the door when Ash drawls, "It's probably for the best that you stay away from her anyway. Harley's getting fucking precious about her and even if she pants after you, she still doesn't want to fuck you."

My spine snaps straight and I give him a look over my shoulder. "What the fuck is that supposed to mean? Don't tell me you're that fucking obsessed with her that you've tripped into petty fucking jealousies now."

His lip curls and I think we're about to fucking fight.

Harley will have fucking kittens if he comes back from his classes early and catches us.

"She told me. She said that it doesn't matter how much she's into your music, she doesn't want to fuck you. Apparently she really does only spread her legs for Mounty slum trash."

I don't know if I'm pissed at her saying that or for the way that he's still talking down about her, but I shove the thoughts out of my head and slam the door on my way out of the room.

His words bounce around in my head the entire way to Haven and back. When I make my way up to the girls' room, I try to look both innocent and studious when Avery opens the door for me but she's not buying it at all, which is dumb because I really am just here for the tutoring.

She still doesn't want to fuck you.

Why the hell is that bothering me so much and why, exactly, did Ash sound so fucking smug about it?

"If you so much as breathe wrong in her direction, I will make your life an absolute misery, Blaise Morrison. I will *ruin* you."

I roll my eyes as I brush past her and into the room, lifting the pizza boxes up like they're evidence. "Why would I feed her if I'm planning shady shit? I just need to pass my classes. You should be happy about this! I'm on your team about her joining our little circle… we'll finally be a circle too, not an oddly misshapen square."

She huffs at me and delicately pulls on a pair of pristinely white dancing shoes. "Yes, and when was the last time you sided against Ash? Never. Never in more than a decade of you two being attached at the hip and following each other into the depths of hell, so excuse me for not believing that you're here to start something that I will end. Because I will end it, Morrison, and I'll take your will to live with it."

Jesus fucking Christ.

"Avery, she's the only person who has ever been able to explain math or biology to me without my brain fucking frying. That's it. That's the whole story."

Her eyes narrow at me as she watches me set myself up on the floor and even though I'm careful to follow all of her meticulous tidiness rules, I can feel the judgement radiating toward me.

By the time I'm finally set up, she hesitates at the door for a second before saying, "She doesn't want to fuck you so don't try anything because if you make her uncomfortable, I'll tell Ash about your little crush. We both know this isn't a notch-on-the-bedpost thing."

Why *the fuck* is everyone pointing out just how badly this girl doesn't want me?

I'm too busy fucking fuming about that to notice that she's gone but the sound of keys in the door again snaps me out of it.

I didn't think her rules would be so fucking hard to stick to on the very first fucking day, but here we are. I take a deep breath to try to calm the hell down.

"You're late, Mounty."

She rolls her eyes at me but there's a little smirk on her face that softens it. "Just let me get changed and then we can start."

I nod and shove a slice of the pizza into my mouth. She starts the coffee machine on her way to the bathroom and it only takes her a second to come back out in a pair of yoga pants and a sweater. They're huge on her and when she pulls her hair back up into a high ponytail, I shove the rest of the slice into my mouth and start messing around with my papers so I don't say something fucking stupid like 'hey, Mounty, why do you stare at me like you want to know what my cum tastes like if you don't actually want to spread those fucking perfect legs for me?'

Jesus.

Stop thinking about her legs.

Yoga pants are the devil.

She sits down and hands me a cup of coffee, perfectly made. I push her pizza box over to her and when she opens it, her eyes narrow.

"Did you ask Avery to get us dinner?"

I feel like I've won something here. "Nah, I drove into

Haven to get it. She told me what you'd eat though. You didn't tell her I was studying here?"

I scratch at my chest and when her eyes drop down to the movement, I see that same hunger there. Why the fuck is she the most confusing girl I've ever been around, and why does that make me want her more?

I'm in deep shit here.

I need to just admit that so I can figure out what to do about it.

She takes a deep gulp of the coffee and says, "I forgot. I'm busier this year and there's more to do now that I'm keeping Avery safe."

Shit.

She does look tired as hell. "Is she safe?"

"As safe as I can get her. Look, I've had a rough day. I appreciate you grabbing us dinner, I wouldn't have eaten otherwise. Can we get into this so I can try to get a few hours of sleep?"

I nod and we fall into a quiet studying session, the hour passing quickly as she gently walks me through everything I've done wrong without any judgement or teasing. I never feel like shit when she does it, even when I've fucked up so badly that it takes longer for her to undo the mess than it takes for her to take me through it the right way. I'm almost pissed when Avery texts to say Ash is walking her back from dance and she clucks at me to get out of here to avoid a fight.

When we both stand, I decide that I might not be able to have her, but I can work at actually being her friend. A real one. So I pull my iPod out of my pocket and offer it to her. She stares at it for a second before she takes it hesitantly.

"What's this?"

"A playlist. If we're going to be friends then I'm taking advantage of your good taste in music. Give it a listen and let me know what you like. I'll grab it next week so wipe it and make me a list."

I can literally see the thoughts fly out of her head as she blanches. "How do you know I have good taste?"

Fuck.

It's too easy not to take the opportunity to flirt, even if it goes against my plan to lock that shit up, so I grin at her and suck on my bottom lip, rolling it between my teeth. More freaking out and averting her eyes, my head gets too fucking big about it.

"Well, you like Vanth. I'm assuming your taste must be decent."

Then I leave, lighter than I have been in days.

BREE

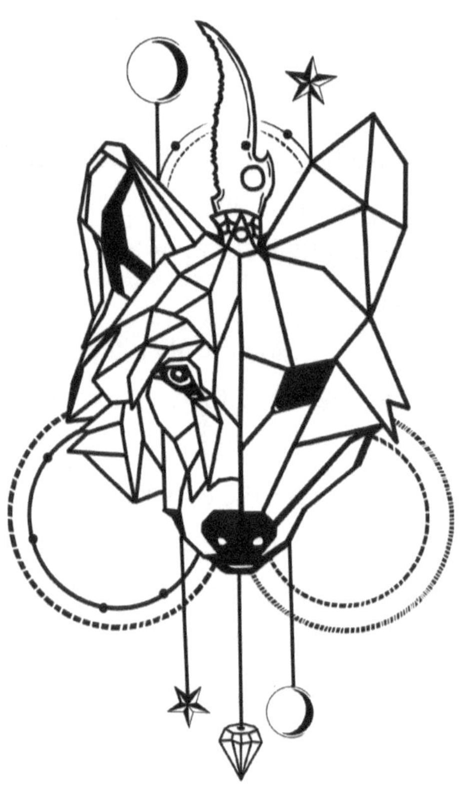

Eight

HARLEY

The good thing about being a Mounty is how fucking easy it is to find someone who wants to be bribed.

The students from Hillview Academic School are all rich by Mounty standards but fucking *nothing* like the assholes here at Hannaford. I feel bad about pulling cash out from the account that Avery set up for me to pay the linebacker to take Rory out, but I can't think of anything else I'd rather spend the money on than fucking destroying that asshole.

Daniel Carmichael Jr. was cut off by his parents back in his junior year for sucking his boyfriend's dick in the locker room in full view of the security cameras there. Fuck, he could've walked three steps further into the showers and never been outed in the first place, but he had something to prove to his high profile lawyer daddy.

Fucking rich kids.

Ash joins me on the walk down there, frowning at his phone the whole time while he tries to track Morrison down.

"Should I be worried about the two of you breaking up?"

I shouldn't sound so smug but the pouting that Ash is doing over this is completely fucking pathetic. He's always been cold and a little standoffish, even with me and Avery, but the icy cold fucking attitude on him these days is next level.

"Joey and his little parade of ass-licking dickheads are worse than ever and Blaise said he was walking Avery over here when he was done studying. If you weren't so busy chasing after the Mounty, you'd know this."

I shrug and walk down to the locker rooms, ignoring the look he gives me even as he follows me without hesitation. "She was studying with Lips. I haven't seen Joey or his dumbass friends get past her once. Fuck, I'd trust her with Lips more than I would with Morrison these days. He's still too wrapped up in obeying his daddy, and he pulls his punches."

That gets his full attention. "You don't know what the hell you're talking about. Just because he's not eager to bury people like you are doesn't mean he won't get the job done."

I scoff but I keep my mouth shut because, well, I'm

only really poking at him to rile him up.

I know what Morrison did for him.

Daniel takes the money with a grin and a wink, eyeing us both like we're dinner, and Ash sneers at him before stomping off. I'm a little less of an asshole about not being interested, because I need the guy to do the job right, but I make my point nonetheless.

I buy hotdogs from the cart on the way past, scoffing at the sneer on my cousin's face at the sight of them. Of course the caviar-eating asshole wouldn't like anything that wasn't served on fine china or that wasn't cooked by his sister just the way he likes it.

Typical.

We get back up to the bleachers and into some decent seats just as the others arrive. All three of them. Together.

Lips looks like she wants to jump out of her own fucking skin to get away from us all, Avery is a blank slate—which is a huge red flag, and Morrison has never looked so fucking guilty in the entire time I've known the asshole.

Ash clearly thinks so too.

Lips scurries over to sit next to me and as much as I'd like to think that she's finally warming up to me, it's definitely a strategic move to get the hell away from Ash and Blaise.

Avery watches her and then her eyes flick between

the rest of us before she sighs and snaps, "Morrison let Annabelle drool all over his neck in the library while he stood there like an idiot instead of shoving the skank-bitch off and telling her to find some other neanderthal to trick into fatherhood. His inability to tell her to *fuck off* is going to fill my planner up, and he's going to owe me more than he's worth by the end of the year."

Ash smirks at him and Morrison bites back immediately. I ignore them, handing Lips a hotdog and enjoying the shock on her face as she takes it. There's something so fucking Mounty about her getting choked up at being given food that my chest aches with the memories of that fucking hellhole of a city.

How do I convince Avery to keep her the hell away from there next year for summer break? How can I talk her into coming up the coast with me so we can spend the time together, safe and fed and happy. Fuck, it isn't even about getting to have her there with me. I've watched all of the girls I grew up around end up on street corners. The only reason my cousins didn't end up there is because my uncles wouldn't let it happen. Not that they'd feed them properly or give a shit about them, nope, it's all about the family name and reputation.

They haven't figured out yet that the name O'Cronin is a fucking embarrassment.

It only takes a minute before Morrison distracts Ash

with random stats about the players, and they ease up a little on their cutthroat banter.

"We're not going to have to sit through the whole thing, are we?" Avery whines, cringing at Lips and I as we eat the hotdogs.

Her words catch Ash's attention again and he throws us both a filthy look, pissed beyond all measure that Lips parked her ass right next to me. I don't know why he's so fucking worried about her, even without her obvious protection of Avery, she's still not going to change our family dynamic all that much.

Lips frowns at Morrison lighting up a blunt and I nudge her gently to distract her. "Relax. No one here gives a shit, Mounty."

She shrugs and looks out over the crowd. She looks... worried. Sad. Anxious? Fuck, unless there's a fucking blush over her cheeks she's impossible to read, and even then she never acts the way I expect when she's looking fucking *ravenous* at one of us.

I could fucking kill Joey for starting that stupid fucking bet.

I don't know if that's the reason that she never follows through or if there really is a slum drug lord in the Bay that owns her, but none of that stops me from wanting to fucking gut anything that's getting in the way.

I don't want to face the idea that maybe, just maybe, she

has no fucking interest in any of us and all of the blushing is... something random that happens to her.

Fuck.

Avery starts bitching me out again, just fucking going to town on me over being forced to sit in these stands with rowdy football fans, but Ash takes the opportunity to fawn over his sister again for a minute. I've never seen the two of them go this long without figuring their shit out. They're like magnets, always finding a way back to each other no matter how much they bicker and fight over useless bullshit, and it's fucking jarring to see them like this.

He tucks her under his arm and murmurs quietly in her ear, probably fussing over her about being here and being around Rory in any little way. We've made it clear to that rapist cunt that if he so much as bumps into her in the hallways between classes, he's dead. Not beaten or socially ruined or even put in a coma.

Fucking *dead*.

None of us would hesitate to do it and, even though Ash doesn't want to accept it, the Mounty girl he hates so much would do it too. I'm so fucking sure of it. The way she watches over Avery and their surroundings, it's protective and like she's ready to start fucking swinging if someone tries anything.

There's guys behind us fucking around and it only takes one jab in my back before I turn around to let them know who the fuck they're bumping into, because today is not the fucking day. It's never the fucking day, and when they settle down Lips looks relieved for a half second before she starts cracking her knuckles and staring out at the crowd again.

She doesn't like being around this many people here, this many rich prep kids and their asshole families.

I don't blame her.

I interrupt Avery's latest rant about football, waving my food in her face. "We'll be gone by quarter time, Floss. Just get a hotdog and enjoy the show."

She gags at me as Morrison hands the blunt to Ash and after my cousin has taken a drag, he offers it to me. It only takes me a half second to decide against it, waving him off.

Lips murmurs at me grumpily, "Don't turn it down because I don't like it."

Huh.

So she does care just a little bit about me... or at least her place in the little family that we are.

I shove the last of the hotdog into my mouth and grab the uneaten half of her hotdog that she's abandoned. I raise an eyebrow at her and, just to fuck with her I say, "I want to remember every second of this and I need a clear head."

There's that fucking blush of hers again.

Someday, some-*fucking*-day, I'll figure this girl out.

I just don't think it'll be any day soon.

She nods as the players march out onto the field and Blaise starts critiquing their movements, a high rambling of words that's more talking shit about them than it is about the sport itself, and Ash ignores us all for his phone. Avery reads his texts and they murmur to each other quietly, a sure sign it's their fucked-up father sending them pain and chaos.

As soon as the game starts, I keep my eyes on the players. I pick out Daniel and Rory and then I watch them both obsessively, not wanting to miss a goddamn thing. Lips fusses and fidgets next to me, clearly bored as hell to be here, but it works out in my favor because she also spends a lot of time looking me over.

I know she likes what she sees.

I know because so long as I pretend I can't see her checking me out, she keeps doing it like she can't keep her eyes off of me.

It's fucking distracting and as much as I want it to go on forever, when she fixates on my mother's necklace I have to say something to break the moment, otherwise I might do something fucking stupid and I'll never hear the end of it from Avery and Ash.

I clear my throat and say, "A senior tried to get it back for Joey during a fight. The leather won't break like the chain did."

She scowls and crosses her arms, a slight shiver running

through her body. "I hope you made him bleed."

I don't like her being cold.

Fuck, I don't like her being uncomfortable for any reason, but this is one case that I can actually do something about it without risking her either running away from me or punching me in the fucking throat. I shrug my coat off and drape it over both of the girls' laps, tucking one side under Lips' thighs so I know she'll stay warm. She thanks me with a quiet murmur and I shrug. Like it's nothing, keeping my eyes off of her because she handles shit better when there's less attention on her.

It's lucky too, because I spot the play before it happens. "Fuck, Aves, this is it."

Daniel runs across the field like a fucking freight train, taking Rory down with one of his teammates in a maneuver that will easily break the asshole's spine. Three other players pile on and I'm fucking positive that Rory will be fucked.

The crowd falls silent.

I struggle to keep the grin off of my face. I glance down at Lips, but she's watching every fucking move on the field as the medics all run out in a panic.

Blaise whistles and murmurs, just loud enough for us to hear, "He'll be lucky to walk again."

I take the opportunity to whisper in Lips' ear with a chuckle, "I paid enough to make sure he won't."

She smiles, a real and fucking beautiful smile, and I ignore my chest tightening up over it. Avery tucks her arm into Lips' and gives her a smug smile, all confidence and ruthlessness now her would-be rapist is broken in half on the field.

Rory never returns to Hannaford Prep.

Nine

ASH

Going back to the Beaumont Manor for the fall break is a fucking nightmare.

Joey spends the entire break too fucking high to function, which is a great thing, but it only means that Senior is pissed about his protege failing to perform and I end up facing the brunt of his anger on our first night home.

I don't like letting Avery know when I'm in pain, but it's pretty obvious that most of my ribs have been broken when I can barely fucking move. I sleep in her bed that night and I plan to every fucking night that we're going to be stuck here, guarding her in case he finally decides that he's going to come after her and drag her to his rooms, all the way to that fucking table that haunts my dreams.

The anticipation of that moment, the fucking showdown that will end with either Senior's death or mine, is almost unbearable.

Almost, but I'd do anything to keep my sister safe, including spending my time in this fucking Manor with broken ribs and rationed bourbon because Avery is too worried about my blood thinning out while I'm injured to let me drink it properly.

It's my own version of hell.

Thankfully, Senior has to take a flight to the East Coast the next morning and we get a reprieve for a few nights, meaning we're sitting in the formal dining room eating dinner under the watchful eyes of Senior's bodyguards when Avery gets the video call.

The Mounty never calls.

They text each other all the time but, then again, Avery texts everyone all the time. Everyone. Harley, Blaise, even that asshole Atticus—her phone is always charged to full power and in her hands for a reason, but the Mounty isn't a phone call kind of girl and she *definitely* isn't a video call person.

Avery glances at the bodyguard standing in the corner as she answers, lifting a finger to her lips as she gets up from her seat and takes off toward her room.

I stalk after her, trying not to look as interested as I am but I'll be fucked if I'm letting the Mounty manipulate her while I'm around.

Not that Avery gives a fuck what I think about any of

this.

The moment the door to her room shuts behind me, Avery grins at her phone and drawls, "Miss me already, Mounty?"

The Mounty doesn't say a thing, not a single thing, and Avery's eyebrows slowly inch upward. "Harlow, Annabelle, or Joey?"

Still not a single fucking word but whatever is happening on that screen, Avery lets out a squeal.

Fuck this.

I swoop down to have a look but it's just… shoes. Avery's Louboutins, the couture ones she had specially crafted that she loves more than all of her other shoes combined, that she's been fucking raging about for weeks.

The Mounty grimaces at the sight of me on the screen and says, "Can you forward a picture onto Morrison for me? I've recovered his missing shirt."

Avery shoulders me away. "Of course. Who had them?"

I can't see a thing on the phone with the angle Avery is holding it at but when it buzzes in her hand, she shudders and frowns like she wants to peel her own skin off. Not a great sign. "Who lives in that cesspit?"

The Mounty huffs. "Harlow. She's stealing and hoarding from other students. Should I call the student hotline or will you deal with the bitch?"

There is nothing on this Earth that Avery loves more

than fucking with Joey's little ass-licking flunkies, so it's no surprise when she practically purrs, "I'll do it."

They hang up and I head for the stash of bourbon, rolling my eyes when Avery clucks at me like that will stop me from drinking what little is left.

I'm not fucking happy about the Mounty going snooping around Hannaford while we're not there. What if she gets caught and drags Avery into shit? I mean, there isn't anything that school or the attending students could do to touch her but it's the principle of it.

My ribs hurt enough to have me feeling fucking vicious about it.

Avery disappears into the bathroom to make calls and get ready for bed. I try to lose myself in the glass, to forget about the sharp pains when I breathe and the fucking mess waiting for us back at school and the sounds bouncing down the hall of Joey trashing the fucking Manor in a drug-fueled rage. I try but I fail because I've never been good at lying to myself.

My phone buzzes in my pocket and I consider ignoring it.

All I've heard today is a running commentary on the Morrisons' fucking disgusting behavior toward Blaise from Harley, and it's making me reconsider my position about not going on a killing spree, like Senior so desperately wants from me. I hear Avery scoff and laugh in the bathroom and something tells me it's to do with the message.

Mounty, I'm sending you something as a thank you for finding my shirt.

It's a group message.

Avery has put us all together in a group message so that I can witness firsthand as the Mounty worms her way into my circle and ruins *everything*.

My phone buzzes in my hand and I find Harley's simpering after her. She would have to be blind not to know how hard he's chasing her; this game she's playing with him instead of just telling him one way or another.

She shouldn't be sneaking into other students' rooms without backup. The shirt isn't worth that much. Wait until we're back, Mounty.

The bathroom door opens and Avery walks out dressed and ready for bed. She looks so fucking fragile, so *breakable*, as furniture shatters down the hall at our brother's hands. The same hands that choked the life out of her back before freshman year started.

I still see it every night in my sleep.

Don't get Avery involved when Harlow finds out you were in there. She doesn't need to be cleaning up your mess.

Avery rolls her eyes at my text as she climbs into bed, sliding between the sheets and propping herself up on the mountains of pillows. "Please don't ruin my night with this. Please."

Fuck.

I set my empty glass down on the side table and slump down onto the pillows, scrolling through the slew of messages Harley has sent about the Morrisons.

We're going to have to deal with them at some point, but Blaise is still holding onto some stupid hope that his father will change his mind and love him.

It's stupid but I can't say a word about it, because Harley is just as desperate to get rid of Joey and I won't give them an answer on why I won't let that happen. Even when it almost tore us all apart, I didn't say a word.

I don't want them to know how bad the Manor really is.

It'll only put them in danger to know.

Avery smirks and my phone buzzes with her input into the group message.

Welcome to the madhouse, Mounty. Now your phone will blow up all day long and you'll hate me for adding you when they start talking about who has the nicest tits or who fucked which girl first.

I roll my eyes at her and she smirks at me, both of us fully aware that she's stirring shit up with Harley because even though we might not have talked about it, we both know he's infatuated with her.

Can't wait.

I turn my phone onto silent, ready to fall into a fucking shitty sleep with one eye open the whole night and not wanting to be disturbed by Blaise's drunken rambling all night long.

Avery is busy tapping away, working on something, but when she giggles maniacally, I can't help but check my phone again.

Seeing as we're all banned from Annabelle and Harley's apparently taken a vow of celibacy there will probably be more complaints of blue balls than anything else.

Fucking Morrison.

Of course he's fucking fallen for her as well.

I knew she'd do this; I knew she'd ruin everything.

The beatings only get worse when Senior gets back from his meeting.

I manage to keep Avery away from him, and I pay off one of the bodyguards to get more coke for Joey so he's subdued and mostly out of our sights. Either way, I'm counting down the days until we can head back to Hannaford and I can sleep in my own bed.

Avery thrashes around in her sleep too much.

The first night back at Hannaford, I take two of the little prescription pain pills that Avery's private doctor prescribes me and I sleep like the dead. I wake to my alarm and Blaise's snoring because he can sleep through fucking anything if he's hungover enough. Harley is already gone for the day which is both normal and a good thing, because it takes me three tries to get out of bed. I avoid looking at the damage in the mirror until after I've showered, as if the water will dull the bruises and I'll stop looking so fucking battered.

I look as though I've been in a car accident.

I'm sure there are many men who would be hospitalized if they were beaten like this but this isn't even the worst I've had before.

The year I went after Joey for choking Avery… Senior almost killed me too.

I don't like to think about that time.

My phone buzzes as I'm buttoning up my shirt, my chest tight as I force myself not to flinch or wince in pain as I move because it'll only make things worse.

Breakfast at the dining hall. Stop avoiding us just because Ash is a dick.

I roll my eyes at Harley's fucking dramatics. He thinks he's going to change my mind about her, that throwing us together all of the time will make me see that she's genuine.

It's fucking stupid.

I drag Blaise down to breakfast with me, mostly so I have someone to roll my eyes with when Harley starts swooning over the Mounty. The girls are both already there when we arrive, and I ignore the Mounty altogether. It's better that way and when Harley sits down with a shitty look on his face aimed in my direction, I think about getting in the ring with him just to beat it out of him.

I can barely move though, so he's safe for today.

A freshman kid next to the Mounty bumps her as he takes a seat and she jolts Avery in the process. The Mounty glances down to where she's bumped Avery and then death stares the freshman, but he's a cocky little fuck and just offers to let her blow him as an apology.

Harley doesn't take that very well.

He threatens him with a butter knife and, though it does the job and I still fucking hate the Mounty, I'm not going to let people around here think that it's okay to disrespect someone even adjacent to my sister.

I lean forward until I can make eye contact with the asshole, watching him gulp as I sneer at him, "You don't win the sweep for getting your dick sucked anyway, Javier. You'd have to be able to get it up *and* slip it in, and we all know you have problems with that."

The kid leaves the table to the sounds of all of us laughing, except the Mounty, who slides straight back into ignoring us all the moment he's gone and digs into her breakfast.

Blaise refills the Mounty's glass with a shit-eating smirk and drawls, "Did you like your present, Mounty?"

Avery grins down at her phone. "She hasn't even opened it, Morrison."

The smirk falls off of his face. "Why not?"

She sighs and pushes her half-eaten plate away. "I don't want to have things bought for me."

Blaise frowns and stares at her like he's fucking heartbroken.

Jesus fucking Christ.

"It was a thank you, Mounty. Jesus, I wasn't bribing you."

She shrugs and takes a bite of her apple, casually fucking with him like she doesn't notice how rarely he shares anything of himself and just how deeply this might cut him. "Most people say thank you with words. I don't want your money."

Avery spots it though and defuses the moment before it can turn into an absolute fucking brawl, flicking a grape at him and saying, "She threw a tantrum at me last week for buying new sheets for her bed because I hated the color of the other ones. She's as weird about money as Harley is."

There's quiet for a moment as we all eat, Blaise groaning over the viciousness of his hangover and the pain in his ego from the Mounty rejecting his little gift.

I'll have to pry what he got her out of him later.

"Junior or Senior?" the Mounty murmurs, and Harley's head jerks up to scowl at them.

Avery looks over to Joey so I can't catch her eye because what the fuck is the Mounty talking about? When she looks back, I finally fucking see the smudge of a bruise on her collarbone, just barely peeking out from her shirt.

Fucking Joey. It had to be, he's gotten to her sometime after we'd arrived back at school and she hadn't called me. For fuck's sake.

"Senior."

What the fuck?

I didn't leave them alone together, not fucking once. How did he get to her? *How the fuck did he get to her?*

I stand abruptly and tug Avery to her feet. "I'll walk you to class."

She doesn't look happy about it, but she tucks her arm in mine and walks out with me.

Senior waited until I was showering and patching myself up in Avery's room from my last beating to find her and terrorize her.

He's never laid hands on her like that before.

Every time he's offered me the choice—me or her— I've taken everything he's had without a single fucking word. He's broken almost every bone in my body, he's covered every inch of my skin in cuts and bruises, and not once have I thought about having my sister take the pain for me.

Not even when he beats me day after day, his fists fucking raged on my body, not even then have I broken.

It doesn't matter.

It never fucking matters because no matter what I do I can't protect her and he came for her anyway.

I'm fucking livid about it and it's almost impossible to go about my day afterward without losing my goddamn mind. I don't even attempt to hide it, either, and the other students don't just avoid me in the halls like they normally do, they actively turn and run away from me.

It makes things slightly easier.

I don't go to the dining hall for lunch because if I see Joey, I'll beat him to death without being able to stop myself so, instead, I head up to my room and down a bourbon.

I might just skip the rest of my classes and get fucking wasted.

Well, I would except Harley arrives soon after I do, and there's something off about him. My hackles rise immediately, on edge and ready to shed blood at the slightest fucking thing today.

I crave it and I hate myself for that.

My cousin takes a deep breath before letting it out slowly, scrubbing a hand over his face roughly. "I need your keys, the set with the Maserati keys on it. Unless... do you have plans tonight?"

What the fuck is he planning? "My plan is to keep Avery safe from Joey, the same as it always is."

He nods and then he shifts into his own version of Avery's power pose, feet shoulder width apart and his hands on his hips. I don't like it because I know whatever comes out of his mouth isn't going to be good.

"Lips has something planned for your dad. I don't know what it is, but she's heading down to Haven tonight to sort it out. I think—I think she's going to use her shit to try to keep Avery safe. If you want to know whatever it is then you should drive her. If you won't then I will, someone has to go with her. That's how this works—we protect our own."

I'm not sure what I was expecting, but it definitely isn't this.

I stare at him for a second and he shrugs. "Say whatever the fuck you want to but the moment she saw those bruises on Floss she fucking went for it, and I don't need the details to know that she's throwing something big his way. Look, I get it. I do. Joey has made shit fucking complicated here but I'm asking you to just go with her and see whatever it is firsthand and decide for yourself if she's as bad as you think. One night. I'll keep an eye on Avery; Lips is trying to keep her out of it because shit might go bad and she's protecting her."

He's never spoken about anything this... honestly before.

All of us carry our secrets, even as protective and close as we all are. Fuck, it's because we're all protective of each other that we don't. Harley never talks about the ticking time bomb hanging over him thanks to his grandfather, I never talk about what happens in the Manor, and Blaise… Blaise never says how bad shit is back home with the Morrisons when Harley isn't there to chaperone.

None of us want to admit how close we all are to plummeting off of the edge into the fucking abyss.

And that honesty in Harley is how I find myself leaning against the Maserati when the Mounty appears in the darkness, almost falling over her own feet at the sight of me.

Interesting.

"Harley sent me."

She huffs at me in frustration and snaps, "You can't stop me; I have to go. I'll explain later."

So Harley obviously didn't have the same little heart-to-heart with her as he did with me. I unlock the car. "I'll drive."

She stares at me like she's waiting for the punchline and I stare right back at her, but there's no fucking way I'm going to just trust her.

There's nothing she can do about Senior… but I want to know who the fuck she's going to be meeting out here and who the fuck it is that she thinks can go against Senior and survive.

Finally, she sighs and slides into the car, a frown on her face that looks different to the one she wears at school.

It catches my eye.

When we'd gone down to the docks in the slums of Mounts Bay to pick Joey up from her the night before school started, she'd been the same way. There was nothing glaringly obvious that was different about her, but there was this hardness, this fierce *blankness* to her that hadn't just shocked me when I'd seen it, it had changed something.

I'm watching her too much.

I'm thinking about her too much.

Even when I was getting the shit kicked out of me by Senior, I only really had two thoughts in my head: protect Avery.

And what is the Mounty girl doing to us all?

Because Avery is a different person now. I was fucking terrified of what that meant at first because she's been the one true thing in my life, the one person who is unshakably mine, and the idea that anything could hurt her or even come between us is unacceptable to me.

Harley is in love with her.

Blaise is a little too fucking interested, no matter how much he's fighting to ignore it.

And no matter how hard I fucking try, I can't stop

thinking about her and I'll hold onto this hate I have for her with everything I have because if I let it go? What do I have then?

Nothing but the fact that she might just love my sister like I do.

I keep my eyes on the road the entire way to Haven, no matter how tempting it is to watch her as she struggles to stay calm.

As the lights of the town come into view, she sighs again and says, "You have to stay in the car. I'm just going to talk to someone about a job. You can't be seen with me."

There's a black Escalade parked up the street with blacked-out windows that couldn't look more out of place in this little falsely idyllic town, with the bullshit fairy lights and the cookie-cutter boutique stores.

This place used to be called something normal and had the usual stores of a small Cali town, but when Hannaford was built and wealthy privileged students started shopping down here, everything changed until it became a bullshit town that caters to bullshit teenagers spending their trust fund dollars.

The only good thing here is Rita's bar.

The Mounty's unwavering stare at the silhouette on the park bench is all the confirmation I need. There's silence in the car for a second but when she unbuckles her seatbelt, I grab her wrist to stop her.

I might not know who she's meeting, but no one can take Senior on and survive. His pockets are too deep and there's too many politicians, feds, and cops in there for anyone to survive him.

"You can't have my father or my brother killed. Harley seems to think that's what's about to happen. You can't."

She stares me down with that perfectly blank face, and it pisses me off that she's not taking this seriously. If only she knew.

But she can't.

"I'm not ordering a hit," she says as she wrenches her arm out of my grasp and gets out of the car, pausing for a second before walking up to the bench and sitting down.

It goes against all of my instincts but I stay put.

There are at least three men sitting in the Escalade. I can see just enough movement through the tinted windows to make that assessment, and I have no fucking clue who they are or what weapons they have. I'm assuming the Mounty has that little knife of hers, but I don't carry.

Mostly because I know if I do, I'll fucking use it and Joey would be the first to die.

Senior has already made it clear to me what he'll do if I kill my drug addict brother.

The little meeting lasts ten minutes at most and I spend every last one of them watching everything. Watching the car, watching their backs, watching the three cars that drive past like there isn't some clandestine meeting happening here in fucking *Haven* of all places.

It doesn't matter how hard I look, there's nothing I can see that'll tell me what's happening here. The person she's meeting is a guy wearing all black, and he's a lot bigger than her. It's dark enough that I can only tell that he's probably got dark hair and that's about it appearance-wise.

He doesn't so much as breathe in her direction.

Fuck, he doesn't even face her for most of the conversation and it's only toward the end that he moves at all, turning slightly to face her.

I tense as she stands, but she just gives him a curt nod and walks back to the car, slow and steady like this is nothing to her and, fuck, maybe it's not. Maybe I've been sitting here watching her back and expecting the worst and she's just catching up with an old friend.

Fucking Mounties.

My eyes flick back to her mystery contact but he doesn't move an inch, just sits there on that bench, even after she slides back into the car and the door gently slams shut.

He's clearly not going to move until we're gone.

I start the car to get us out of there and it's only then that I notice just how badly she's shaking. Whatever this was, it was terrifying for her.

She did it for Avery.

It's that fact that keeps my mouth shut even though there's a lot I could say right now. I don't say a fucking thing the whole way back to Hannaford and into the buildings, up the stairs and down the hall; I wait until she's inside the room she shares with my sister and handing the keys back to me before I finally break.

"Whatever you've done, if he finds out—"

She cuts me off. "He won't. He won't the same way Harley's grandfather can't come after him. I'm not going to explain it, you'll just have to trust that it's taken care of."

There's this tired look in her eyes that tugs at my chest, even as I push the sensation away.

"Go get some sleep, Ash. Just forget tonight ever happened." Except there's no fucking way I can do that.

No way.

Ten

BLAISE

When Harley arrives back to our room and threatens me to get me to distract Avery, I think about arguing with him until Ash gets on board with it and decides he's going to fuck off to Haven with the Mounty.

I decide it's worth a night of pain to get him to change his mind about her.

I don't realize just how fucking jealous I'm going to be over the two of them spending the night together in my Maserati. Fuck, if it were any other girl I'd be betting on him fucking her over the hood because there's something about cars that just gets him climbing over a piece of ass, but I don't want to think about that.

It makes me really fucking jealous.

Jealous of him fucking the Mounty, the one we all spent freshman year hating and taunting and throwing every little bit of abuse at because she was below us and worse.

She was a danger to Avery because she caught Joey's eye.

Now she's a danger to us because Harley might kill us all if we try fucking *anything* with her.

So instead of dealing with any of this spiraling fucking bullshit, I do what I do best.

I get fucking wasted.

I drink so much that Avery has something new to bitch me out about, because she has to make sure I don't choke on my own puke all night when I finally pass out. Harley only drinks enough beer to deal with Avery's bitch-fit with nothing but patience and kindness so he's really fucking laying it on thick.

I wake up to a glass of ice water poured over my head and a seething tone in my ear snarking out, "Get your ass up. I need you to walk me to choir and I'm not going anywhere with you stinking like an alcoholic homeless bum someone picked up off of the roadside."

Ash snickers at his sister like this is all so fucking funny, but when I finally drag my ass out of the shower, Harley dips his head in my direction in thanks and I know that I've done the right thing for us all… even if I don't really know what it was that I was so instrumental in making happen last night and it'll still be hours before I can ask Ash what the fuck went down.

So I just grit my teeth and bear it when Avery looks down her nose at me for shit I didn't do and I walk down to our class with her, smirking and snarking at the other students as we pass them. It's the only thing that can help the pounding fucking hangover that's taken over in my head, until my eyes are watering and my stomach is churning.

We arrive before the Mounty and take our seats, still snarking about the latest round of bullshit that's being whispered about in the halls.

Mainly Harlow's latest conquests to grab Joey's attention, the brainless fucking skank-bitch. She's a fucking cunt and the only upside to being forced to be around her is hearing the vicious rumors about her and knowing how much of it must be going back to her parents.

They care a little more about her reputation and well-being than mine care about me.

Lips arrives with about three minutes to spare, looking a little tired and rumpled, and Avery assesses her every move. I'm sure she's taking in just how tired her friend is, but we all know how much the Mounty studies so we should be safe enough.

Lips sits next to Avery and smiles over at some of the other girls in class, rolling her eyes when Avery snarks at her, "Stop being nice to the sheep."

"Your green-eyed monster is showing, Aves. You know you're my favorite."

Avery giggles back and bumps her shoulder with the

Mounty's. "The only green-eyed monster around here is Morrison and he's too hungover to be any trouble."

Fuck.

Does Avery know— no. She's talking about my actual eye color, not the secret jealousy that's slowly worming its way into my gut every time I see someone else fall for the Mounty's charms.

Fuck.

I'm so screwed.

I roll my eyes to cover my ass as Lips looks me over. "Drinking on a school night? How very rock star of you."

I groan and slump down in my chair like my head is killing me… which, to be fair, it is. I spin a little story, just to make sure we're all on the same page. "I had no choice. Ash borrowed my car to go fuck a Haven chick and Avery cornered me about my own *evening activities,* so I tried to drown her out with bourbon. I think I'm going to join Harley in celibacy because I haven't found a pussy yet that's worth dealing with Avery's lectures."

Avery makes a gagging noise and Lips stares at me with this gaping look, stunned at my crassness. I guess I've covered my ass a little more.

Miss Umber walks in and starts the class, drawing the attention away from me.

Thank fuck.

"I have some exciting changes in your syllabus to

announce! Usually your final assignment for choir is to perform in front of the class but this year we're joining forces with the music students and holding a concert for the entire school!"

She's too fucking excited about this lame-ass idea, but I go with it, another distraction and an opportunity to hear Lips sing.

I want to know how the fuck she beat me… how she's still beating me.

"What the fuck is Miss Umber's obsession with individual performances?" Lips hisses at Avery the moment Miss Umber's back is turned.

Huh.

The Mounty really is shy about her voice then.

Come to think of it… I've never heard her sing.

Interesting.

Avery hums under her breath at her, lifting a shoulder in a nonchalant way, but Lips is looking sick, wiping her palms on her skirt and swallowing like she's got bile creeping up her throat.

What the fuck.

Miss Umber hands out her usual useless worksheets, designed to help the plebs pick which song they'll sing, and then giggles like she's flirting when I smile at her. I do it to distract her away from Lips because it's clear to me the Mounty is either about to puke or have a full-blown panic attack. Avery scoffs and rolls her eyes at me, but I'm determined to keep her away from the Mounty.

I can't undo how I treated her last year, but I can make amends.

The sweating gets worse and worse as Miss Umber continues talking, "The concert will be held at the end of the school year; choir students will sing in front of the entire school. Then the musicians will perform. So I hope you all take this very seriously, as always the majority of your mark will be determined by your performance. No exceptions. If you're not there, you're not passing this class."

Fuck.

She's really fucking panicking. Avery notices it, but only after the warm-ups start and Lips whispers in her ear again.

I glance at them both but I can't hear a thing they're saying so I focus on distracting the entire class away from whatever the hell is going on with her.

When Miss Umber notices that they're not joining in, I kick it up a notch and flirt mercilessly with her until she forgets why she ever walked over to our group.

I try to plan out what I can say to Lips when the class is over but anything I can come up with will be a giant red flag to Avery and my ears are still ringing from the last lecture I got from her. When the class finishes, I walk them out to their next class.

As I turn to leave them there, Lips hands me the iPod and I nod back to her.

We communicate better with lyrics than with words.

I find out why Lips was looking so fucking rattled after class when I get back to my room to find Harley and Ash in a fucking raging argument.

At first I think it's over last night, that maybe Ash didn't enjoy his little joy drive with the Mounty and things are only going to get worse, but no.

No, this is about Joey and his bullshit again.

Fuck.

"You can't go there by yourself; he's going to have at least ten guys with him. Do you really think you can take them all on at once?" Ash snarls, derision dripping from his tone, and I wince.

I've seen enough of these arguments in my time to know how this is going to go. I'll be breaking the two of them up in no time and getting my ribs broken in the process in a hot fucking second.

I throw my bag down on the ground and pull my blazer off so my arms aren't restricted, ready to dive in, but Harley's words bring me up short.

"Lips went to Haven to help Avery but she also went for you. Now she's going to the party to deal with Joey too and if I try to stop her, she'll just figure out how to go without me. If I don't go with her and have her back, I'm no fucking better than any of the rest of these assholes here. She's had our backs, even when we fucking hated her. I'm going. Deal with it."

And that's the end of that.

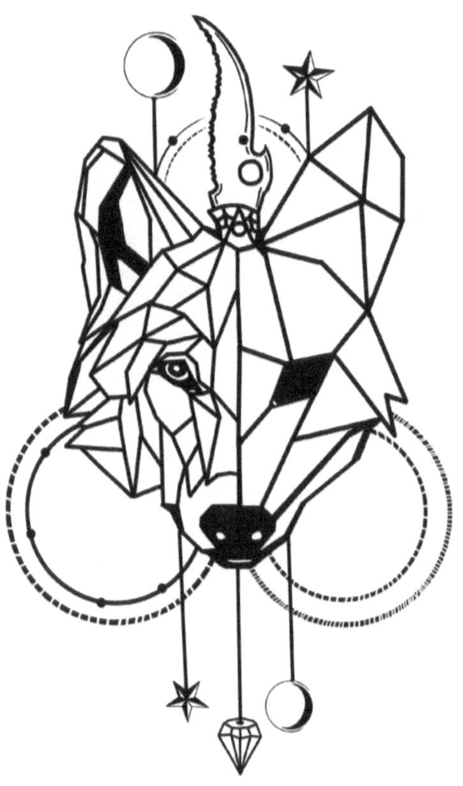

Eleven

HARLEY

There's no way Ash can talk me out of going to Joey's little party with Lips.

I shower in the girls' bathroom just so I can leave my shit there and have an excuse to come back up with the Mounty afterward. I'm glad I decided to when she opens the door to me, dressed for comfort but with her hair pulled back and makeup on.

She's unbelievably hot.

Something about not being a bag of bones anymore has softened her face, and she's gone from striking, to fucking gorgeous. Every time I look at her I feel like the air has been knocked out of my lungs and it's getting harder and harder to play it cool around her.

I'm pretty fucking sure everyone knows I'm fucking panting after her too now.

Tonight is the goddamn night. No matter what, I'm not

leaving here without making a move.

My entire body is buzzing as I lean on the wall while Lips locks up, angling my body into her and enjoying the sight of her shivering at how close I am. Fuck, I want her. I want her so fucking bad, it's kind of pathetic. I mean, I know it's pathetic already but Ash doesn't let me forget it either.

He shuts up real fucking quick when I point out how obsessively he watches her too.

The thought of her picking him or Morrison over me… fuck.

I need to make my move on her tonight but she's so fucking… jumpy. Literally, if she watches me for too long she startles like a rabbit caught in headlights and scurries away. Floss won't tell me a thing about her, nothing to give me a clue to why she's like this, but at least the blushes and shudders let me know she's into me too.

Something catches my eye and I curse under my breath.

I don't want to fucking deal with Annabelle's bullshit right now. I'm pissed at myself for ever touching her in the first place and now she won't fucking leave me alone.

"It's bad enough I have to watch Blaise leave here most nights now you're here with her too? Come on, Harley, what are you thinking?"

My skin crawls at the sound of her voice.

The attitude is just as bad, I know she doesn't give a

fuck about Morrison. He's nothing but dollar signs in her mind and that alone has my teeth clenching.

Lips stalking away, ready to bail on me over this has me fucking *livid* at the slut.

I grab the Mounty's hand and tug her back over to my side. There's no way I'm having her doubt me, not over this bitch. Not over anything, I've never been so sure of anything in my life as I am about her. Whatever it takes, she's going to be mine.

"We're heading out to Joey's party. Have a great night with whichever dumbass you're all dressed up for, Summers," I say, scathing sarcasm dripping from every word.

Annabelle's bottom lip drops and she looks like a fucking child, none of the integrity or backbone of the Mounty. Not a fucking inch of it.

She simpers at me, reading me out a list of shit that she thinks will get her back under me but the second she puts Lips down, the second she starts to throw shit at her, what little restraint I had for this clueless cunt snaps.

"I was born in the same city as Lips. I spend all of my summer breaks there. We have friends in the same circles. When I leave Hannaford, I'm going back there. I'm as much a Mounty as she is. Give up, Summers. I'm never touching you again. I never should've touched you in the first place."

I keep a firm hold of the Mounty's hand as we walk off, even when she tries to tug it away, never once looking back at Annabelle. Lips finally relaxes when we make it down the stairs, still alert but the tension in her body has eased.

I'm still fucking furious at what the cunt said about her, so I'm sure I look positively murderous.

The party is always held in the clearing, Joey likes his shit in the same place because he's a creature of many habits, and I grab whiskey for us to share.

She drinks it without a single flinch and fuck me, it's the hottest fucking thing.

The eye rolls at Joey's friends is even fucking hotter.

She deals with them like they're *nothing*, something even Floss struggles with, and then we move on to dance together and actually enjoy a little of this night.

There aren't many perks to growing up in Mounts Bay.

Knowing how to dance with her is definitely one of them.

Fuck me, that ass of hers grinding back into me… it takes all my fucking self-control not to just say 'fuck it' and bend her over right the fuck here. The grins and gasps that come out of her are like nothing I've ever heard before. I'm addicted to it, filing them away to think about and obsess over once the night is over.

If I don't have her by the end of the night, these

memories might just hold me over while I figure something else out.

She's fucking killing me here.

Finally she spins in my arms, her chest pushing up into mine so I'm panting, and says, "Let's get this over with."

For a second I think she's on the same page as I am, ready to leave this party and find the closest surface to fuck on, but then her words actually filter into my brain and nope, we're dealing with Joey.

Fuck him and his psychopath plans.

I nod and we weave our way through the other students dancing, none of them with half the skill or grace that we have, and further into the forest. There's couples fucking everywhere, a few of them definitely cheating and I make a note to tell Floss. It's always good to have ammo on the other students.

Lips comes to an abrupt halt and I plant myself behind her, the widening of her stance telling me a whole fucking heap about this situation.

It's the same stance she had down at the docks.

So as much as it kills me, I stay behind her, just for now. The second Joey so much as flinches in her direction I'll get around her and beat the living fuck out of the dickhead.

"This guy bothering you?"

Who the fuck is that guy? His hand slips behind his back. Fuck me, he's offering to kill Joey for Lips?

What the actual fuck?

Every time I think I know what the actual fuck is going on with her, something like this happens and I'm back to square fucking one with no idea of who the fuck she is.

"He's just a guy with too much money and too little respect for how things are done in the real world, boys," Lips says, her voice strong and confident. She sounds cold and calculating though, none of the girl I know showing through.

The second guy is shitting himself. He's standing there like he needs to climb out of his own skin to get away and his eyes are anywhere but on Lips.

"What'll it be then? You need me to take care of him?"

Fuck, I wish we could say yes. I almost hope Lips does say yes, but Floss and Ash would never forgive her. The twisted mess of a web that their family is in would give a saint a fucking headache.

"I'm here to go to school, not start a war. Head home, boys. Hannaford isn't the place for you."

They leave immediately, not a single question for her once she's given them the order. The guy who was doing the talking comes over and shakes my hand. I frown at him but, fuck, I guess this is what happens when I *belong* to the Mounty.

Once the car is gone, peeling away from the back parking lot with squealing tires, Joey turns back to us, completely fucking clueless to how close he's just come to his brains being blown the fuck out.

"Who the fuck are you, Mounty?"

Isn't that the million-dollar fucking question.

We should've gone straight back up to the girls' room after we'd finished with Joey and his shitty little attempt at calling Lips out, but all of that dancing went to my head. I don't want to admit it, and I've drunk enough to push it right out of my head, but I drag her back to the dance floor because I fucking crave the feel of her grinding up against me and if the rest of the night goes to shit then at least I'll have that memory.

By the time we do finally head back, there's barely anything left in the bottle and Lips doesn't even notice that I'm holding her hand again. She just threads her fingers through mine and accepts my help when her leg gives out a little. The alcohol stops her from putting up so much of a front and I'm fucking *praying* that means she trusts me.

Fuck, I'm getting desperate for a sign that she actually gives a fuck about me. Something I can work with, because she's the first thing on my mind every morning and the last thing running around creating chaos in my head—on the rare occasions that I get some fucking sleep.

I hate when I have to drop her hand so she can fumble

around with her keys, mumbling a little under her breath, but I take a second to clear my head before I fuck this up.

"I'm sleeping in Avery's bed tonight. If Joey comes up here again, I don't want you alone."

She startles a little but the door finally clicks and swings open, distracting her enough to get us both into the room. I stalk in before she can poke holes in my plan and strip out of my jacket.

Thank fuck for the whiskey.

She's not wasted and she definitely still has her head about her, but the jumpiness in her has eased off a little and I'm not worried about getting dick punched just for fucking talking to her.

We stare at each other for a second but she doesn't show any signs of making a move, good or bad, so I take one last shot straight from the bottle.

She watches my every fucking move with this longing, this hunger, that I could always feel simmering away under the surface of her skin, even when I wasn't entirely sure it was aimed at me.

There's no mistaking it now.

I offer her the bottle and she blinks at me, finally snapping out of the little trance she's in to walk over and take it. She downs the last of it in one go and carefully sets the empty bottle on Avery's custom coffee table, clearing her throat a little.

"Do you have pajamas here or do we need to go back to—" Her voice disappears as I reach behind my head to pull my shirt off because fuck no, this isn't a fucking sleepover and I'm not letting either of us puss out of it.

I've waited too long and played my cards too close to my chest to fuck it up now.

Her eyes stay fixed on mine as I unbutton my jeans and fuck me, the little moaning sound that comes out of her as I kick them away and stand there in nothing but my boxers almost has me nutting myself. There's no fucking way that she can deny it now, she's practically dripping all over the floor and I've never been so fucking relieved in my life, never been so fucking glad that every person we care about is miles away at some pretentious dance for wealthy assholes just trying to look important around each other.

I'm not leaving this room until she's mine.

Her chest starts heaving like she's been running a marathon, and her hands shake so bad that I start to worry she's about to talk herself out of this before I get the chance to show her just how fucking badly I want her, just how good I'm going to make this, so I taunt some of that signature fire of hers back into her.

"Are you just going to stare, Mounty, or are you gonna do something?"

A shiver runs down her spine and she licks her bottom lip, just a little movement but enough to have my dick joining the fucking party.

It almost takes me to my knees when she finally grabs the bottom of her shirt and yanks it over her head, unbuttoning her jeans and shoving them down her legs like she has something to prove until she's standing there in just her bra and panties, tiny little scraps of lace that barely cover anything. I swallow roughly and fight to keep my eyes on her, but it's hard when there's so much I want to finally look at, touch, taste, and fucking worship on display.

She's too fucking hot.

If she's not in uniform she's always wearing these big, ugly sweaters that look like they're swallowing her whole, so I hadn't noticed how much she's changed since we found her at the docks in the Bay.

Fuck.

I wonder if she has that outfit lying around somewhere?

I force myself to just stand there for a second, to give her every opportunity to back out or talk some more shit at me, but when her breathing just gets heavier, I finally break and just fucking lunge at her. I grab her by the backs of her thighs and lift her into my arms, pressing her into my chest like I can fucking keep her there forever if I get her close enough. She doesn't hesitate to wrap her legs around my waist, her arms looping around my neck as I finally get my lips on hers again.

This time, I'm not going to stop.

She groans into the kiss, that fucking sound that's going to rattle around in my head for the rest of my goddamn life, and bites my lips as I finally get my hands on that ass of hers, squeezing and pulling her in even closer to my chest. She's fucking squirming in my arms, rubbing against me, and if I don't get her on the bed now, I'm just going to end up fucking her against the wall.

She pulls away from me to take a breath and I mumble against her lips, "Bed?"

She doesn't hesitate to nod and kiss me again so I get my ass moving, stretching out on her bed with my back against her pillows and only pausing for as long as it takes her to get comfortable.

Then she looks up at me, her eyes a little unfocused as she pants slightly, and it hits me in the chest again just how fucking perfect she is. She wasn't lying when she tore Blaise and me down on the first day back, she is a broken little Mounty, but she's so much more than the shit from her past. I don't need to know all of the details to know that she's fucking it for me. She's everything I want and now I have her, I'm not going to fuck this shit up.

I cup her face in my hands, gently because she's fucking tiny in my arms, and when her breath hitches a little in her throat, I pull her back into my lips.

She kisses me like she's with me in this worship and, fuck, I'm done for. This is it. This is the only girl I'm ever going to fucking want.

Fuck. I can smell how badly she wants me back—she's fucking drenched, dripping down her panties and onto my cock. I want her so fucking bad; I'm at the point of begging. I've never begged for a goddamn thing in my life, never lowered myself like that and yet this girl has taken me to my knees.

Her hips start to move, grinding down onto me, and I have to break away from her lips to catch my breath before I finish too fucking fast. It feels too good, too much and not nearly enough all at once, and I try to distract myself by kissing and sucking at the skin just below her ear but that just makes her hips rock even more, every grunt and moan that I gasp out like fuel to her fire. She tugs at my hair and moans right in my ear.

Her hands thread into my hair and she tugs a little, pulling until I feel lightheaded.

Fuck.

How much did we have to drink?

I don't want to forget any of this and, fuck, if she tries to play this off later as being just a drunk hookup, I'll fucking break something. Fuck, I'll call her out on it too because I've never had a girl fucking drip for me like this before and there's no way she can say she doesn't really want me.

She fucking can't.

"Fuck," I mumble as I drag my lips away from her

shoulder. "This isn't how I wanted to do this. You've had too much to drink."

Her freakout is immediate and so fucking obvious that I react to it instantly, for once doing the right thing around her and not royally fucking this up, so when she pulls away from me sharply, snatching her arms back from where they're pressed into my chest, I keep my hands circling her waist as I pull my knees up to push her back into my chest where she belongs. I reach out to gently stroke the hair away from her face.

My voice is nothing more than a rasp. "Don't freak out. I'm just saying I don't think we should be doing anything more than making out when we've finished a bottle of whiskey between us."

She blows out a breath and I know I'm doing the right thing, even if I feel like I'm going to fucking die, when her eyes slide around a little like she can't focus on shit.

"You're right. We should stop."

Right.

That's what I need her to say, but hearing it doesn't exactly feel great.

One last kiss won't hurt.

Except, the moment our lips touch again, her hips move and I can't keep holding myself back like this. It's the hardest fucking thing I've ever done, but I pull away.

"Nope. No. We'll stop. If you can't kiss me without

grinding on my dick like that, we have to stop," I ramble on and she groans at me as she slides away, collapsing on the bed. Fuck. Her tits look like they're going to spill out of her bra and I didn't even get the chance to taste them.

Fuck.

She pouts up at me but her eyes are already fluttering shut. "You're the one that stripped off."

I scoff at her as I slide out of the bed to get some space before I change my mind, mumbling under my breath, "I had to get your attention somehow."

I rummage around until I find a blanket to pull over her, smirking at the little frown on her face because I stupidly think that she's just as fucking gutted about stopping as I am.

In the morning we'll be sober.

In the morning we can finish what we've started.

I'm telling myself that right until I move to tuck the blankets up around her chest and she whispers, right in my fucking face, "I can't fuck a Hannaford boy."

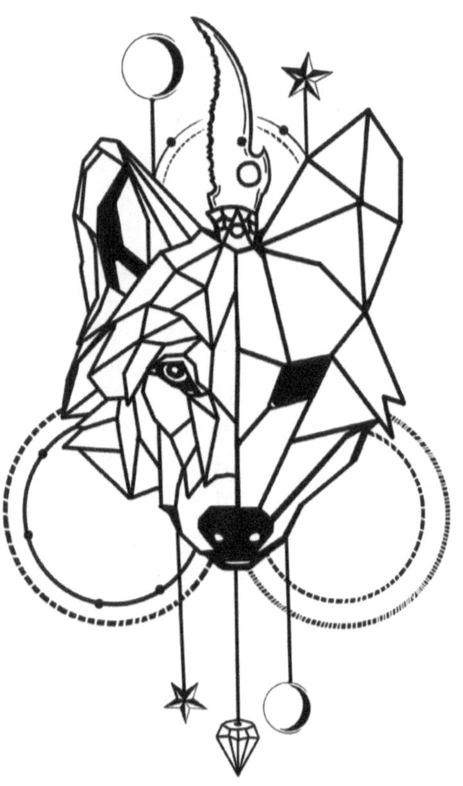

Twelve

ASH

Avery dances in the ballet like a dream, all of her hard work paying off, and she stands out as the star of the entire show.

Senior doesn't show up, for the first time ever he misses an opportunity to see us both and do his usual brand of terrorizing us both, because he beats me to get to Avery, and he reminds me of all of the things he could do to her to fuck with my head. It's not exactly original but it's fucking effective thanks to all of the times he's forced me to be involved in the sick games he and Joey play.

I can't help but wonder if this is what the Mounty did for us both, but there's no way some girl from the slums of the Bay could have arranged that.

We arrive back with Blaise and we walk Avery to her room together, helping to carry all of her dance gear. Blaise is looking hungover as fuck, thanks to his night of trying to escape his fucked-up family dynamic by finding the bottom of a bottle of bourbon, but he still manages to carry a bag and grunt along with our conversation.

The smell of whiskey hits us the second Avery gets the door of her room open.

Blaise's eyebrows shoot up, looking alive for the first time today, and Avery startles a little before slipping her shoes off and creeping into the room.

The Mounty drank at Joey's party last night.

Fucking *typical*.

Fury pools in my gut, but Avery knows me better than she knows herself and turns to give me a savage glare as my mouth opens to wake the Mounty the fuck up and chew her out. Blaise rocks on his heels for a second before he drops Avery's bag to the ground, with just enough care that it doesn't make any noise, and then he leaves without a word. I get a look at his face as he leaves, even as he ducks his head to attempt to hide the *gutted* look he's now wearing.

Fucking Mounty.

I turn back just as Avery steps over a pair of jeans that are definitely not hers or the Mounty's, and I almost bite my fucking tongue off to stop myself from unleashing a slew of vitriol.

Then Harley staggers out of the bathroom in nothing but a pair of black boxers and a queasy, pissed off look on his face, and I'm glad Blaise got the hell out of here. Fuck, the fight we'd be dealing with if he'd gotten an eyeful of this walk of shame… it would be catastrophic, and it's the entire fucking reason I didn't want the Mounty anywhere near any of us.

She's fucking poison.

Avery's eyes narrow at him and it's only when she points one perfectly manicured finger at her bed that I notice it's unmade.

"What the hell are you doing sleeping in my bed, dressed like that?" Even whispered her words drip with acid.

Harley shrugs and walks over to the walk-in, flicking open one of the drawers and grabbing out one of my shirts to pull over his head. "What the fuck else am I supposed to wear while I sleep? Even Ash's pompous ass doesn't wear silk to bed like you, Floss."

She huffs and props her hands on her hips, her eyes narrowed like she can smell the bullshit wafting off of him. "Why the fuck were you sleeping in my bed to begin with, Arbour? You had a room to yourself for the night, you could've found some slut to bend over."

She's baiting him and we all know it, but it slides right off of him without so much as a clenched fist or gritted teeth as a reaction.

He steps into his jeans and pulls them up, ignoring

Avery's huffs of indignation. "What, you think I should've left Lips up here by herself, drunk and passed out after we'd seen Joey and pissed him off? I had her back while you were gone, just like you asked. She's going to be hungover as fuck, you should let her sleep it off."

Huh.

I share a look with Avery because that's not at all what either of us were expecting.

He doesn't stick around for any more questions either, just grabs his jacket and shoves his feet in his shoes as he hightails it out of there. I kiss Avery's cheek and then follow him out, determined to not make this whole thing worse than it has to be, mostly because I've enjoyed the time away with my sister and I miss the hell out of her thanks to our arguing this year so far.

I head back to our rooms to unpack and grab a shower before dinner. Harley spends the time studying, looking worse and worse as the time goes on. I ignore it because hangovers will do that but when we make our way down to the dining hall for dinner, Blaise still nowhere to be seen, he knocks my arm with his to grab my attention.

"Who do you think is still giving Lips shit? Other than you."

My eyes narrow at him but his own are steady staring back at me. "Why? Who the fuck cares?"

There's a tick in his jaw as he clenches his teeth. "Me,

obviously. Someone is still giving her shit and I want to know about it."

I roll my eyes but I'm saved from trying to rein in my vicious answer by finding Avery waiting for us at the bottom of the staircase. She brushes me off when I remind her that it's not safe to be walking around alone and tucks her arm into mine with a grin.

"Lips is still out cold. I've messaged her to get her ass down here for food though, she needs to get out more."

Harley's face shuts down and when we get to the dining hall doors, he stops and says, "I need to talk to her about last night, go ahead."

Avery's eyes narrow at him but she finally shrugs and tucks her arm into mine. We grab food and take our usual seats, Avery distracted by her phone the entire time. It's probably fucking Atticus on the other end and I might have to talk Blaise into skipping class tomorrow so we can drive over to the asshole's place in the Bay and beat the life right out of him so I never have to see his smug, bullshit face again.

I completely miss Harley and the Mounty arriving until they both slide into their seats. Harley looks like he might flip the table at any second just so he can destroy something.

And here I was thinking he'd been pissed when we found him hungover in Avery's bed.

I turn to the Mounty to see if she's looking just as pissed off, but the sight of her bruised lips and the hickey on her neck smacks me in the fucking face.

She didn't just drink at that party.

She hooked up with someone.

She fucked someone at Joey's goddamn party.

I'm out. I stand up and leave before I can even really think about it, stalking out of the room and away on legs that can't move fast enough.

I don't want to think about whoever the fuck she was making out with at that party. I don't want to think about who won the bet, who's tasted her, who she finally decided was good enough at this school to mess around with.

I don't want to think about any of it.

I go straight to the track to try to run out the churning feeling in my gut but even when my legs are shaking and my chest is heaving I can't stop fucking thinking about the Mounty.

I hate her.

I hate her more now than I did when Joey called all of his social-climber asshole friends off of her, because Avery is fucking obsessed with her, Harley is in love with her, Blaise is doing everything in his power to stay away from her, and me?

I can't stop fucking thinking about her.

When I get back up to my room to shower, Harley is already there, getting dressed for fight club. Whatever happened in the dining hall after I left, it wasn't fucking good, because he looks like he's heading in there for more than just a fight, he's going there to take one of the guys out.

I drop my bag on my bed and head to the shower. "So the Mounty told you who she fucked, then? Are you going to kill every guy who touches her in a jealous rage or just when she does it under your nose?"

He doesn't say a word so I scoff at him as I shut the bathroom door behind me. I should stay in tonight and finish up my homework but, fuck, if running didn't get her out of my head maybe breaking some asshole's face will do the job.

When I come out of the bathroom after my shower, Harley is still standing in our kitchen, pulling a jacket on with that blank look on his face that says he's locking his shit down tight. Jesus.

Someone might die tonight.

"You coming? Morrison is MIA."

Of course he is.

I don't know if he's out there sneaking around with Annabelle in an attempt to forget about his little crush, or if he's found some new pussy to chase. I send him a text but he brushes me off with some bullshit answer that I'm going to call him out for later.

I glance up and Harley is scowling at me. "Are you coming or not?"

I smirk at him slowly, the type I know pisses him off the most. "Do you really think I'm going to go and watch you make a fool of yourself, fighting some asshole over some Mounty trash? You should really just get over your obsession. If she wanted you, she'd fuck you."

His jaw clenches and he gets this look on his face that I haven't seen directed at me since Joey took his mom's necklace, like he's actually thinking about taking a swing at me for real. We've always been good about keeping that shit in the boxing ring, mostly because Avery would chew us all out if we didn't, but he has taken a swing at me twice before.

I should've guessed insulting the Mounty like this would trigger his response but I can't help but push him, test him, poke at him to see just how far he'd go for her because I've never seen him like this about a girl. Fuck, of course he'd fall for the same girl as Blaise and of course she'd be the the bane of my existence.

Nothing is ever simple in our family. *Nothing.*

"Listen, I get you fucking hate her, and that shit is on you, but I don't and neither does Aves. If she finds out you're talking about Lips like that she'll fucking cut you out again. Do you really wanna spend the whole year fighting with her?" Harley grits out, the words squeezing through his clenched teeth.

Fuck.

He's really trying to convince me, which means he actually gives a fuck about keeping us all together. Avery would be so goddamn proud.

I pour myself a bourbon and salute him with the glass, sarcasm dripping from me because I can't fucking believe it's come to this. "Fine. But you didn't answer my question, are you going to fight every guy who fucks *Lips*?"

I down the glass and listen as he grinds his teeth some more, hating me and the air I'm breathing right now because even if I stop calling her Mounty trash, I'm not going to back down about her.

Finally, he grabs one of Morrison's leather jackets and walks over to me, a smirk back on his face. "She didn't fuck anyone at the party. She stayed with me the whole time. Someone is threatening her and making her fucking jumpy as hell. When I find out who it is, he's fucking dead. You in or not?"

He fucked her. He fucked the Mounty, or at the very least got off with her.

There goes the churning in my gut again. I set my glass down and take the jacket he's holding out to me.

We're fucked.

We're all fucked.

Thirteen

BLAISE

Lying to Ash about where I am is getting harder and harder.

I don't want to break Lips' trust but, fuck, Ash and I have been close since grade school and I'm fucking shit at keeping anything from him. He sees through it all and even if I can avoid him for a few days, after weeks of disappearing three nights a week he catches on to the fact that it's girl related.

When I refuse to tell him who it is, he tells Avery I'm running off to fuck Annabelle on the regular. When she doesn't *ruin me,* he figures out it has to be Lips.

I stay the fuck out of his way while he gets pissed over it. I'm too fucking busy curating playlists and sketching in my new lyric books. I'm a little fucking heartbroken the Mounty hasn't opened my present yet and these lyric books are still too *new* and *fresh* for my liking.

I gave her all of my favorite ones.

It's as confusing as hell as well because she refuses to open the box, but then when she thinks I'm distracted she'll stare at me like she's craving something only I can give her, like I'm the one person in the world that can fill the need that she has, so why the fuck isn't she doing something about it?

Avery warned me about upsetting her little Mounty friend when we'd first started studying together so instead of doing what I want to do, which is spread her out on the cushions and eat her out until she screams, I take her little pieces of my soul on paper to try to coax it out of her.

It's all of the little things that I never talk to anyone about but that Ash, Harley, and Avery all somehow know. It's the broken and bleeding parts of us all that somehow call out to each other until we're all circling the same fixed point in time. It's all the pieces of me that I find so fucking ugly but am completely fucking engrossed by and even though it's fucking hard to share it with her, the way that she takes them without a word is oddly comforting.

The problem is that the more time I spend with her, the harder it is to ignore the looks that she sends my way. We've spread out on the floor where I'm most comfortable on the cushions in front of the TV. I'm dressed for comfort with my shirt unbuttoned and she can't take her eyes off of me, not even when I look over at her in an attempt to get her to stop.

I'm only human, and I want her so fucking bad.

"Fuck, Mounty, don't make this even harder for me than it already is," I groan and she looks up through her eyelashes, licking her bottom lip like she wants a taste, and I'm going to fucking break if she keeps it up.

"What's hard?" she says, her voice dripping with sex, and I just about nut myself. She blinks at me and I assume she's just fucking with me, this is some new sort of torture she's thought up for me as a punishment for the bullshit that was last year.

Right.

Calm the fuck down, Morrison, she's definitely off limits. I tip my head back and let out the breath I've been holding trying to keep myself in check. When she clears her throat, I look over to find her blushing worse than ever and focusing on my homework again, mumbling under her breath a quiet, "Sorry."

She looks fucking mortified and I'm fucking lost here.

Does she want me or not?

Fuck, it doesn't matter if she wants me. Off. Limits. Morrison. I need to get my fucking head together and forget about this girl who is the only person in the fucking world who has ever looked at me and seen all of me without fucking hating me. Fuck, she sees parts of me that I don't even show Ash or the others and not once has she judged me.

Even when I was a fucking asshole to her.

Maybe that's the real reason I'm not chasing her like

Harley is, because I know I don't fucking deserve her. Fuck, none of us do. After everything Harley did to her last year, she used her secret connections to sort shit out with his family. She saved Avery from Rory even when they still hated each other. She's tutored me without ever accepting money or social status for doing it.

I try to focus back on my homework but it's fucking impossible now, especially with her sitting so close to me without actually touching me. Fuck, even that feels like a tease.

Am I going fucking crazy here? Probably.

Even blushing and twitching like she is, Lips puts together a page of notes for me for an upcoming test which I'm already pretty confident I'll do well in. Fuck, I've never felt this prepared for classwork, and while my grades aren't what my dad wants them to be, I'm going to ace them this year thanks to these tutoring sessions.

Her phone buzzes with a text from Avery to say she's heading back from ballet practice and I watch as she packs up all of her supplies. She's doing everything she can not to look at me and I decide that I really don't give a fuck about consequences anymore. I just can't fucking help myself.

I clear my throat but she ignores me, picking up papers and stacking them for no good reason but to look busy, all little movements that she does when she's trying to blend in when inside she's filled with that same chaos that I am.

You learn a lot about a person when you're spending this much time with them.

Yeah, fuck it.

I push up onto my knees and she startles, her head jerking up to finally meet my eyes, and I take the chance to push her gently back into the cushions until I'm covering her body with my own. She stares up at me, holding my eyes with hers for a second before she glances down to my lips, her breath stuttering in her chest as she makes this little gasping sound that fucking breaks me.

As I lean down, her head tilts so her lips meet mine and, even though that's all the permission I need here, I take it slowly at first.

Mostly because I can't fucking believe I'm kissing her finally, after *months* of trying not to think about it. The second she kisses me back, her mouth opening and her tongue dancing across mine, I lose myself in her lips.

She pushes back into the kiss, squirming underneath me, and I try to hold back a little, try not to put fucking everything into this kiss, but she comes alive underneath me.

She parts her legs and rocks her hips just as I break away from her, panting. Fuck. I feel like I should say something here, just so we can acknowledge the fact that Harley is going to freak the fuck out and then there's Avery and Ash, but my brain hasn't caught up to just how fucking *right* kissing her is.

I aim for joking but it falls flat when my voice comes out as a sex-filled drawl. "Is that better?"

I should have kept my fucking mouth shut.

She blinks at me for a second and then it's as though the little bubble we're both in shatters, her face blanching as she scrambles out from underneath me so fast I barely notice she's moving.

The moment she's on her feet she starts shaking, taking another hasty step away as she shoves her hands in the pocket of the sweater she's wearing. "Avery is going to be back soon. I need to get ready for bed."

Her voice is all croaky from the kiss, but she's back to looking anywhere but me.

Fuck.

Fuck, I've ruined everything.

I only stick around for as long as it takes to grab my shit, shutting the door on my way out and stomping my way back to my room.

Thank fuck I don't see Avery on the way.

That's my only saving grace.

I wake up the next morning from a fucking terrible night's sleep in an awful mood.

Okay, yeah, it's definitely guilt because I keep playing

everything over in my mind to see where exactly I went wrong, to see some cue that I must've fucking missed, but nothing jumps out at me.

I've never had a girl run away from me like that before.

Things only get worse when Avery arrives at breakfast with a look on her face that tells me exactly how fucked I really am. She doesn't say a word to me, doesn't look at me or attempt to call me the fuck out, she just lets me sit there and sweat about it like the true evil freaking dictator she is. Harley eats his breakfast next to me, completely oblivious, and Ash is too busy snarling about something that went on in fight club to notice.

Lips doesn't join us to eat.

I don't know if that's a good thing or a fucking terrible sign that my life is about to be ruined, all over a kiss that ended too goddamn soon thanks to my fat mouth. Fuck, I'd spent half of the night trying to forget how she felt underneath me and just how badly I wanted to strip all of those layers off of her to taste her skin.

Jesus.

I have to try to discreetly adjust myself so I don't have a glaringly obvious boner at the fucking dining table. I shouldn't be thinking about this again and definitely not now with Harley sitting next to me and Avery's harsh judgement hanging in the air, invisible to everyone but me.

I stupidly think that Avery is going to leave her vicious

scolding until later when we don't have an audience, but *fuck* am I wrong about that. When Ash leaves to head to his class with a kiss to her cheek, she only waits long enough for him to be out of earshot before she finally looks at me.

I stand up like there's a chance I can get the fuck away from her before she starts, but we have choir together and I'll be walking her down there to make sure Joey doesn't attack her.

Again.

Harley finally notices something is up, his eyes darting between us as a smirk stretches across his lips.

"You fucked Annabelle again, didn't you? Fucking *idiot*."

It kills me to keep my mouth shut but the smug, shit-stirring air rolling off of him will disappear pretty fucking quick if he finds out what the real reason is.

Apparently me keeping my mouth shut isn't good enough for Avery. "It wasn't Annabelle so he gets to keep breathing for now, but if he ever attempts to touch my friend again, I will end him in the most cruel and creative ways."

My teeth clench but I manage something close to a nod at her, stalking a little faster to class so I don't have to see Harley's reaction to this.

It doesn't work.

"What the fuck is that supposed to mean? Floss, what the fuck did he do?"

He gets a hand around my arm and yanks me back until we're facing each other. I stare him down because I'm not afraid of him and even if we weren't friends, I can hold my own.

Avery wedges herself in-between us and gives Harley a little shove. He barely moves because he's a fucking wall of pent-up anger issues but her scathing tone gets his attention. "Neither of you are allowed to kiss her. Don't throw stones, Arbour, now get to class."

Harley clearly doesn't want to let this go but Avery is a force of very deadly nature when she wants to be and she finally convinces him to get to his own class. She doesn't say another word to me for the rest of the walk but when we walk into the classroom, she tucks her arm in mine and smiles at me, a show for the other students because there's nothing she hates more than gossip about us all fighting.

Neither of you are allowed to kiss her.

Her words bouncing around in my head are enough of a distraction to get me through choir without losing my fucking mind about Lips pretending I don't exist. She just stares at the floor the entire time and I start to obsess about everything that happened last night because, Jesus fucking Christ, she's making me feel like I was a fucking predator or some shit.

Was I?

Fuck.

I need to just stay the fuck away from girls; this shit always blows the hell up.

Why did she have to be so fucking… perfect. Why did she have to be everything that I needed, everything I didn't even fucking know that I wanted, and also be completely unattainable? So fucking off-limits that I might lose my dick if I can't get my shit together.

Because even if she had've reacted well, we'd still be fucking doomed.

I make it through my morning classes without hearing a word my teachers are saying and when lunchtime rolls around, I head straight back up to my room because there's no way I'm sitting through another meal down there.

I'm supposed to go study with her tonight.

I'm not fucking going.

I decide that there's no point in going back down for the rest of my classes, because I'm not fucking getting anything out of them, and I'm about to get absolutely fucking hammered when the door opens and the person I least want to see walks in.

Well.

The friend I least want to see.

I really don't want to see any of our parents or guardians.

Harley doesn't look surprised to see me, slinging his bag onto his bed and kicking his shoes off.

"I'm going down to the gym, grab your gloves."

It's more of a demand than an invitation but I stupidly think that this means we're cool.

Boy, am I wrong.

My eye is fucking killing me when I get to the girls' room.

Fucking Arbour and his shitty temper.

Avery sent me a text while we were in the ring to say that I had to show up to my tutoring, so my mood goes from fucking abysmal to borderline reckless nihilism. I shouldn't be around people, let alone being around the girl I'm not allowed to like and her fucking keeper.

But I'm not a pussy so I show up, shit mood and all.

Avery takes up watch on her bed like she thinks I'm going to molest the Mounty against her will if she leaves us alone which only makes things fucking worse but I ignore her entirely.

It's a hard thing to do when she's glaring fucking daggers into my back the entire time.

Lips and I sit on the floor like we always do but everything is different now. Her eyes dart around everywhere like she doesn't quite know where to look and my gut churns over it. I'm pissed off, I'm embarrassed, I'm fucking gutted, but I can't say any of that.

There's silence as we work, thank God.

When the excruciating hour is almost finally over, Avery

gets a phone call and ducks into the bathroom for privacy. I shouldn't do it, I know I shouldn't, but I finally fucking snap, "You're such a hypocrite. You ran straight to Avery."

She blushes like an innocent little fucking maiden as she nods, and my heart squeezes in my chest. "I know. I told her exactly how embarrassed I was with my actions and I owe you an apology."

What the fuck?

She clears her throat and fumbles over her words a little. "Look, I'm sorry I was staring and making you uncomfortable. I was tired and not thinking straight. I'm also sorry Avery yelled at you for the whole…thing, I was embarrassed that you had pity kissed me and I moped to her about it. You know how she gets when she's in protect mode. Can we just forget it and move on?"

Pity kiss?

She thinks I'm uncomfortable?

When am I ever going to understand what the fuck goes through this girl's head? I'd put good money on never.

I can't help but gnaw on my lip as I think. I can't just say whatever pops into my head because that's how we got into this mess in the first place.

She kissed me back before I opened my fat mouth.

"That's not what I was expecting you to say," I finally murmur.

She shrugs, her eyes dropping back down to her hands

in the perfect pose of sheepishness.

I get one chance to fix this and make her mine.

But the moment I open my mouth again, Avery walks out of the bathroom and pegs me with a *look*.

Fuck.

Fuck.

I don't want her meddling in our shit, there's already too many people involved in this, so I play it off. I raise an eyebrow at her, all of my cocky attitude back in spades now I have a little more of the story.

"Where did you get that lovely black eye from, Morrison?" Avery croons, poking at me to start a fight. She struts into the kitchen and begins to make hot cocoa. Two mugs, so I'm not getting one, but I don't drink the shit anyway so no skin off of my nose.

I deflect her question, because it's both true and none of her business. "Arbour was defending his love. He thinks I'm trying to steal his girl out from under him and he can be a jealous shit."

Lips starts to fumble around with her supplies, avoiding both of our eyes, as Avery snarks back to me, "I didn't know he had a girl."

He doesn't and maybe, just maybe, she might pick me instead. I grin and pack away my textbooks and notes. "Try telling him that. Have a good night, girls. I'll see you both tomorrow."

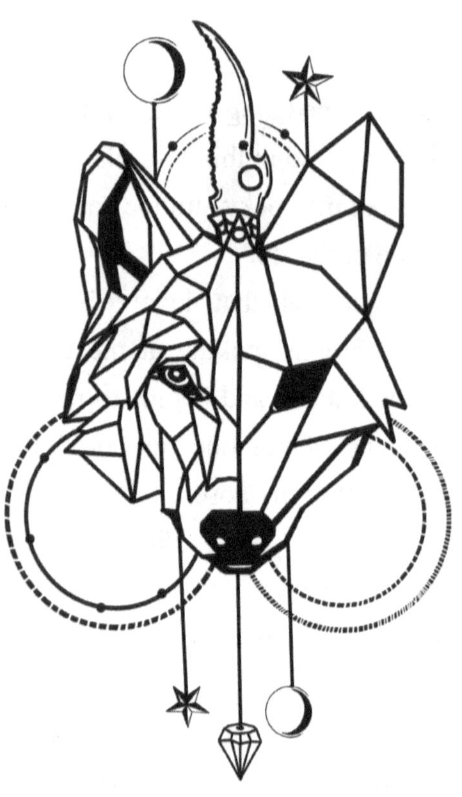

Fourteen

ASH

Father called, he has a new crop of sluts coming in from Europe. I've picked one out for you already; she looks so much like the Mounty slut that you might just break and play with her too.

I don't understand how exactly it is that I spend all of my time trying to stay the fuck away from Joey but he can still read me like a fucking book.

The morning I wake up to that text only gets worse as the day goes on. It's almost impossible to push down the blind *rage* inside me, the need to walk over to my brother's room and just fucking slit his throat so consuming that I take an hour in the shower. The cold water does nothing to put the burning in the pit of my stomach out. Fuck, *nothing* is going to calm it down today.

Nothing.

I eat breakfast with everyone and thankfully the

Mounty doesn't join us. I can't fucking look at her right now, not without seeing that text in my mind over and over again, until I'll lash out and fucking ruin everything.

I get angry at her for being here all over again.

I can't afford to have something else for Joey to use against me. Protecting Avery is a full-time fucking job, even sharing some of the load with two other people, and adding another vulnerable girl to the mix just isn't fucking smart.

Even if she has invaded every aspect of my life like some sort of insidious disease.

Fuck.

The worst sort of attraction is the kind that you hate because it really does become all-consuming. All. Fucking. Consuming. I hate her and I hate that no matter how fucking hard I try to stay away from her she just keeps drawing me back in.

I'm fucked.

I barely notice the absence of Harley and Blaise all day, or the fact that the Mounty doesn't show up for lunch or dinner at the dining hall either. It's not until I've showered and sat down with a glass of bourbon to take the edge off my anger, that Harley and Blaise get back to the room from boxing and I find out the drama I've missed from the day.

The second the door swings open I realize something has shifted in our family that won't ever shift the fuck back.

Fucking Mounty.

Morrison stalks over to the freezer and grabs an ice pack to hold against his eye, glaring at Harley like he's going to slit his throat in his sleep.

"What the fuck happened?" I snap, though I already know exactly who this is about.

Harley looks at Morrison without a fucking inch of remorse. "He knows what he fucking did. He needs to back the fuck off."

Morrison drops the ice pack and snaps back, "You haven't actually said that you're interested, you just sit around obsessing about her."

My hand tightens on the glass in my hand, the ice clinking.

Why the fuck do I care so much about his answer? There's nothing that I can do about it.

"Well, I am… so back the fuck off."

I knock back the whole glass and reach for the bottle.

I don't fucking like that.

Not one bit.

And from the look on Morrison's face he's just as pissed.

Fuck.

It would be too obvious to just tip the whole bottle back and start chugging so I pour out another glass and fix a sneer onto my face. "If you're so fucking *interested* why don't you grow some balls and fuck her? Oh wait, you did and she didn't want to keep you around. Maybe you should do us all a favor and just forget about her, cousin."

Blaise's eyebrows hit his hairline and, fuck, the seething jealousy in him is impossible to miss. I knew he wanted her but he looks like he wants to choke Harley out for claiming her first.

We're all fucking doomed.

Harley completely misses all of this because he's too busy staring at me like he wants to crack my skull open with the bottom of his boot. I know the look well, it's the same one Senior throws my way whenever I'm forced to breathe the same air as him.

I stare right back at him like none of this matters to me at all because I refuse to admit that I might hate that Mounty more than I want air at the moment but I'm just as invested as they are in her.

I fucking hate it.

Finally, he blows out a breath and then gives me a look. "I didn't fuck her at the party. No one did because she's being threatened."

I fight to keep my face blank but Blaise frowns at him, his face an open book like always in our room. It's the one space that we're all just *open* and *ourselves* in the world.

"By Joey? Who else would dare, we've been clear about that stupid fucking bet?"

Harley shrugs as he grabs a pair of sweatpants off of the clean pile on his bed and stalks toward the bathroom. "I don't know yet and Avery won't tell me a fucking thing, but when I find the guy he's dead."

Blaise frowns and readjusts the ice on his eye and I can't help myself from calling out to Harley, "So you didn't fuck her but you got a taste, right? Is she really worth all of this to you? Seems like a lot of work just to get laid when there's dozens of girls gagging for it just down the hall."

I don't point out that none of us have been taking that option, not for *months*.

Fucking Mounty.

He glances back over his shoulder at me. "This isn't a fucking game for me. She's not some piece of ass I'm chasing just for a fuck so don't treat her like that. I know exactly what went down that night and the only complaint I have is finding out some asshole is trying to fuck with her. We find him and we deal with him."

I feel like if there is anyone at Hannaford with a special interest in the Mounty, it's Lance. Well, him and Joey but I already have a close enough eye on my brother to be confident in ruling him out, so the little scholarship creep is definitely it.

Even though I don't really want to help Harley clear

the obstacles in the way of him dating Lips, I don't like the idea of anyone who isn't me threatening her.

The fact of the matter is that she's Avery's best friend, and everyone in our group is obsessed with her in one way or another and there isn't a person walking these halls who isn't aware of that fact so anyone daring to threaten her is going against us.

I'm not about to let that happen.

It's bad enough that Joey and his fucking stupid little friends all keep trying bullshit with us and none of us have time to deal with someone else.

Especially not some grinning idiot from Mounts fucking Bay, sitting across the desk from her and ignoring all of the giant screaming warning signs she has written all over herself that says she's uncomfortable in his presence.

Harley would bleed him out if he ever saw it.

"I'm the school photographer. I've got a good shot of you at a football game a few weeks ago. It's the only one I've seen you at."

The flirty grin he gives her makes me want to puke. "You sound like a fucking stalker. Lay off a bit or she'll realize how desperate you really are."

Lips' jaw clenches as her eyes flick over to me for a second before she looks at the Mounty. He's still grinning at her and looking deranged in her direction as he hands over his iPad for her to look at the photo. It's a shot from the only football game we've all attended together, the one that Rory was taken out on Harley's orders.

The last time the cunt walked.

It's a great memory for us all.

Lips stares down at it for a second, then she swallows and says, "I need a copy of this. Can you email me one? The highest definition you have please."

He smiles at her like he's trapped her into something, and it only makes me more certain that he's the fucking creep threatening her.

Why is she being nice to the asshole then? I've seen her punch a senior twice the size of her out before. Fuck, she took down Rory for Avery, the Mounty fuck is nothing in comparison.

When Lips hands him the iPad back, his hand brushes hers and he runs a finger over the back of her hand.

She freaks the fuck out.

I see red.

"Don't be a creepy fuck."

He smirks back up at me. "You're the one watching her like an obsessed boyfriend. Maybe she should be worried about you."

I'm killing him.

I might not do it here and now where she'll see and read into it, but the freak is fucking *dead*. "Run along, Mounty. I'll see you back at the dorms."

Something in my voice finally gets through to him that he's in mortal fucking danger and he gulps as he leaves.

Lips quirks an eyebrow at me that I ignore as we both pack our shit away. I'm ready to be done with today so I can go follow the creep and drag him to fight club to die in the most public way possible but then Lips says, "Avery wants us both to meet her for dinner in the dining hall."

I don't want either of them guessing what I'm doing.

Harley or Blaise.

I want to do it myself.

So I nod and wait for her to get her shit together, frustrated as fuck. I want her to tell me what the hell he's been doing, and I'm pissed at how badly I want it. I flick a hand at his empty seat and snap, "Did you really have to encourage him? You obviously aren't interested."

She sighs as she slings her bag over her shoulder, both of us heading to the dining hall together. "How did I encourage him? I never flirt back."

Maybe it's just the stark comparison of how she treats him even at her most uncomfortable or maybe Harley's claim over her has me spiraling, I'm not sure, but I'm fucking seething at the whole situation.

A group of seniors get a little too close to her as we get closer to the dining hall and, without thinking, I grab her elbow to pull her in closer to my side where I can knock someone out if they so much as bump into her. "You asked for a copy of the photo and you don't snap at him like you do when I speak to you."

She rolls her goddamn eyes at me like I'm overreacting here. "I snap at you because you piss me off. You get under my skin, you hurt me, you say stupid shit to me all the fucking time to get a rise out of me. But you don't creep me out. I'm never worried about you taking things too far."

My spine snaps straight as her words shatter my brain like a fucking bullet. I finally realize I'm still holding her elbow, and I drop it.

Why does she never react to things like I think she will?

She huffs and rolls her eyes again. "Settle down, Beaumont, I'm just saying you're a decent human being when you're not being an asshole to me."

A decent human being.

Fuck.

"Are you blushing right now? What exactly has you swooning? The word asshole?" The teasing tone she's using makes me want to die.

I glare at her and roll my eyes right back. "Shut up, Mounty, I'm not fucking swooning. No one has ever called me decent before and my reaction is one of shock. It doesn't happen often so you wouldn't have seen it before and don't expect to see it again."

I aim for scathing but clearly I miss because she stops and grabs my elbow, a mirror of my own actions. "You are decent, Ash. You're loyal to your friends and you protect Avery fiercely. You even protect me when you think I'm in danger even though you don't trust me. You lost your mind over the thought of your brother hurting me. Being related to Joey, and your father, doesn't make you bad."

The sincerity in her voice is too much. It's too much for me because I hate her, I've done everything I can to prove that to her, and here she is opening up to me with nothing but insightful kindness and I feel the overwhelming urge to prove her wrong.

To break her because nothing ever lasts and I'd rather be the one ruining things than having my world turned upside down for some Mounty girl from the slums with eyes that haunt my dreams.

She's the ache in my chest that I can't cure, no matter how hard I try.

When we get to the dining hall I stare down at her for a second, thinking through all of the ways that I could ruin this moment, and then I decide I'm too fucking tired for it today. I grab us both a tray instead and when she moves to grab one for herself, I snap, "Don't be dense, Mounty, what do you want for dinner?"

The Mounty fuck avoids me.

I can't keep tabs on his every movement without telling

Harley and Blaise about what I'm doing, and I'm not ready to share his death yet. He doesn't eat at the dining halls or hang around anywhere on the school grounds other than his room, which not only has a lock but a fucking deadbolt.

Pussy.

I seethe about it so much that Blaise assumes I'm still pissed at the Mounty and takes to getting me high as often as possible considering our classes. I'd love nothing more than to just drown myself and my anger in all of the alcohol and weed that I can, but I'm too worried about running my fucking mouth so I make sure to ride the line, never getting so fucked up that my lips loosen up.

We're all keeping secrets about the Mounty these days.

I find out about some of Harley's when we go down to his swim trials. We never miss going because Avery has her mind set on us showing a united front at all times and, with the competitive nature in us all, there's nothing quite like watching my orphaned son-of-a-mobster cousin absolutely annihilate the spoiled trust fund babies in the water.

He's *fucking* good.

Blaise and I arrive at the girls' door to walk them down and the Mounty is looking both grumpy and unprepared as she answers the door, her blazer half on and her feet bare.

Blaise does a once-over of her, subtle enough that she misses it but Avery and I share a look over it. He's fucking hopeless about her and I'm predicting a showdown between him and Harley in our future.

I'm not going to be a part of it.

Over my dead fucking body.

The stands in the pool are packed out and Blaise has to threaten someone to get us seats with a decent view. I sit in-between Avery and Blaise with the Mounty on Avery's far side, muttering and mumbling in a mood.

"What are the trials for?" she says as she openly fucking drips over Harley in a speedo.

The ache in my chest gets worse.

"A spot on the state team. Harley wins it every year and then when they offer it to him he turns them down," Avery murmurs, sipping her coffee before she hands it to me for a sip, a sign that I might just be back in her good graces.

"Why?"

Avery shrugs back to her. "He enjoys winning but doesn't want to take it further. I told him he should do it for scholarships for college but, until you got here, he assumed he'd be dead by then."

I don't want to think about the fucking O'Cronins and their bullshit family politics. Liam and Domhnall need to die for what they've done but so do Joey and Senior, and I have no fucking clue how we're going to make that happen.

Harley steps onto his starting block and gets into position.

All of the other swimmers keep glancing over at him, loathing and jealousy in their eyes because we've all seen this show before. None of them stand a chance, which in itself is bad enough for them, but Harley does it and then refuses the prize.

He just swims to remind them that his last name means nothing in the pool, they're all fucking plebs compared to him.

Avery straightens, jabbing me in the ribs sharply and I look over to find fucking Harlow sitting next to the Mounty.

Just what we fucking need.

"How the fuck do you know Joey's dealers?" she murmurs, quietly enough that I miss half of it but I get the gist of what she's mumbling about. Joey's dealers.

When the fuck— *the party*. Fucking Harley keeping secrets.

"His dealers or yours?" Lips says back, her voice louder and Avery snorts, muttering, "Typical," under her breath.

Fucking junkie bitch, here to try to threaten us on behalf of my junkie brother.

We should drown her.

Harlow flicks her hair over her shoulder and says, blithely, "Does it matter? They sell the best and they're rough guys. Joey's concerned at having his baby sister rooming with the wrong sort of girl."

What an utter load of shit.

I throw my head back and laugh because it's been years since I heard something that fucking hilarious. Blaise just glares at Harlow like she's a ticking bomb, here to ruin everything. Fuck, he looks ready to pounce on her if she makes a move at the Mounty who's stolen his senses.

"You better not be here at Joey's request because I've already warned him twice about provoking me. If he does it again, I'm not going to play games with him, I'm going for his throat," Lips says in a flat, no-bullshit tone.

It's my favorite one she uses.

Avery tucks her arm into her bestie's and holds her hand where Harlow can see it, a clear statement of cutthroat loyalty. "Run along, Roqueford. Go snort your lines somewhere else so I can enjoy watching my cousin wipe the floor with your brother. Oh, wait, you did know Andrew Wakes was your bastard brother, didn't you? Everyone knows you come by your slutty nature from your father. I hope you use condoms a bit more than he does or you'll have your own horde of bastards in no time."

Harlow curses viciously under her breath as she leaves and we turn back to the race just in time to see Harley touch the wall first, a full body length in front of his competitors. The savage pride I'd usually feel is gone because there's too many unanswered questions here.

"He really should join the state team," the Mounty says, and Avery hums her agreement.

Blaise clears his throat, his jaw clenching. "Are either of you going to explain what the hell she was talking about?"

Lips looks over at him, startled. "Didn't Harley tell you?"

Like she doesn't know. I snap, "He doesn't tell us anything that involves you."

She sighs like the world is on her shoulders. "Joey brought some of his dealers to the school and thought he'd be able to out me as a gang member or dealer or whatever. As I am none of those things, he was pissed when they left at my request."

My brain has trouble processing her words.

Left at her request?

I blink at her like a fucking idiot. "You asked his dealers to leave and they did?"

She shrugs. "I asked nicely."

Avery giggles and changes the topic, an attempt to distract me from that little bombshell.

It hasn't.

Not at all.

Fifteen

HARLEY

Someone at this fucking hellhole of a school is fucking with my girl.

I will kill the asshole, I will fucking gut him, but first I need a clue because after weeks of chasing down guys in the hallways, beating the shit out of half the male student population in fight club, and straight up stalking Lips around the school… I've got nothing.

Fucking *nothing*.

Everyone goes home for Christmas break and, like always, I stay behind.

Lips refuses to leave her room, no matter how much I try to coax her out over text, and it progressively drives me fucking insane. When she doesn't come down to the dining hall for the giant spread they put on for us both on Christmas Eve, I take matters into my own hands and text Avery for the spare key.

She always hides one in our room for emergency purposes but this year, thanks to her roommate, she didn't tell us where it was.

She's obviously worried enough now that she actually tells me where the fuck it is while chewing me out about being nice to Lips.

Like I need to be told.

She doesn't move from under her covers when I walk in. I hover by the bed for a second to make sure she's actually fucking breathing, my own chest going tight at the thought that maybe she just decided to take a handful of pills and end it all.

I know just enough about her past to be worried about that and not enough to be sure.

When I know for sure that she's alive and just sleeping, I get to work in the kitchen. This girl is fucking obsessed with food. I get it, I am too in my own way. It's like the Mounty kid trauma toolkit; we all have weird issues about food, money, and loyalties. Don't ask us to snitch on shit and don't ever, ever touch our food.

I once broke a guy's skull in three places in juvie for touching my hamburger, and it tasted like garbage.

But food is food.

I switch the TV on while I wait for the pan to heat up, the coffee machine doing its thing, when I hear the first signs of life from the sleeping beauty.

The groan is fucking obscene.

I have to swallow to get my voice to come out right. "I'm making French toast. Aves said it's your favorite, consider it a peace offering. I'm only good at breakfast so you're going to have to figure something out for us to have for dinner."

She doesn't reply, doesn't move, doesn't attempt to engage with me at all. For a second I think that maybe I've fucked up big time coming here and I try to explain myself a bit, as hard as that shit is. "I get you don't do Christmas but this is the first chance I've had to spend the day with someone since my da died. I've been trapped in boarding schools ever since and teachers really don't give a crap about orphaned mobster kids."

I turn back to the stove and start frying up the French toast, my fingers sticky with the eggy mixture. She groans again but this time she climbs out of the bed, fumbling around in one of the drawers for something to cover up.

Even though I've already seen her in next to nothing, it kills me not to turn around and get a look at her.

When she joins me in the kitchen, she has one of her ugly, oversized sweaters on that goes down to her knees. I hand her a giant cup of coffee as a peace offering and she rummages around in the cupboards for syrup and sprinkles, mumbling under her breath, "It's Christmas, we deserve some fucking sprinkles."

It's too fucking cute.

When the food is ready I make for the breakfast bar, but Lips redirects me to the floor in front of the TV instead. She puts on Nightmare Before Christmas instead of the carols and then we argue for the entire movie. Let's just say one of us thinks the movie is a Halloween movie and the other person is wrong.

She moans softly over every bite and I feel like I've fucking won something.

When she stands up to clear our plates, my gaze catches on her bare legs because I can't fucking help how badly I want to be between them, have them wrapped around my head as I eat her out every fucking day for the rest of my life.

She stumbles a little, her cheeks turning scarlet as she rushes to find some pants. I laugh at her because it's a little too late for that shit.

I'm already hooked.

While she's busy in the closet covering up, I head to Avery's stash and pull out a bottle of whiskey. It's the good shit, not that bullshit fancy crap that Blaise drinks when he wants to die. The shot glasses are a little harder to find because Floss deeply disapproves of taking shots, something about it being below her to binge drink her issues away.

It's definitely not below me.

I sit on the floor where we've just eaten breakfast because she seems most comfortable down there, like things are less of an issue when you're lying around on cushions in sweatpants and that's the mood I'm going for here.

I'm going to find out who the fuck is after her.

When she finally comes out, wearing a pair of yoga pants that mold to her ass so fucking good that it's still a win, her eyes take me and the alcohol in warily. I grin and hold up a shooter glass like a peace offering, praying she'll take the shot.

There's a pause and then she rolls her eyes and downs it like a real fucking Mounty as she slips down onto a pillow next to me, so fucking close but not actually touching me.

I take a shot and chase it with a beer, not wanting to admit to myself that I need the liquid courage. Well, courage isn't exactly it but I need to keep my fucking cool when she starts getting evasive and weird about… *fucking* anything I ask her.

"Aves told me you guys swap truths. I want to give that a go."

She arches an eyebrow at me as she rubs her palms on her yoga pants, a nervous reaction that's one of her tells. "We also choose our own truths. I'm assuming you want to ask me questions?"

I nod and refill the glasses. "We take turns asking. If

you want to pass, take the shot."

She pulls a face at me. I think that I've pushed too hard and lost her already but after a second she nods, and I can't help the wolfish smirk that spreads over my face.

Fuck.

I'm supposed to be playing it cool here.

"Ladies first."

She snorts. "There are no ladies here, just you and the Mounty trash. But fine."

She pauses and stares around the room, her eyes anywhere but me before finally going with a cop-out question, although the flirty tone is fucking amazing. "First kiss?"

I flick the lid from my beer at her. "Lame. Some chick in fifth grade. I can't tell you her name, I honestly don't remember. Yours?"

It's such a dumb question… until she takes the shot.

What the fuck? "You've got to be kidding me? How is that classified information, Mounty?"

"It's my turn to ask a question." She refills her shot glass, her eyes never straying from the glass and there's *no fucking way* I'm letting this go.

"I'll give you a freebie. You can insist I answer something if you answer this one."

When she finally answers, her voice is nothing but a throaty whisper. "You. Well, one before you but I don't count it because… well, I just don't. Just you because I also don't count Blaise's pity kiss."

A punch to the dick would've been less shocking to me.

I was her first kiss except… fuck, Joey attacked her last year. She threatened him with a knife to the dick to get away from her but that would mean—

Surely not.

The girl from the slums of Mounts Bay is a virgin?!

She didn't fucking feel like one when she was sitting in my lap wearing tiny fucking scraps of lace and grinding on my dick like she was made for it. Fuck. *Fuck.*

I grab the bottle of whiskey and drink it straight because I need more than a tiny fucking shot glass will give me right now.

Fuck.

Get your head together, Arbour. Because, even if she's a virgin, there's still someone out there threatening her and now I'm beyond fucking pissed about it.

There's a vulnerability about her now in my eyes and I will gut any man, woman, or child that might be a threat to her without fucking hesitation.

I try to save face with her, leaning back against the coffee table and smirking.

She looks startled but relieved, clearing her throat. "My turn. Why get a face tattoo? I know you have the chest piece but most people fill up their arms and even their necks before getting one on their face."

Fuck.

Knowing it's coming doesn't stop the wrenching in my gut at the idea of talking about it but I was hoping for a little while longer before she asked.

"I didn't choose the tattoo. Or the placement."

She blinks at me for a second and then when she opens her mouth for details I cut her off, "That's your answer. You want another question, wait your turn."

She nods and waves a hand at me to take my turn. I don't go for the throat like she did but I up the ante. "Worst memory?"

"Pass." She takes another shot.

For fuck's sake.

I roll my eyes at her. "Worst memory you're willing to tell me?"

She sighs and drums her fingers against her leg as she thinks. I'm sure she's about to tell me to fucking shove it but then she sighs and whispers, "What's yours?"

Fuck.

Laying everything out for her might be the best way to get her to trust me but this shit is like poison to me. Thinking about it, talking about it, fucking dealing with it makes my whole system shut down until I'm nothing but rage and loathing and misery.

I tip back the bottle of beer, draining it before saying, "My da being killed. My grandfather shot him, point blank, right between the eyes. If I close my eyes I can still feel the heat of his blood hitting my face."

She swallows.

She doesn't offer me condolences or any of those bullshit pretty words people say to make themselves feel better, she just sits there and really fucking hears what I'm saying. Fuck, I'm sure she's hearing what I'm not saying too.

Then she speaks and my chest feels like it's being ripped open at her own story.

"I'm pretty good at getting into places no one else can. I was given a job to take something from a well-known marksman. Gun for hire. Assassin. Whatever you want to call him, he was the best of the best. I was terrified but I was also hungry. Lonely. Depressed and lost. I snuck in, got what I was paid to get, and I made it to the back door before he woke up. I sprinted to the gate but my leg had only been put back together for a few months at that point and I wasn't quick anymore. Diarmuid pointed a gun at me and told me to give up my employer or he'd shoot. I turned and stared him in the eye. I thought maybe seeing how young I was would be enough to stop him but he stared at me with steady, cold eyes. So I turned and ran, and he shot me. I had to run for two miles with a fresh bullet wound, then I got sewn back together with no pain relief by some nurse turned crackhead. It got infected and I nearly died."

Fucking Diarmuid.

Just thinking about him has me pissed off. The way he'd looked at her the one and only time I've met him still gets me fucking enraged at the sound of his name. He'd looked at her possessively, like he had this long history with her that I'll never know about or understand, and at the time I was convinced they'd had some sort of relationship. That he'd fucked her and that's why she's fucking jittery around me.

Now I'm guessing the fucker is waiting her out.

Over my dead fucking body.

I nod and rub at my chin, enjoying the way her eyes are glued to the action. Her cheeks are a little flushed, enough of the alcohol in her system to give her some color but she's not anywhere near drunk yet.

Do I even want her drunk? Do I trust myself around her if we do get fucking wasted? Shit.

"Who forced the tattoo on you?" she says, a little hesitant but I'm ready for it this time.

It doesn't stop me from keeping my eyes away from hers, running a finger over the rim of my shot glass as the words tumble out of me a little easier than before. "My uncle. My da was the oldest in the family. He had nine siblings, four full blood and the rest were from my grandfather's second marriage. Domhnall was the next boy born and he's set to take over now that I'm out. There was a threat made against me and Ma. My grandfather didn't give a shit. He said casualties were the price they paid for being in the business they were in and Da should just deal with it. Da didn't trust his gut and Ma was taken. She was left outside my grandfather's house a week later but the damage was done. She now lives in an institution for the mentally ill. It broke Da and he left, took off and left me with my grandfather. When he came back to get me, he told the family he was out. They killed him. Then, they held me down and tattooed me. The family creed is actually '*Blood, Honor, Faith*'. They said that Da had put Ma before his blood, which he did. It's not something he was ashamed of but they tattooed me to try and shame me for what he did."

Fuck.

That's more than I've ever told anyone. More details than I even told my cousins who saved me from that life.

I take another swig from my beer, draining the bottle before I continue, "I found out later that my grandfather was the one who took Ma. My uncles all helped…torture her. They kept saying Da put his honor, his pride, before his blood. They're fucking crazy. The tattoo was shit, looked awful because I was only nine when they did it, and I was screaming and trying to get them to stop. When I grew it got even worse, stretched and faded out. Two years ago, Ash and Blaise dragged me to a parlor and we had it redone. None of us have good families, blood doesn't mean shit, but we chose the family we have now. So, when I got mine they both got our new creed tattooed too. Avery keeps saying she's going to get it done as well but she's an absolute fucking sissy about needles so I'm not holding my breath. I don't need her to get it anyway, I know she's one of us."

She gets this pissed off look on her face, like the idea of the O'Cronins just rubs her the wrong way which I more than understand.

I take my turn, asking a question I shouldn't be so fucking focused on but I am. "How did you go from being shot by Diarmuid to being friends? He hugged you like… like he had a right to. I'd swear that you'd slept with him if he hadn't made that stupid comment about your tits."

She rolls her eyes at me, blushing a little more. "Our mutual acquaintance put him on the books. We met in friendlier circumstances and he kept asking how I'd gotten through his security. When I finally realized he was impressed not pissy, I told him and then he started acting like we were best friends. I haven't slept with him, and I won't ever in the future. Even if my tits do fill in."

Her tits are fucking great.

You can hardly tell from the way she dresses but, thanks

to all of Avery's mothering and obsessing about making her bestie eat, the weight Lips had lost over summer break is back and she doesn't look so… fragile anymore.

And the ass on her would tempt a fucking monk.

I scoff as I open another beer. "Your tits don't need to fill in, they're fine. Da used to go on and on about how good of a shot Diarmuid was. I wanted to learn from him. I wanted to be just like him."

She huffs a little and then fidgets again, picking at the hem of her sweater. "Who are you dating? She seems to be causing waves in your tight-knit family."

I will *kill* someone for the gossiping bullshit of this school if she's hung up on this. "I'm not dating anyone. Who told you that?"

She shrugs. "Blaise. Avery asked about his black eye and he said he'd been making a move on your girl. No, wait, he said you accused him of moving in on your girl."

Fuck.

My head tips back as I exhale so fucking deep. *Fuck my life*, maybe the virgin thing makes a little more sense the more I think about it. She has no idea, no fucking clue about how badly I want her. I've been chasing her ass around this school all goddamn year and she has no fucking idea.

I need a different response to my usual shit.

"I gave him the black eye in the ring. He was mouthing

off and I got pissy. We usually don't aim for the head but I lost my cool and cracked him."

She fights a grin back at me and I think I've won. "Oh. So, no girl?"

I give her a flirty look. "Not yet."

Clearly she sucks at this because her face drops as she says, "Let me know. I'm running background checks on everyone we get involved with from now on. I do not want another Annabelle or Rory getting close ever again."

Right.

New tactic; I'm just going to start fucking saying shit and hoping she opens the hell up. I nod and take another long mouthful of beer for luck. She watches me and her thighs squeeze together subconsciously. Fuck me, I guess this shit is karma for all of the reckless shit I've pulled with the girls that came before her, because I'm going to have to work hard for this shit.

That's fine.

I'm playing for keeps this time.

"I'm fairly observant, I think sometimes you underestimate that," I say, my tone warm and coaxing, as I pour her another shot.

She clears her throat twice to answer me, "Oh yeah?"

"You're a virgin, aren't you?"

She panics.

I'm fucking right, the freakout that's etched all over

her tells me fucking *everything*. She's hard to read but I've been watching her since she showed up here and I think I've finally got her figured out.

I hold her gaze as I continue, "Yep. I'm observant enough to realize that Joey had to be your first kiss. You told me and Blaise at breakfast on the first day back after summer break, you said you held a knife to his dick. Now you've just told me I was your first real kiss and that the other one didn't count. So, unless you're out fucking guys like the chick in *Pretty Woman* then I'd guess you've never had sex before."

"How have you seen *Pretty Woman*?"

I roll my eyes at her because of course that's what she's focusing on. "When Aves sulks over guys she watches three movies; *Pretty Woman*, *Dirty Dancing*, and *Ghost*. I dunno, it has something to do with Aunt Alice. Stop avoiding the question. Answer it or take the shot."

She looks around the room and I start to fucking freak out with her because it looks like she might start screaming or crying or something.

Fuck.

What if— "If Joey touched you, I'm driving to his place tonight and I'm setting it on fire. I will burn that fuck alive."

She shivers at the viciousness of my tone, biting her lip a little. "No, it's—he didn't. He tried but I've found a sharp knife nestled against a guy's dick is usually a good deterrent. I'm more worried about the bet. How much bigger do you think the payout will be if they find out I'm a virgin?"

Fuck.

Fuck, I didn't even think of that shit. *Fucking Joey.*

I groan and rub my eyes. "I forgot about that stupid fucking bet. So you spent your first year here being accosted by horny guys trying to talk you into a quick fuck for money and every single one of them assumed you were up for it because you're a Mounty girl."

Fuck, we all thought that. How often has Ash called her a slut? Blaise was constantly on her about being a groupie, like she'd lie back and spread her legs for him given the chance.

Maybe that's the fucking threat she's so scared of?

We fall back into silence, only the sounds of us drinking to be heard. Her phone pings and she ignores it, a bad idea considering how freaked out Floss has been.

"You should get that. Avery is freaked out that you haven't texted her back."

She panics again but this time it's the type of panic I can laugh at, the type that's all about just how much she loves my cousin.

The moment the phone hits her ear she cringes and I burst into laughter, loving the savage looks she throws my way.

I don't even mind the interruption because now I finally have a plan.

Kill anyone who put money in that fucking bet.

Sixteen

ASH

We get back from Christmas break to Harley beating the shit out of every single senior in fight club.

Even with Senior missing I spent the entire time we were back at the Beaumont manor for Christmas dealing with Joey and keeping his twisted fucking fantasies away from Avery, so even though I'd usually be the first in line to help him destroy anyone with zero context needed, I sit this one out.

Blaise is all in for the bloodsports.

I'm on high alert for the first week back and I refuse to let Avery out of my sights, following her to every class and only leaving her if Blaise or Harley are with her at all times.

By Friday, Avery is sick of sharing her bed with me and kicks me onto the couch. It's comfortable enough except that the Mounty gets up at fucking stupid times and even though I managed to sleep through Harley's insomnia, there's something about her that has me on high alert and the second she sits up in bed I'm awake.

Frustrated and fucking savage about it.

There's something about today that's different than all of the other mornings though because instead of tiptoeing around meekly like a fucking tease she slams a drawer shut and stomps over to the bathroom like she's trying to wake the goddamn dead.

I cuss her out more viciously than I have in months, mostly because living together like this has fucking broken my will to live and if I have to live with that then so can she.

She snaps back at me, "Sleep on your own fucking couch then!" and slams the bathroom door behind her.

My eyes finally peel open and when I drag myself up onto my arms I find Avery staring me down from her mountain of pillows and linens.

"Do you have to be such an asshole to her? She hasn't said a single word about you being here all week and the one time she's in a mood you tear into her. For Christ's sake, Ash… she's not a bad person."

Maybe not but she's the worst type of person. The type that could ruin everything I hold dear in my life. "I am an asshole, Floss, to everyone but you."

She stares me down for a second and then sighs, sliding

out of her bed and pulling one of her dressing gowns on over her pajamas as she heads into the kitchen. She flicks the coffee machine on and starts to mess around with the cupboards and fridge.

The way that she's not bitching me out is fucking evil because it makes me feel like the scum of the Earth, something that doesn't normally bother me but today seems to be the exception for every-fucking-thing.

So I get up and pack away the pillow and blanket I was using, folding them neatly, then I join her in the kitchen to pour us both cups.

"Someone is taking her underwear. That's why she got angry when she got up, she's once again running out because some idiot is stealing from her to mess with her."

Fuck.

I don't like that.

Not at all.

I keep my face neutral but there is no-one on the planet who can read me quite like my twin can. Her eyebrow goes up and I hand her a cup of coffee with a stern, "Don't even think it, Floss. Just because I fucking hate sexual predators doesn't mean *shit* about her."

She smirks and takes a sip, crooning over the rim at me, "Sure it doesn't. Do me a favor and kill whoever it is when we find them? Not because you're just as smitten as the other two are, just for me."

Smitten.

I've never felt the urge to strangle my sister before but I imagine it feels a little like *this*.

The smirk on her face only gets wider as the bathroom door opens and the Mounty walks out and stops me from snarling something I would probably regret to my beloved sister.

I stalk to the bathroom, barely acknowledging her murmured, 'sorry' because I'm too fucking… *raw* this morning. I don't want her seeing anything on my face that should be there in the first place.

I hear Avery murmur to her in her most gentle tone, "I'll have some more delivered today and we can go see the ladies in the laundry to find out where they're disappearing from."

I close the door of the bathroom behind me and instantly get hard at the smell of her fucking soap which is utterly pathetic. Kind of gross too, considering Avery buys it for her and uses it sometimes, so I'm stuck staring down at my dick not knowing if it's fucked up to be jerking off right now.

Avery would kill me if she knew.

But then my mind supplies me with all sorts of images, of the Mounty in here covered in that soap just minutes ago, and my dick fucking *throbs*. Fuck, every night she wears yoga pants until she goes to bed and the soft fabric clings onto her ass until she might as well be naked.

I'll never fucking admit how badly I want to pull them down and bury my face in her pussy, my dick in her ass, and my tongue down her throat. I want to cover her body with my own, mark her up, fucking ruin her until there's no questioning that she's mine.

As I strip down and step into the shower my hand is wrapped around my dick, squeezing and pumping as I bite back a groan, before I even realize how close I really am to coming just from thinking about her.

It's so fucked up.

I've always told myself I was nothing like Joey or Senior because I've never wanted to own someone before, never coveted them like this, but once again the Mounty fucking ruins everything. My hand moves faster, my fist tightening as I chase the feelings curling in my gut until I tip over the edge.

I blow my load all over the tiles, my arm braced and my forehead slumped against them, groans ripping out of my chest at the intensity. Fuck, if jerking off with nothing but her voice inside my head is this good then what will it feel like when I—

Fuck.

No.

Not happening, there is no fucking when. I need to get her the fuck out of our lives before I completely lose my goddamn head over a piece of ass!

I quickly scrub myself down and finish up in the bathroom, my uniform feeling a little too tight and uncomfortable on my skin, but that's probably just a guilty fucking conscience. I'm supposed to be better than this, for fuck's sake!

When I step back out into the girls' room, they're both eating and talking quietly, neither of them taking any notice of me as I grab a plate and join them. The Mounty still looks fucking pissed but she's always so calm and kind to Avery.

Fuck.

It makes me reckless.

The moment we finish eating I grab Avery's laptop and join the Mounty on the couch. If I'm going to be dragged down to the pits of hell by this girl, then I should at least get to enjoy the fucking ride.

Imagining her while I jerk off will be much easier when I know what she's wearing under all of the layers she insists on.

She doesn't take much notice of me until I'm already filling up a cart but the blush she gives me is worth it all. I smirk back at her, drawling, "What? I don't know where Mounties shop. Is there a slum version of Agent Provocateur?"

She elbows me in the ribs but it's so gentle it barely

registers. "I can buy my own underwear, thank you very much."

I hate to think what lingerie Mounty girls buy. I doubt it's even close to my tastes so I shrug. "You can but after waking me up you'll be nice and let me do it. It's one of my true skills in life."

Avery narrows her eyes at me over the rim of her coffee cup, still seeing straight through every word that comes out of my mouth. "What would you know about choosing lingerie?"

Well, I could keep my mouth shut but where's the fun in that? I smirk at her, ignoring the indignation on the Mounty's face. "More than you. You've bought it for one body, I've seen it on—"

"Do *not* give me a number right now, Alexander Asher William Beaumont, I will smother you in your sleep. No sister wants to hear how many sluts her brother has gone through. Which reminds me, when were you last tested for STIs? Annabelle probably gave you herpes."

Gross.

I mean I know I'm clean, I get checked regularly even now that I'm fucking celibate. The bile creeping up the back of my throat is more at the idea that I'd ever touched Annabelle. I can't even blame being desperate because there were plenty of other girls available and I fucked them all.

It was just… fun to share someone with Blaise and Harley.

She wasn't the right girl for it, we all knew it from the start and never really did anything with her beyond the usual quick, rough fuck, but I think we'd all entertained the idea of sharing someone.

Fuck.

I'm too busy in my own thoughts so when the Mounty starts choking and trying to wrestle the laptop away from me, I almost let her take it, until she snarls, "I do not fucking need corsets, suspender belts, or a crotchless bodysuit!"

She does though, she really does.

I raise an eyebrow and continue to fill the cart up. "How very vanilla of you. All cotton granny panties then?"

The Mounty pouts like a child, arms crossed and huffing, while finally shutting up and leaving me to pick items out. Avery comes over to perch on the armrest and point out pieces she likes. I add them to the cart, her taste impeccable as always but ruining the experience a little for me because it feels weird to fantasize about things she likes.

Christ.

When I'm finally done, the Mounty finds her card details and I process the payment for her. I would've paid for the lot but she gets this stubborn look on her face and Avery discreetly shakes her head at me.

I don't like it and I hate that I feel that way.

I'm fucked.

"Why are you doing this? You don't even like me," she says finally, the pout still over those tempting lips of hers. Avery pats her head like she's the densest girl alive, which might be true here, and heads to the coffee machine for round two. It makes it easier to lie.

"I know you're going to fuck us over at some point, I figure why not have some fun until then?"

She glares back at me and Avery calls out from the kitchen in a sing-song voice, shit-stirring like always, "Baby steps!"

My phone buzzes in my pocket and I already know it'll be a text from Harley, checking the girls are both okay. His campaign to murder anyone who's ever looked sideways at the Mounty pops back into my head, and I can't help but wonder if her missing underwear is another symptom of whatever the fuck is going on.

She packs her bag together, her shoulders hunched under my gaze, until finally she snaps, "What?!"

"Who do you think is stealing your underwear?"

She groans dramatically and flings out an arm. "If I knew, it wouldn't be happening anymore. I'm fucking sick of replacing it. Whoever it is, they're taking them when I send them out to be washed. Avery thinks it's a prank and someone in the laundry is in on it. I think it's Harlow being a snotty bitch because I found Avery's shoes."

Fuck.

This is worse than I thought.

I frown at her. "They're taking underwear you've already worn. It sounds like a desperate guy taking them to sniff."

Horror fills her face and then her usual fiery rage kicks in as she snaps, "Guys are disgusting. Seriously. I'm putting a fucking camera on the door and I'm washing my own shit from now on. Fuck this!"

She storms out, the door thumping shut behind her in a temper. Avery hums from where she's drying plates, her hands steady even though I can see she's in full planning mode.

"Floss? Put the underwear thief on the planner."

She smiles at me like I hung the moon just for her.

"He's already there."

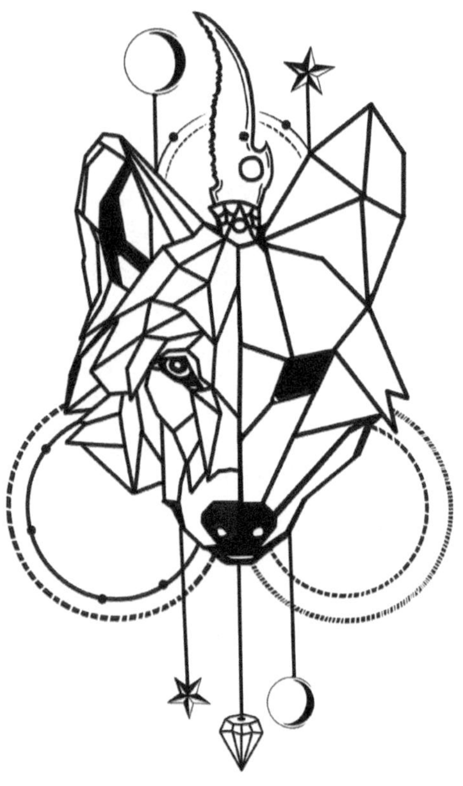

Seventeen

HARLEY

There isn't a senior walking the halls of Hannaford who isn't aware of the brutality of my vendetta against the whole fucking lot of them for starting that goddamn bet.

Sure Joey might've been the one to start the fucking thing but there's over two mil in the pot now and he's not that flush without his fucked-up daddy's permission, so there's a lot of trust funds pouring into this setup.

My original plan was to shut it down, but the first guy I approach is a fucking dick about it so that gets thrown out and the new plan is make every last one of them bleed until Lips feels safe in this hellhole again. I get angry at myself for last year all over again because things would be different if we had've just left her the fuck alone.

Fuck, what if we'd missed her altogether?

If she'd been some shy kid at the back of the class, her head down and completely fucking invisible, I might have missed her altogether. Fuck, without her around I don't even know where we'd all be now. I don't know what the protection she's giving me is, but Liam didn't even try to contact me over the summer break and he never fails to hold my inheritance over my head.

I fucking hate the cunt.

Ash and Avery both spent Christmas without Senior for the first time in their lives, the best present either of them could ever ask for, and Blaise is passing all of his subjects thanks to her tutoring. Fuck, he told us all that his shitty father kept his mouth shut over the break for once.

She's changed things for us all.

She's slowly changing all of the worst things that we face, the heavy burdens we all carry, and even Ash can't argue with that anymore. He might be a stubborn asshole, and not want to admit it yet, but he's watching her. It's both a good and bad thing. I want him to ease up on her.

I don't want him to fall for her.

Going up against Morrison is bad enough. The way she looks at him when she's sure he won't notice… fuck, my gut churns just thinking about it. I don't know if she turned him down over the kiss because she didn't want him or because of all of the extra bullshit she's dealing with, and the not knowing is killing me.

So I'm a grumpy fuck about it.

The grumpiest fuck, which is saying something

because Ash exists.

I'm beating the ever-loving fuck out of three of the most pretentious, arrogant fuckwit seniors when I get the text from Avery.

911. Meet at my room now. Lips was jumped by Devon.

My heart just fucking stops.

I'm about as far away from the girls' room as fucking possible, out behind the gym where there's no cameras and very little teacher monitoring, and there's blood down my shirt from Theo's nose exploding all the fuck over my fist.

He's unconscious on the ground. Ryan is groaning and wheezing next to him and Dean is swaying where he's kneeling, blood bubbling at the corner of his mouth. I barely think about consequences or not breaking his fucking neck, I just grab Dean by the back of his head and smash his face into my knee, knocking him out cold.

I leave without another word.

Also a mistake.

What's the point of beating them up if they don't know for-fucking-sure who to stay clear of? I mean, they know. Everyone knows. There isn't a kid at this school who isn't flinching away from me in the hallways, all of them fucking terrified because each one of them has done something to her.

Gossip, bets, beatings—they're all fucking guilty.

I have enough functioning brain cells to wipe my hands

and button my jacket up, covering most of the mess. My pants are wrecked but the charcoal color helps to hide that shit a bit and the fact that no one wants to look at me helps too.

Jumped.

That's not enough fucking information, not even close. Was she hurt? Did she kill him? Which part of this is the 911 because if she's hurt, I'm burning this place to the fucking ground.

I fucking *sprint* up to the girls' dorm.

Running isn't my thing and I'm nowhere near as quick as my cousin but I make it in a decent clip, shoving the door open and inadvertently taking Morrison out at the same time.

"What the fuck happened!?"

Lips is sitting on her bed, tugging her shoes off, and I can't see any damage to her but that shit is beside the fucking point. There's a whole lot of skin under her clothes that could be damaged.

Avery huffs at me from the kitchen, wiping down the counter without a word, and I'm about to call her the fuck out about it when Morrison holds up a hand like an offering.

"When I got out of the shower I heard Devon threatening someone. Then I heard him mention Joey and the bet I realized he was talking to the Mounty and I came out to find him pinning her to a wall by her throat."

I see red. There's no other way to describe the pure, unadulterated *rage* that enters my body. "What?! He had his hand around your throat? I'll gut him."

Blaise smirks back at me. "Oh, don't you worry, the Mounty was going to. Pretty sure he'll end up with a nasty scar. Really, I saved his life with the beating I gave him."

That's my girl.

That's my fucking girl.

Ash startles and jerks around to look at her, underestimating her to the bitter fucking end. She raises an eyebrow at him. "What? He's twice the size of me and grabbed me from behind like a little bitch. He deserves to lose his intestines."

Avery starts to straighten up the coffee mugs, compulsively and without even fucking looking because she's done it so often that it's all muscle memory at this point. "I think I should get one of those knives too."

Fuck.

I've never heard a better fucking plan than that.

Lips nods emphatically. "I'll get you one and teach you how to use it."

Ash grabs her hand to distract her away from her ritual, tugging her until she's standing with him. "Agreed."

She smiles at him, the type she knows will get her whatever the fuck she wants because Ash loves her more than he needs air. "Stay for the day? I'll cook something for dinner later and we can watch something Blaise picks so he doesn't whine at us. Like old times, but better because Lips will side with me when we pick snacks."

I discreetly check my knuckles for blood and Ash raises an eyebrow at me. I shrug; there's no hiding from him what I've been doing all fucking day.

Blaise huffs and fucking *whines*, "I don't whine, you guys just have shit taste."

I really want to hang out but the thought of dealing with him simpering the whole fucking time has my jaw clenching already. Mostly because every time he does it the corners of Lips' mouth quirk up like he's so fucking funny.

I hate it and then I hate myself for how much I fucking hate it.

I kick my shoes off, close enough to the door that I can ignore the daggers shooting out of Avery's eyes, and say, "If he's picking I'm going to need a beer."

I head to the kitchen to wash my hands and Ash covers for me by rifling through the cupboards and saying, "Fuck it, I need something stronger than beer to get through this. Where are you hiding the good stuff, Floss?"

Lips doesn't notice what we're up to, or it's not important enough to register in that super genius brain of hers, and she stalks over to get settled onto the couch.

Avery fucking preens with satisfaction, homemaking joy just fucking *oozing* out of her at us all being here together.

She glances down at my knuckles but doesn't say a word about it as she messes around with the coffee machine and gets shit together for her and Lips. She already knows that if she doesn't hand the kid from Mounts Bay food, she'll just starve.

They all broke me out of that shit years ago.

I grab enough beer to deal with whatever bullshit Ash and Morrison are going to pull on us all and then park my ass on the couch next to Lips. Floss leans forward to give me a look but I ignore it easier than breathing at this point.

I pointedly refuse to look Ash's way and catch the seething jealous judgement from his hypocritical ass.

I get started on the beer and even grab a handful of the popcorn in Lips' lap, trying not to get pissed the fuck off at how uncomfortable she seems to be jammed between me and Floss. She wasn't at all fucking uncomfortable when she was grinding on my dick but, for my own goddamn sanity, I let it slide.

Until she sighs and nudges me gently.

"Can you grab me the blanket you're sitting on? My nipples can cut glass at this point and I'm not ruining my new bras."

Fuck.

I can't be thinking about her tits right now or her

nipples, which I was fucking robbed of seeing by a bottle of whiskey and my own fucking conscience.

Avery giggles as I scoff, shifting and handing her the blanket. Ash watches the three of us like we're prey and then gives Lips a sly look, drawling out, "Which ones are you wearing today?"

She chokes on her coffee, sputtering, "Uh no, my underwear choices are not going to be a daily conversation starter."

Two things become very clear to me.

Lips and Ash have been hanging out without me being aware of it, and I don't fucking like it. This feels like Ash's warped version of flirting and there isn't enough beer in the fucking world for me to sit through it without breaking his fucking jaw.

Ash shrugs. "Might help me like you."

"Hard pass," she snipes back and I thank small mercies that at least she's not playing along. Fuck's sake.

"They say women pick their colors according to their moods, so which is it Mounty. Red? Are you feeling feisty today?"

She throws a pillow at his head which saves his life because Avery uses the distraction to text me all of the ways I'll fuck everything up if I say a goddamn word right now. I hate her almost as much as I hate Ash right now, but I keep my mouth shut and let my Mounty girl deal with him on her own.

"Black, now fuck off."

"Depressed or horny?"

Blood explodes in my mouth as I damn near bite my tongue off to stop myself from butting the fuck in. To her credit, Floss is just as pissed but the biggest surprise comes when Morrison steps the fuck up and snaps, "Lay off, man. She's not here so you can poke and prod at her for your own enjoyment."

Ash shrugs and drinks his bourbon like this is all nothing.

It's not fucking nothing.

I ignore the look Avery shoots my way, and snap at Ash, "Why are you asking her about her underwear?"

Lips panics.

She fucking *panics* as Ash smirks at me and says, "We picked out her entire collection together this week. Why do you care?"

I'm going to kill him.

Lips nudges me again, always so fucking gently like she thinks she'd actually be able to hurt me, and says, "He decided our path to friendship is going to be paved in lace. I decided he's a perv and it's easier to let him go than fight it."

He fucking would too.

"Crap, we haven't gone down to the laundry yet to ask

about the thief," Avery mumbles but she doesn't look up from her phone.

Thief?

Blaise looks up from the floor at us. "Someone is stealing your underwear?"

"Her *used* underwear," says Ash.

What.

The.

Fuck?!

I glance down at her but she's staring up at me like this is all so fucking normal, like I didn't just find out that there's a whole new fucking subset of bullshit going on with her that I need to sort out. "Are you a magnet for fucked up shit and psychos?"

Avery laughs. "Why yes, Arbour, she is."

Eighteen

BLAISE

The first time my father told me I was a mistake was the day my manager came home with a NDA he'd forced out of a groupie who'd taken photos of me eating her out after one of my first gigs. I was too fucking drunk, and young and stupid, to do a decent job of it and she was out there in the world talking shit about me.

My straight-laced, incredibly bigoted father almost dropped fucking dead on the spot.

Sometimes I imagine that Blaine Morrison must only have bland missionary sex in the fucking dark on a night that's been marked in the calendar for the last six months, because that's the good and proper thing to do. It makes me sick to my fucking stomach.

So I already know exactly what the fallout is going to be when my agent calls me with the news of what Annabelle has done. It has to be Annabelle, she's the only bitch who hasn't given up on chasing us all. Fuck, she's still panting after my trust fund and Ash's billions every chance she gets.

Explaining this to my father doesn't fucking work, all he sees is his fuck-up son once again making mistakes, so I do what I always fucking do when I know I'm going to have to deal with this.

I get fucking wasted.

I head back to my room from the dining hall before anyone can stop me and I start with Ash's top-shelf bourbon, sculling that shit down until I find myself at the bottom of the bottle.

Then I start in on Harley's whiskey.

He keeps this shit for emergencies, some Mounty fucking quirk he has that none of us question because that's what friends do, but it barely touches the sides as I chug it down.

"*Jesus fucking Christ*, I told you there was something wrong."

The bottle is wrenched out of my hands. I'd put up a fight to keep ahold of it but the perfume is Avery's and I'd never, ever fucking disrespect her or Ash like that. If she broke a nail in the struggle? No fucking thanks, the fallout isn't worth the shitty whiskey.

"What the hell are you doing letting that fucking snake into your room? Morrison—"

"Drop it, Floss, he's already in the fucking hole."

The hole.

The deep, dark place inside of me that swallows me until there's nothing fucking left. Sometimes it feels fucking pathetic to be here because Harley watched his dad's brains get fucking scrambled and Avery was choked to death by her own brother.

Why do I get to be this depressed over my asshole father?

Words aren't that fucking bad, Morrison, for fuck's sake.

"Just shut up and put your fucking arm around my neck. We're going to the girls' room. Hold the hell onto me, I'll be fucking pissed if you eat dirt right now."

My words are slurred and running into each other as I fumble out, "I'm fucking pathetic."

We're about the same height and Ash is a fucking solid wall when he wants to be, draping my drunk ass over himself as he walks for both of us. "He's pathetic, not you. You were drinking and having fun in the photos, they're nothing. If he's pissed about the letters then that's his own shit, not yours."

My legs stumble underneath me but Ash's grip never falters, muttering under his breath about how all fathers should just be wiped off of the face of the Earth, and I guess I can get behind that sentiment.

I finally open my eyes back up when we stop, Avery furiously texting in one hand and unlocking her door with the other.

I wonder if Lips will be here?

Ash probably wouldn't let her come here but I wish she would be. I wish she could just… be here.

The door finally shoves open and Avery stalks in, leaving Ash to move me by himself. "Sit him on the couch! I'll grab the bed out and then I'll deal with this."

Except Lips is here, and she gets to work rolling the spare bed out from under one of the beds, frowning and glancing over to where Ash sets me down on the couch.

I feel both pathetic and relieved she's here.

Avery collapses on her bed and starts furiously texting.

"Can someone please explain to me what the fuck is going on?" Lips says, hesitant even as she witnesses this new low of mine for the first time.

Oh no.

Nope.

Goodbye whiskey, my stomach starts to heave right as Arbour saves the day by shoving a bucket under my nose. Ash parks his ass next to me, ready to jump in if I pass out in a pile of my own puke, and this right here is the reason why I won't jump off the roof.

This lot are worth the pain of living, even if I am in the goddamn hole again.

"Didn't you read it? See the photos?" Ash snaps and if I wasn't swallowing bile down, I'd call him out for being an ass to her.

"Obviously not. If it's personal then I'm not fucking looking."

That's pretty fucking nice of her.

I puke.

I puke so hard I feel the blood vessels around my eyes burst, and I want to *die*. Downing two bottles of spirits like that wasn't fucking clever. It was a shit decision and maybe I do need to grow the fuck up a bit, get over this self-destruct mode I've built into my being. Harley grabs a bottle of water out of the fridge and presses it into the back of my neck. He's an asshole most of the time, but he's still one of my best fucking friends.

Dammit, now I want to fucking cry over this like a pussy.

I need a beer.

"It's Annabelle right? It has to be; she's the only one who's been in our room. Dammit Morrison, I told you not to let her in there! She's a fucking snake," Harley says as he starts to pace again.

Ash groans. "Drop it. It's out now; all we can do is deal with the fallout."

Then my goddamn, fucking asshole of a phone rings and the entire room stops breathing.

We all know who it is.

I'm fucked.

"Just leave it; you can speak to him tomorrow," says Ash, in a tone he usually only uses at Avery. A knot forms in my stomach.

"I'll get it out of the way now. No use putting it off," I mumble and then I hit answer, the tirade of vitriol starting down the line before I get the phone to my ear.

"—incompetent, selfish cunt! You're paying someone to take your tests for you, aren't you? I knew it. I told your mother there's no way you'd get your GPA up on your own. My God, is it too much to ask for you to think about someone other than yourself for once? How was I cursed with such a fucking useless excuse of a son?"

I should hang up.

I know it, but sometimes I think I'm addicted to this kind of pain… like something in me is so fucking twisted and perverse that the gut-wrenching feeling of my own father telling me how fucking terrible I am soothes me.

I mean, if by soothing I mean tearing my soul up into strips, lighting that shit on fire, and then burning it to the ground.

"Do you have any idea how shameful it is for me to see these photos? I'll have to deal with the fallout at the next Kora board meeting; I have important stakeholders who respect me, and now they're going to be too busy fucking gossiping about my delinquent son to focus on what's happening in my business. If you can't pull your fucking head in then I'm cutting you off. Say goodbye to every last luxury in your life; I'm done bankrolling your deviant lifestyle."

That doesn't faze me at all really. He only pays for my phone on the regular, and Ash will get me a new one the second my dad cuts it off. It's more the idea of him cutting me off that stings.

I should really tell that to Annabelle to get her to leave me the fuck alone.

"I suppose we should be grateful it's not that Beaumont boy with you; I suppose you have *those* photos locked down tightly."

Of course.

Because I couldn't possibly offer Ash or Harley or Avery anything but my fucking body in my father's eyes. It doesn't matter how many times I tell him that I'm straight, I must be a fucking defect in his bigoted eyes.

"If I find out you've shown those letters to anyone else, boy, I will ruin you. I'm already trying to get rid of you, the succession plan has changed, but if you try this shit again to drag me to hell with you, I will ruin you."

Finally he gets sick of listening to his own goddamn voice and hangs up.

I throw my phone at the wall.

If he's going to cut it off anyway, why the fuck not?

"Well, that'll shut him up," Ash drawls, opening the bottle of water and pressing it into my hand.

It won't though.

Nothing ever shuts him up.

I drink myself into an oblivion all day Thursday.

Lips doesn't drink with me—annoying as hell because a drunken hookup is exactly what I need to get me through this—but she skips classes to babysit me. Only, it doesn't really feel like the usual suicide watch that I'm put on when I'm in the hole.

She wakes up before I do, and she makes me French toast for breakfast. I don't want to eat, because it'll take me longer to get wasted later, but the syrup and rainbow sprinkles are so fucking out of place that I find myself taking the plate from her and digging in. They're delicious and in the quiet of the morning room, I find myself calm for the first time in what feels like weeks.

Doesn't stop me from chugging back the drinks all day.

She studies and cleans, folds laundry, scrubs at a pair of her Docs, paints her toenails, reads a book… she does everything possible in this tiny fucking room while she watches me slam back drink after drink.

I can't remember passing out, but I wake up Friday

morning lying in the rollout bed with my head over one side, heaving into a bucket while Avery mumbles curses and threats at me as she wipes down my sweaty brow.

When I stumble out of the shower later, the alcohol is gone, disappeared, *poof* into thin air.

I'm like a fucking crackhead chasing a hit, and this is not the bullshit I signed up for. When I finally find the stash, Lips narcs on me to Arbour and the fucking traitor comes running for his little love, taking all of the booze with a smirk my way.

I think about killing them both.

By Saturday, I'm climbing the fucking walls and even Lips is sick of listening to me rage about sobriety. It doesn't make her give in though, fuck my actual life. Her answer is always fucking *coffee*.

"Fuck coffee, haven't you ever heard of the hair of the dog? I need tequila."

But still she doesn't break.

I refuse to admit that the only reason any of this is fun for me is that I get to be here with her, messing with her and watching her rein herself in. She always holds back around me, and I find myself poking and prodding at her more and more just to see if she'll snap.

It backfires on me when the others get home to see it.

Ash smirks when he sees the look on Lips' face, joy oozing out of him at the thought of me pissing her off. It gets my hackles up, like me pissing her off is fine but him enjoying it takes shit too far.

I'm completely fucked in the head.

"How is suicide watch going? Have you hidden the bed sheets from him yet? Why are you still using real forks? You should switch out to plastic until he's come down from the ledge."

Harley walks in with arms full of my shit, including a guitar so at least I'll have something worth doing tomorrow.

"He's better. He spent all morning whining before I left so progress is being made." I almost miss the cutting edge to Avery's voice as I watch Lips and Harley circle each other.

Fuck.

I think she likes him too.

Fuck.

If they're going to start dating I need more alcohol, like fucking *now*. "I wouldn't be whining if you let me fucking drink. The Mounty is practically a fucking AA sponsor and she needs to lighten the hell up. Let's go to the bar in Haven; they do the best cheese fries."

Lips glares over at me as Harley hands over stacks of paperwork, notes he's taken just for her.

Fuck, she really is falling for him and his nerd brain.

"Drinking is making it worse. Harley brought your guitar, write a song and chill the fuck out. Eat ice cream.

Watch your shitty movies. Do homework. Do *not* drink and do *not* get high," Lips drawls, and Ash glances between us all like there's a love triangle going on… except there's not.

Lips and Harley are in love, and I'm fucking *worthless*.

I kick the coffee table.

Dumb move. I know the second the thump reverberates through the room that I've royally fucked up and, sure enough, Avery cusses me the fuck out.

She marches over to me and jabs me in the chest sharply. "Just so you know, you ungrateful little shit, I've had the posts taken down and I've contacted your agent to release a statement on your behalf claiming the entire thing was a slanderous hoax concocted by a jilted ex. He doesn't give a shit about the photos and the press is lapping it up. You've even had a spike in sales! I've also burned the letters and sent your father a gift basket with a lovely note telling him to choke on the fucking pretzels. Ash and Harley will now be opening, reading, and destroying any correspondence from that man before you see it. So get up. Eat something substantial, have a shower, do your homework. No one fucking cares that your dear old daddy is scum. I don't, Ash and Harley don't, and, if she were honest, Lips would tell you to tuck your vagina back into your jeans and get over it."

Well.

I guess I should suck it up then.

It's impossible to properly mope and wallow with Lips around.

For one, I hate looking fucking pathetic around her, even if she doesn't judge me fucking once the entire time I'm here, but I also can't look at her without fucking craving her. I want to wrap myself around her when she's studying, I want to listen to her hum quietly under her breath while she's flipping pancakes, and I for-fucking-sure want to see what noises I can coax out of her while I'm fucking her raw on the couch.

I need something to fucking distract me from how badly I want her.

So, when she offers me a joint if I'll take a shower, I fucking jump at it. She opens all of the windows like the idea of sucking in any secondhand smoke is a crime but I'm too fucking eager for it to give a shit.

The shower really does make me feel better.

She's too fucking good at this caretaker shit.

Then I eat the pancakes like an obedient little fucking worm, gulping down the coffee that she makes fucking perfectly for me. When I'm done, she hands me a bowl of ice cream, the same way my mom used to after my dad would yell at me, like our own little secret. It always made me feel like we were together in dealing with Dad.

It was before he broke her down, before she chose her marriage over her son, and before I decided to stop hoping she'd leave the fucking asshole, just run away from him together and be broke but fucking happy.

I don't want the ice cream now but she's so fucking invested in it that I take it.

I try to distract myself from the bullshit threatening to take over in my head again. "What's your earliest memory, Mounty? No wait, don't answer that. It's probably really fucking bad and I'll feel like a pussy for comparing."

She laughs at me quietly, the raspy sound washing over me like some kind of communion. I finally light the joint, sucking in a great lungful and blowing the smoke out the window. I'm not addicted but, fuck, it helps chase away some of the shadows playing around in my head.

Lips clears her throat. "My mom rolling joints on the back steps to our house. It was too hot to move and I kept crying and pissing her off so she filled a bucket with water and dumped me in it. I think she was trying to be cruel but it was the best feeling ever."

What a cunt.

But bonding over shit parents is what I do best. "My father's office. A modernist nightmare of cold steel and crisp white boxes. I've fallen asleep on his weird couch, that doesn't even have cushions, under his suit jacket. I wake up but I keep my eyes shut because even at five years old I know that when my parents talk in that hushed secret way they're talking about me. My mom is telling my dad that 'normal' children can't read by age five and to lower his expectations. My father says he's sure I'm actually retarded. His ethics board would shit themselves if they knew how he speaks to me. He has a whole list of words he likes to use in my direction because he was born with an IQ of 190 and I'm…so fucking average. I remember I cried and he looked so disgusted at me. Said I'd probably turn out to be a faggot too. Imagine every derogatory word in the book and that man has thrown it at me and the worst part…the fucking stupidest thing is I still care. I *still* hate that I don't measure up."

She stares at me for a second and I lose it, I lose the last tiny scraps of my soul that she didn't already own because when Lips Anderson *looks* at you she sees everything. Every-fucking-thing. And the terrifying thing is that she likes what she sees in me. All of the cruel and handsome and broken and true—every little piece of it that she finds, she likes.

She fucking owns me.

Arbour is going to murder me.

"Eat your fucking ice cream, Morrison. Do we need to hug? It's not really my thing but I'll give it a go for you."

I burst out laughing, because I'm fucked and if I hug

her I'll end up kissing her too, so I dig into the ice cream.

It doesn't taste like heartbreak anymore.

When I finish the bowl, and I have more control over myself again, I sling an arm around her shoulder and whisper in her ear, "How about a song, Mounty? Sing me something with that voice of yours that's so good you can beat me in choir."

Because there's nothing I want more than to finally hear this voice of hers, the one that even Avery fell in love with while she was on her warpath.

I'm shit out of luck there though because she blanches, the color seeping out of her skin entirely as she gulps and squeaks out, "Ah, sorry. I have severe stage fright. Avery and I are working on it."

I groan, but if I'm not going to hear it for myself then I want to at least enjoy the rest of our afternoon together so I hunt down my guitar and lyric book instead and watch the light start up in her eyes when I sit back down.

"I'll have to give you a private concert then, Mounty. I've been working on some songs, tell me what you think."

She fucking melts.

I'm doomed.

Nineteen

HARLEY

Morrison comes back from the girls' room with an attitude.

The type of attitude that'll get his fucking face broken if he's not careful and Ash takes note of it too. When I get back to the room on Monday from my swim practice, he's already awake and messing around on his guitar, his lyric book out in front of himself on the bed and a pick tucked behind his ear. I sling my bag onto the bed and he glances up at me with a glare, not even attempting to hide how fucking confrontational he really is, so I stalk into the bathroom for a shower.

He's always been an asshole, but not like this.

When I get back out, Ash is back from his run and gulping down more water in the kitchen. He's spent more time than ever pounding the pavement and I think we're all a little too fucking pent up for our own good because he glares at me too.

"If either of you have something to say then just fucking say it. This bullshit moodiness is getting on my last fucking nerve."

Ash slowly lowers the bottle to the kitchen counter, his eyes fucking savage, but it's Morrison who answers me.

"When are you going to stop being a pussy and actually make a move on Lips? Where have your balls gone, man? Because if you don't then I'm going to."

Nope.

I swing around to level my own pissy fucking look his way. "It's not that fucking simple."

Morrison laughs at me. Fucking tips his head back and just roars with the kind of laughter I know is all scathing wit. "What's not simple about walking over there and shooting your fucking shot? Either she wants you back or not. Maybe you should fuck her out of your system and then leave her for the rest of us who want a taste."

Nope.

Not a fucking chance.

I'm at his bed with a fistful of his sweatshirt before any of us have the chance to blink. Ash curses under his breath and stalks over to pull us apart as I drag Morrison up to his knees on the bed.

"Don't you ever fucking talk about her like that. She's not some piece of ass and I'll fucking take you out if you keep that shit up."

I'm expecting him to let it go but his eyes narrow my way. "You don't date. You've shut down every girl who's ever wanted more than a quick fuck; how am I supposed to know you want more than just the chase here?"

My jaw cracks as I grind my answer out through my teeth. "She's different. Why are we going over this again, I've already fucking told you to stay away from her."

He huffs and jerks himself out of my grip. "Yeah, and then you didn't do a fucking thing about it. You're holding up the fucking line."

Nope.

Don't like that either.

Except this time Ash is close enough to grab me and even the extra muscle mass I have on him doesn't stop him from jerking me back from killing Morrison.

He grunts and snaps, "Just fucking do something about it or get over her. Is she really worth all of this?"

Morrison slides off of his bed and snarls, "I've given you time to do something! Fuck, how long does it really take to ask her out? Or have you already been rejected and you're guarding her ass like the crown fucking jewels? Pathetic, man."

Killing them both seems like the only option right now, but then Ash's phone starts fucking ringing and with one last glare he lets me go to answer it.

It only rings for Avery, and he *never* misses her calls thanks to last year.

"I'm a little busy right now, Floss… sure, we can come over… I can get dinner tonight… order in, we'll grab it on our way… do you need anything else… don't go anywhere without me."

I stare Morrison down as he starts to pull on his training gear. Getting into the ring with him now is too fucking dangerous, not something either of us should be doing with the headspace we're in, but I'm feeling reckless.

When Ash hangs up, I think *fuck it* and just lay it out there. "Someone is threatening Lips. She won't tell me shit about it, and neither will Avery, but something is going on with her. I've taken out half the fucking senior class trying to find out what's going on but they're all keeping their shit locked down tight."

And if I wasn't already so sure that they're both panting after her, I sure-as-fuck am now.

Both of them look at me like I've been holding out information from them that is life changing.

"Who the fuck is threatening her and why the hell didn't you tell us?" Morrison snarls, his shirt half on as he stalks back over like maybe he's about to take swing at me.

I roll my eyes at him. "You really want to go there? I didn't tell either of you because neither of you gives a shit about her, right? She's just some girl from Mounts Bay that you like messing with. I'll fucking fix it."

Ash doesn't say a word, he just picks up his workout bag and walks out. Morrison stares at him and then turns back to me.

"Don't fucking keep that shit from me. I don't give a fuck how he feels about her; if someone is messing with her then you come to me."

Fuck.

The backup would be good but clearly he's not going to let his infatuation with her go easily.

Fuck.

Ash doesn't go down to the gym.

Morrison and I spend half the day beating the shit out of each other in the ring, clearing up some of the pent-up rage without aiming for the face, but he doesn't show up.

It's not until Avery summons us to her room for dinner that we find him, freshly showered with busted-up knuckles, and I figure out where the fuck he's been.

"Yes, all three of you need to sit your asses down and explain to me what the hell is going on. Eight seniors have dropped out, three are hospitalized, and the rest are running away screaming from us all in the halls," Avery snaps the second she sees us eyeing off the damage.

I glance around, but Lips is nowhere to be seen.

"She's at tutoring with the Mounty dickhead," Ash mumbles, but he's sitting at the table with a bourbon and zero fucks about any of what Avery has just thrown at us.

Clearly he's already heard half of it.

"Don't worry about it, Floss. We're dealing with it."

Her eyes narrow at me but Morrison stalks forward and grabs us both beers, slumping into the chair next to Ash and sliding a beer across the table to me as I take a seat with them.

None of us say a word.

It doesn't take Avery long to lose her shit at us in the most *Beaumont* way. Her eyes narrow, her lip curls just a little, and she very slowly slides into the seat next to mine.

She doesn't speak for another minute, just slowly staring each one of us down, and Morrison gulps down his beer so he doesn't have to make eye contact with her.

Such a fucking pussy.

"You're going to tell me what *the fuck* is going on or I will make your lives so miserable you'll be begging for my forgiveness."

There are a lot of ways she could ruin us all and only half of them are off-limits.

I try to catch Ash's eye but he's still fucking drowning in denial over the whole mess so I tell my own truth of the situation.

Well… I tell the bare minimum.

"The bet is still going about fucking Lips and I don't like it. The seniors started it and they'll fucking end it too."

Avery stares at Ash but he just stares back at her, his face giving away *nothing*. I start to get this feeling that shit is about to go really fucking badly at this table when there's scratching and fumbling at the door before it finally flings open and a fucking *livid* Lips stalks in.

I've seen her angry before but that was a cold and deadly thing; I've seen her take guys to the ground before but even that was a flash of rage that burned out the second she struck. This is something different altogether.

We all watch her, transfixed and fucking hypnotized, as she sheds her bag and shoes, silent even as her blazer gets torn off, but when I realize we're about to get the angriest striptease of our lives, I clear my throat to stop her.

She swings around to finally see us all sitting here fucking gaping at her and Avery arches an eyebrow at her with a little smile, one that would usually have her smiling back but, nope, it just sets her the fuck off.

"Fuck today, fuck this school, and fuck every fucking knuckle-scraping, chest-beating, egotistical piece of shit guy in this fucking hellhole!" she screams as she stalks to the bathroom, slamming the door behind her.

"What the fuck was that?" Morrison sputters, and Avery giggles at him, standing and heading after her.

"That was Eclipse Anderson, pushed to the edge by

something and when I find out what it is, you'll kill it for me."

When she opens the bathroom door, the shower is running and Lips lets out this frustrated screaming sound and I'm onboard with straight up murder today. Just bleeding some cunt out for daring to make her feel like this.

"Do you think this is retaliation? Some fucking senior coming after her for what you two have been doing?" Morrison says, getting up for more beers.

He slides another one over to me and I take it because I need to calm the fuck down before Lips gets out here and takes a swing at me for losing my fucking head.

Ash shrugs. "If it is then we'll deal with it."

I scoff at him. "Finally admitting you're into her, then? Am I going to have to stake a claim with you as well?"

His lip curls at me but then the bathroom door opens and the girls walk out together, Avery looking cold and calculating and Lips still looking pissed. She's wearing one of those ugly old man sweaters again, and I make a note to start leaving my shit here again so she has better options.

Not that I really think she'd wear my shit but a guy can hope.

Avery starts dishing out dinner to us all, only Lips refuses a plate and goes straight for a tub of ice cream, no bowl just a spoon. That's not a good sign from any girl.

"You gonna share with the class whose fault it is you're pissy or just attempt a diabetic coma?"

She shoves a spoonful of ice cream in her mouth and flips me off. Ash snorts at her and she glares back at him, talking with her mouth full which should not be so fucking endearing. "Thanks for skipping, by the way. I had to deal with the little creep by myself."

Ash smirks at her but I can see the relief clear as fucking day. "I didn't realize you needed backup, I thought your knife was enough."

She doesn't take that well and if I wasn't keenly aware of just how fucking inexperienced she is, I'd say she was getting back at him with all of the tongue action on the spoon. Morrison has to adjust himself, fucking squirming in his seat, and that sends me over the edge. "Stop tongue fucking the spoon. Some of us are going through a dry spell."

She flicks a cherry at me and keeps going.

I might die of blood loss if I keep watching her, everything rushing to my dick at the sight.

Avery gets sick of all of us panting after her bestie so she tucks her arm into Lips' and says sweetly, "Lance offered his services to end the bet. When Lips declined his offer he took it upon himself to try and persuade her. Alas, the great and complex mind of Eclipse unknown-middle-name Anderson remains an unsolvable puzzle to mere mortal men."

I'll kill the Mounty fuck.

Blaise takes another swig of the beer, trying and failing to cover his moan at what Lips is doing to him right now, completely unaware. "What a dick. Maybe you *should* just fuck someone and get it over with. Might lighten your mood."

Right.

I'm killing Morrison too.

But the second I open my mouth to tear him a new asshole, Lips shoots me a savage look, clearly not wanting details of her private life aired out for us all to see.

Fine.

New tactic.

I grit my teeth for a second before saying, "We decided Lips is in, right? Avery and I vouched for her, Blaise has come around, and Ash may still be a stubborn dick but we all know she's in. So, are we going to accept some dickhead chasing her tail, begging for sex, or are we going to remind the sheep of where they belong?"

Lips looks like she's going to cry over me being decent to her and even Ash can't fucking handle that shit, jumping in with, "We've gone from three people on the planner to pure fucking bedlam. Joey, Harlow, Annabelle, Lance, dozens of little bitches from the stupid fucking website.

We need to get on the same page and decide what our priorities are. Is Lance going to be an issue?"

Lips clears her throat. "No. I'm pissed but I'm not in any real danger."

Blaise opens yet another beer and points the bottle at her with a slow, dirty smirk. "I'll beat the disrespectful little fuck for you."

I scoff at him. "Only if you get to him first."

Avery laughs and leans in to whisper something to Lips that I don't catch but it has her blushing and scrubbing a hand over her face. It's fucking cute and I want to know what set her off so fucking bad.

"Joey?" Blaise asks, and when Ash opens his mouth, Lips cuts him off sharply, "I'm on it. Next?"

Fuck, I need details about that.

"Harlow?"

Avery hums softly and says, "She'll dig her own grave eventually. Same goes with Devon. The real problem is Annabelle."

All eyes are on Blaise as he fidgets with the bottle cap from his beer because he's the weak link here. He's the one who always caves and feels bad about her because deep down his damage has broken him that way.

The rest of us have damage that means she could die and we wouldn't flinch.

Lips clear her throat and then speaks carefully, "Do we

need her to disappear? I…can make that happen."

Fuck.

That's a good option, but I wasn't expecting her to just come out and say it.

"So you really do have gangster connections then?" Blaise grumbles, and she flinches.

She fucking flinches.

I punch him in the arm, wanting it to be his goddamn jaw, and he groans. "Fuck, I didn't mean it like that, Mounty, just…I know nothing about where you come from. I guess Avery does and Harley obviously knows something but I'm trying to figure out how the fuck a sixteen-year-old girl can calmly, casually, offer to end someone's life. Fuck, it's not even the killing. It's the mundane tone, like you've killed a bunch of other girls for pissing in your Cheerios."

She swallows and slowly looks around the table at us all. "I know a lot of people from all different walks of life. Some of them are gangsters. I am not a member of any gangs, I do not fuck members of any gangs, and I do not owe loyalty in any manner to any gangs."

I scrub a hand over the back of my neck and attempt to defuse the situation before Morrison puts his fucking foot in it again. "Whatever, it doesn't matter. We can't *kill* her. She's a dumb, manipulative bitch but she's not Joey. If we're killing anyone it's him."

"No one is killing Joey," Ash snaps, and I guess that's

the end of that.

Twenty

ASH

Lance the Mounty fuck knows he's dead.

He knows it because the whole school knows it and he goes to the faculty to change where he sleeps because he's that fucking scared of what will happen to him when I get my hands on him.

He becomes a fucking ghost.

To make matters worse, Joey finally resurfaces from whatever drug haze he's been in and hears about the fucking warpath we've all been on and starts fucking messaging me again.

Only this time he adds Lips into his little blood-soaked fantasies.

The response I have to those messages shouldn't surprise me at this point but the violent and possessive need to protect her, covet her, and *own* her takes me to my fucking knees.

I'm fucked.

I'm absolutely, without any doubt, fucked. Because she's the worst possible option to feel this way about for so many different reasons. Two of the three most important people in my life are already fighting over her. She's a fucking Mounty street kid who would be eaten alive by the social circles I was born into, and then there's the small factor that both my father and my brother are serial rapists and killers who would love nothing more than to destroy her just to fucking ruin me.

I can barely stay on top of keeping Avery safe.

I can't add someone else to that list… but she's already fucking there.

She's already the first thing I think of when I wake up and the last person on my mind every night. I truly fucked myself over when I picked out all of that lingerie for her because I haven't been able to take a shower without jerking off over each and every item, how it would look on her and especially how it would look coming off of her.

I'd *never* cross the line by looking at those fucking revenge nudes Harlow took of her but fuck do I wish I knew what she looks like under the uniform and ugly sweaters.

I wonder if Harley has seen her and then I fucking loathe him for getting the chance.

I'm completely fucked.

And because apparently I've developed a taste for torture, when Harley says he's going down to the gym to watch Avery's first attempts at learning self-defense, I go with him. I can't even lie to myself and say I'm going to make sure no one goes after my sister.

I'm going because I want to watch the Mounty in action.

I can't deny that her ability to take out guys three times the size of her makes her even more appealing to me, just another part of her that draws me in. It doesn't stop me from wanting to kill anyone who's placed bets on her, threatened her, *fuck*, so much as breathed wrong in her direction. But I can't deny that seeing that streak of viciousness in her is… appealing. Maybe it's the thought of a girl finally fighting back and winning that turns me the fuck on, or maybe it's just all of the conditioning Joey and Senior have tried going wrong, I don't really care either way.

All I know is that she's under my skin now and there's no digging her out.

"Don't be a dick to Lips. She's doing this to help keep Avery safe and, fuck, *alive* so don't give her shit just for helping out," Harley says, his voice tense as we make our way down to the gym.

Blaise is hungover, the normal type for this early in the morning, but he side-eyes the fuck out of both of us like he wants to get a word in but just can't bring himself to start this fight all over again.

I get the feeling.

All I've done this year is fight. With Avery, with the Mounty, Harley, and myself. It's all been for nothing, I'm right where I didn't want to be.

"I'm here to support Avery; I won't say a word to the Mounty so just drop it."

Harley gives me one last disbelieving look and then shoves the door open to the gym. The girls are both already dressed in gym clothes and Lips is running Avery through lessons, ignoring every grumble and whine that comes out of my sister.

I grab a seat to watch, dragging it over to have a better view, and Harley and Blaise both do the same.

The longer the lesson goes on, the more I wonder about exactly where the Mounty learned all of this and what her life looks like back in the Bay because… there's nothing basic about this lesson. Sure teaching my sister not to tuck her thumb in is common sense but the stances and target points aren't at all basic shit. She didn't learn about that level of centering at a youth group self-defense class back in the Bay.

Harley shares a look with me, seeing it all as well.

Someday we need to figure out where *the fuck* she comes from.

When they stop for a break, Avery looks like she's done a four hour hip hop class and isn't at all happy about it. The Mounty is completely unruffled, calm and contained even in the thick hoodie she's wearing.

"Do they teach this in Mounty school?" drawls Blaise, but his eyes are still glued on the Mounty like he wants to fucking jump her.

I don't like it and neither does Harley.

Avery spots it from a mile away and comes trotting over to me, ready to deflect and distract so Lips doesn't get caught in the crossfire. Always the fixer, the caretaker, and the glue to hold us all together no matter what.

We'd be lost without her.

"She's good," I say, and Avery smiles at me like I hung the moon just for her.

"She is, she's the best. If I have to learn this, there's no one better to teach me."

I nod because it's true and I'm tired of fighting everything. I'm just fucking weary, and Avery has always been my safe space to come home to, to be myself and feel whatever the fuck I needed to feel around.

The Mounty changed that and I hated her for it… but it was my own fault.

Lips calls out to us, "We still have more to cover, Aves, so get your ass back over here."

She groans and drags her feet as she walks back over to

her. "I'm not strong like you, Lips. I can't do this."

That's a load of shit.

Avery is one of the strongest people I know; strength isn't just the ability to fight.

Lips sighs and leans her ass against the boxing ring, her arms crossed against her chest as she gives Avery a look that says she sees through her bullshit. "You think that because you've always had Ash or Harley or Blaise around to protect you but you're wrong. You exercise six days a week. Some days you do three sessions. You've never broken a bone, no nerve damage, and when you froze at what Rory was doing it was fear not PTSD. Physically, you are stronger than me. What I am teaching you is the basics of self defense but the most important, the most *valuable* thing you need is something you already have."

Shit.

She's fucking good.

I stalk back over to my seat, ready for them to get back into it.

Lips ignores Avery huffing and crossing her arms as she continues her assessment. "You're observant and intuitive. You can look at a student and make a quick assessment of what weaknesses they have and how to exploit them to take them out. So far you've used that strength to socially ruin the sheep but you can easily switch to reading body language and defending yourself. You're better at it than anyone I've met, you're as good as I am. You may end up better than me at it."

When Lips glances at us like we're going to be a problem, Avery waves her off. "I don't care that they're here. But I need you to show me something real. Walk me through a situation and explain how knowledge will be better than strength or size. I need you to prove it to me so I can stop second guessing myself."

I share a look with Harley because Avery is too fucking good at manipulating situations to get what she wants. I hate it when she does it to me, but when it happens to everyone else and I benefit from it. Genius.

Lips frowns for a second and then sighs like the whole world is resting on her shoulders. The look on her face isn't that of a sixteen-year-old girl. She looks like a veteran who's seen too much death and destruction in this world to ever be the same again.

She grabs a stack of training mats and starts to pile them up until they're about as high as her hip, then she slips her hoodie off and hands it over to Avery.

Avery looks at it like it's grown teeth and wants to take a chunk out of her, but she hesitantly takes it and pulls it over her head. She looks fucking stupid in it, fucking ridiculous, and I can't help but take a photo of her for later use.

Blackmailing my sister just got a little easier.

Lips digs around in her bag until she finds a knife, slipping it into the hoodie pocket while Avery watches her every move. She uses that level of scrutiny on everything in our lives but here and now she doesn't have to attempt to hide it so it's more obvious.

Then she stops and stares at the three of us sitting and watching all of this like it's the most fucking fascinating thing we've ever witnessed. Fuck, it kind of is the best fucking sight because now that she's handed the hoodie over, Lips is standing there in yoga pants and a tank top that molds to every inch of her chest.

It's the most I've ever seen of her and *fuck* does she live up to my expectations.

"Look, you guys have to stay quiet. If she's going to learn how to defend herself, you need to let me walk her through this. If you can't hack it then please leave."

What the fuck is that supposed to mean?

I nod, lying really because if I don't like this I'm going to step the fuck in, and instantly I do want to butt in because her hand shoots out and grabs Avery's wrist. She jumps and frowns back at the Mounty.

Harley's arm shoots out over my chest like he knows I'm about to jump in except… I do trust the Mounty enough to let it go.

Doesn't mean I like it.

"The party that Joey insisted I go to first year. He told

all of the juniors he was going to fuck me, one way or another. He found me walking back to the dorms and I knew he was high but I also knew he could outrun me. He's not as big as Rory or Ash or most of the guys at this school because of his habit but drug addicts are unpredictable. I couldn't just run."

Fuck.

Fuck.

I could handle it being anything, fucking anything, but Joey. Anything but the psychopath who taunts me, tortures me, fucking messes with my mind every chance he gets.

The psychopath who knows just how much I want her.

Lips holds up Avery's wrist like she's making a point. "He held my wrist harder than this. I could feel my bones bending under his fingers and pulling away meant fighting him off with a broken wrist. So…what do you do? Knowing him, reading the situation you're in, what do you do?"

Avery swallows but we both know the answer. "Play along. Get him talking and distract him."

I need to leave before I find out something that snaps the careful restraint I have over myself where my brother is concerned. I can't do anything without risking Avery and I will not let anything hurt her again.

Lips nods and tugs her over to the mats, sitting down and waiting for Avery to settle next to her before continuing, "Now he tells you he can fuck you by force or you can lie back and enjoy it. He kisses you. What do you do?"

I'll fucking kill him.

The second I can kill him without losing Avery, I'm going to use every last brutal lesson I've learned over the years to draw out his death until he's fucking begging me to end it. The simmering rage I've felt for him all of my life finally comes to a boil, overflowing in my veins until I feel so fucking reckless.

It only gets worse.

It only gets worse because Avery nearly breaks as she answers, "Play along. I have no choice, he's still got my wrist."

"Good."

The second Lips shoves her back and covers her body with her own, I lose my fucking mind. I don't even realize the vicious curses are coming out of me until Harley is wrestling the chair out of my hands and shoving me out of the gym.

"Go. Go find someone to bleed out. I'll watch out for Aves."

I can't see or hear a thing as I make my way back up to our rooms because there's no way I can fight right now. I'd kill whoever I went up against, just fucking pummel them into the ground, and it'll be on Avery to cover up a fucking murder.

So instead, I lock myself in my room and drink until I

find the bottom of the bottle of bourbon.

It doesn't help one bit.

Blaise finds me absolutely fucking destroyed on the floor next to my bed.

We've been friends for too fucking long because he just grabs a beer and joins me down there, not a word said between us because there's fucking nothing to say.

I just want Joey dead.

I can't kill him.

If he raped her… if he did to her what he's done to too fucking many other girls, I don't know if I could stop myself.

I need to know.

I'll fucking figure it out if I have to.

I struggle to my feet and Blaise watches me, his eyes wary but he doesn't attempt to stop me. When I stumble a little at the door he calls out, "You can't kill him in that state."

I don't answer him, mostly because I could kill Joey high, blind, and fucking wasted if I wanted to, and I make my way out toward the girls' room. It only takes me until the end of the hallway to get my legs working properly underneath me and half of the students are still doing everything they can to avoid me so I'm not worried about being jumped on the walk over.

I almost just unlock the door, always having a set of

keys on me because Avery would never accept me not having them, but I think better and knock instead.

I want to fucking puke.

The door swings open and Lips stares up at me, the shock melting off of her face quickly and exasperation taking up residence fucking quickly. Without a word, she shoves me toward the couch, mumbling under her breath as she locks the door, "My life is now babysitting drunk, spoiled rich kids."

It burns a little that she thinks of me like that. I'd rather she thought of me as an asshole than a spoiled rich kid.

She sighs and rubs a hand over her face. "Avery is in the shower, if you need to puke please tell me now so I can get you a bucket."

I frown at her but, really, of course she thinks I'm here for my sister. At what point have I given her any reason to believe I'd want to see her instead. She takes a little gasped breath in and tries to step away from me, so I snatch her wrist and tug her down onto the couch beside me. "I'm not here for Floss."

She keeps the shock off of her face but her movements are too rigid as she settles back into the couch. "What's wrong? What do I need to fix now?"

I can't even attempt to soften my words. "Did my brother rape you?"

She frowns at me and I fumble over my words to

explain myself. "I know you walked her through it but I need to hear from you, that you got away from him. I need to know that he didn't get away with it."

She blinks at me. "He tried but I got away from him. Don't worry about it, I'm not losing sleep over it."

That's it.

She's going to fucking hate me forever, there's no coming back from being the brother of that rapist cunt. Even if she did forgive me for everything else that I've done to her. Fuck. Do I want forgiveness? Is there enough alcohol burning through my system to admit just how badly I need her to want me back right now?

I groan and lean forward until my elbows hit my knees and my face is cradled in my hands. How fucking badly have I misjudged her all along and now it's back to bite me in the fucking ass.

"Fuck, how can you even stand to look at me? I look just like that fucking monster. We're all the spitting fucking image of our father." The bitterness I feel leaks through into the laugh I choke out. "Harley looks like my mom. He gets to look like the only good we ever had in our lives and I get to stare in the mirror at the demons who own us. Fuck, now I sound like Morrison. Someone get me another fucking drink before I start singing."

It's quiet in the room for a minute, only Avery's shower making any noise and then she speaks, her voice quiet but firm. "I don't think you look like Joey. I think you look like Avery and she's one of the very best humans on this earth. So yeah, looking like your mom, like Harley, would have been great but looking like Avery is pretty fucking good, too. Stop having a meltdown over shit that doesn't matter."

And in four sentences she grants me the absolution I do not deserve but so desperately crave.

"Where the fuck did you come from?"

She snorts at me and pats my leg like I'm a fucking child. "A drug addict. Or a meth lab, depending on which specific you were looking for."

I try to stay away from Joey.

I try and I fail. Miserably, because when I wake up at 4 in the morning to a rambling text from him about how good the Mounty's blood will look on his dick when he fucks her bleeding corpse, it hits a little too fucking close to home for me, and I get out of bed to hunt the fuck down and end him.

I don't have to go far, he's waiting for me out in the sitting area in the boys' dorms, off his fucking head and rambling to himself about sluts and whores like he always does. His eyes are bloodshot and glassy, the liquid way they get when he's so fucking far out of his mind. I wonder if he's moved on from the cocaine and gone to heroin or meth; I wonder if he's going to burn himself out finally and I won't have to fucking deal with him anymore?

Even off his head he can read me like a book.

"You raise a hand to me and I'll tell Father all about her, your dirty little secret."

I hesitate and it's the fucking worst thing I could do because he takes the action in and digs deeper. "Some little slum pussy from the Bay, no one would even notice if she disappeared. Avery is already on borrowed time, do you really want the little slut to die too?"

So I don't raise a hand to him.

And when he flies at me fists first, I let him. I stand there and I let him burn out some of his own rage against me and it's only when he has me on the ground, kicking at my ribs like he wants every last one of them broken, that Harley's shitty sleeping habits come in handy and he tackles Joey to get him off of me. It only takes one sharp hit to the face to knock Joey out, but Harley hits him a few more times just to be sure.

Or because he wishes he could kill the asshole.

Blaise looks fucking murderous as he helps me up, ducking under my arm to help me hobble back to our room even as my ribs scream at the stretch. "What the fuck are you doing? If he corners you then fine, take the fucking beating to keep Aves safe, but you were safe in our room.

For fuck's sake, Ash, you're getting reckless."

I shrug because it's easier to keep my mouth shut than to explain the intricacies of how fucked I am when it comes to my brother. I could just tell him that he'd threatened the Mounty, then he'd probably drop me and go back after Joey, but I can't let that happen either.

We're all fucking doomed.

I take a shower, slowly and fucking excruciatingly, but at least the pain puts a dampener on my dick for once and I don't find myself jerking off over the Mounty. Any other girl I wouldn't give a fuck about rubbing one out over every morning but when it comes to Lips?

It only makes me crave her even more.

When I finally shuffle out of the bathroom, Harley is waiting for me, sitting on the end of my bed with my phone in his hand and a frown on his face. He doesn't know the password to get into it but I doubt he's looked into it either. I trust him more than that.

"Every morning your phone goes off and every morning I assumed it was Avery but it's not, is it? It's fucking Joey."

I shrug and wave off Blaise because I don't need a fucking ice pack for my ribs. This isn't my first beating and I doubt it'll be the last, so I'm well versed in just how much this shit will suck for a few days. I don't care about the pain.

"Just tell me, Ash. Tell me what the fuck it is that he

has over you and we'll fucking figure it out. I'll go back to juvie to get him the fuck away from you."

I huff at him but it sounds more like a wheeze. "Like Avery would let that happen again. It's nothing I can't handle."

Harley drops my phone and stands up, hands on his hips and gives me a savage look. "You weren't handling it. You were taking a beating and he wanted to fucking kill you. At what point would you have made him stop? Or were you so fucking ready to die out there?"

I glance over at Blaise but he's looking just as fucking pissed off so he's not going to jump in anytime soon.

My ribs hurt too much for this shit.

"You're going to be late for your swim practice, forget about this."

His eyes turn into slits but he grabs his swim bag and slings it over his shoulders. I think for a second that I've won and he's just going to leave but he pauses in front of me.

"I can't forget about it because if I do you're just going to skip fucking merrily off to your own death to keep Aves safe and as noble as that shit is, it's also fucking stupid. Who watches out for her if you're dead, Ash?"

We don't normally do this emotive, open bullshit. I'm more of a sarcastic asshole type.

"You do, and Blaise... and the Mounty. I wasn't

going there to die, I was going there to kill him but then I remembered that Avery isn't the only person he's threatening. She's not the only person I'm trying to keep safe from him."

I refuse to say another word about it, no matter how he and Blaise push.

I spend the day in bed with no intentions of leaving for the day but then Avery blows my phone up the second Harley narcs on me and tells her what went down, so I drag my ass down to the dining hall for dinner. I don't want her going into a full-blown panic over Joey again so I do what I can to keep the pain off of my face.

It's just my fucking ribs that burn.

Blaise and Harley flank me in the line, snarling and shoving at anyone who gets too close to me which makes it too fucking obvious that I'm injured. It's the quickest way to get fucking jumped on my way back to our room later but I'm struggling to breathe too badly to argue with them.

We take our usual seats and Avery slips her phone into her pocket with a concerned look at me which I brush off. I'm fucking *fine*. Blaise cracks a joke to lighten the mood which only makes things worse but at least Avery isn't fussing over me anymore so I'd say it's a win.

The Mounty starts handing out drinks but I barely notice while I'm trying to choke down some food under Avery's watchful eye so she doesn't fucking stalk me over this shit for days. I don't think I should sleep in her room again, the torture of being in close quarters with the Mounty is too fucking much for me right now.

My thoughts are broken by Avery's glass of juice landing in my lap as she gasps and lurches backwards. The Mounty's hand is still raised from where she's smacked it and I snarl at her, "What the fuck is wrong with you, Mounty?"

"The glass is oily. Smell it. It smells like Harlow does after gym class. She rubs down with Wintergreen oil."

What *the fuck* is Wintergreen oil?

The Mounty huffs at us all and snaps, "It's a type of natural aspirin and she's put it in your juice. She's fucking *poisoned your drink*, Aves."

Poisoned her drink.

I can't think or move for a second while those words bounce around in my brain like a fucking pinball until finally I lift the glass out of my lap and sure enough, it's fucking oily. One sniff and the scent is there, not one I recognize but I trust the Mounty to know what she's talking about.

I'll fucking kill her.

"That. Fucking. Cunt."

The Mounty jumps to her feet and looks around the dining hall for the slut and the second he figures out what she's doing, Blaise does the same.

I'm too fucking blinded by rage to join them.

"Did you drink any? Are you sure it was her? I need to know I'm fucking killing the right bitch," Harley says to Avery, his voice almost fucking vibrating out of him as he tries not to completely lose his fucking mind.

"I'll handle this. Avery, go back to our room and get cleaned up. You guys need to walk her up and stay with her until I get back," the Mounty says and then she's gone, stalking away from the table like she's going to actually murder the cunt.

Not without me she's not.

She's quick but even injured I'm faster and I grab her elbow and wrench her around to face me.

"Mounty—"

I'm not expecting the fire inside of her to be aimed my way but she fucking snaps, cutting me off, "How could you ever think I was in on this? How could you think I wanted to hurt her? You've spent the last year watching us together, do you really think I'd try to *kill* her?"

Fuck.

Goddammit, there's no way of talking myself out of this without just fucking saying, "I don't. I… fuck, you're in. You're family now. I'm coming with you and I'm helping you take Harlow out."

She looks at me as though she doesn't trust that at all, but I can't exactly blame her.

I stand outside of Harlow's room for all of ten minutes.

There's nothing that can be heard over the music in Chastity's room, no thumping or screaming, fucking nothing to tell me if I need to go in there and help. Then the door opens and Lips walks out, blood all down the front of her uniform that definitely won't wash out.

Her arms are shaking.

I glance back into the room and Harlow is a fucking mess but she's breathing, which is all that matters here. I have no doubt Avery could cover up a murder for us, but I don't want that shit on her plate right now. It wouldn't be smooth or effortless and I'm fucking positive that Lips would spend at least a little time in lockup which wouldn't go down well with... fuck, *any* of us.

As we start walking she stumbles, and I grab her arm on reflex to steady her. I look down at her, the closest we've ever been, and she stares up at me with nothing but honesty. She walked into that room ready to do whatever it took to keep Avery alive and with zero apologies.

I shouldn't, I really fucking shouldn't, but I can't help myself. "Come to my room. You can clean up there before you see Avery."

She doesn't hesitate to nod and follows me out of the hall.

None of the girls watch us.

When we get to the boys' dorm, every last one of them does.

I'm used to the stares so at first I think it's business as usual until I see the fucking phone. "Take a photo of her right now, Smithson, and you'll never walk again. Do you think your father will still love you if you're not on the State Track team?"

That gets the fucking sheep moving.

I unlock my door and usher her in, locking it back up just in case word gets back to Joey that she's here and he comes looking for round two. I don't think I'd be able to stand there and do nothing this time.

I think I'd fucking kill him.

Lips slowly walks around the room taking everything in. I know for sure that she's categorizing everything, planning out escape routes, and taking in all of the little clues that are left everywhere, because even though she's more subtle about it than Avery is, the look is the same. She does a little double take at the photo of us all in the kitchen, and suddenly I feel so fucking exposed having her here.

"I'll grab you something to change into, the towels are under the sink. Use whatever you need."

She clears her throat but her voice is still raw. "I can go. Aves has seen me worse than this, she's fine."

I snort at her and flick the coffee machine on. I need the caffeine to get my shit together because bourbon would be too fucking risky right now. I'd probably do something fucking stupid like kiss her.

"Just take a shower, Mounty."

I force myself to sit my ass on my bed and wait until she's in the shower before I move. Avery is blowing up my phone, needing more details than whatever Lips had sent her but I have none.

All I know is that she got the job done without flinching, without stalling or second-guessing herself, and knowing that I have someone else watching Avery's back who would kill for her is a weight off of my shoulders. Someone Avery loves and is joined at the hip to, who can also bleed someone out is everything I never knew we fucking needed.

I can't lie to myself anymore and pretend that's the only reason I want her around.

Harley and Blaise have both text to check on Lips as well, and I answer them without my usual cutting sarcasm. I'm just... fucking tired. Tired of being angry and an asshole, tired of living by my brother's psychotic whims, tired of pretending that I don't want the Mounty girl around.

I want her more than I've wanted anything else in my life.

That in itself should be terrifying.

It's not.

When the shower cuts off, I wait a minute and then I knock and hand her a pile of clothes. She barely cracks the door open and I respect her privacy enough not to look, the temptation fucking vicious. I distract myself by making us both coffee. I know exactly how she likes hers thanks to all of the time I've spent in the girls' room watching Avery fuss over the perfect brew.

When she finally emerges I'm drinking my own cup on the end of my bed, trying not to stare at her and freak her the fuck out. I gave her my shirt because I'm fucking weak and I wanted to see it on her, even just this once. I'm sure she'll burn it later, or give it to Avery to get it back to me, but she's obviously not wearing a bra with it and even though the soft fabric dwarfs her tiny frame, I can still make out the curves that have filled in thanks to Avery's cooking.

I want to touch them all.

She grabs her coffee and takes a deep gulp, a total fucking addict like Avery and I both are. She refuses to look at me, her eyes tracing over the rest of the room like she's going to find some magic portal out of here. I can't hold it against her; I only have myself to blame.

I keep my eyes away from her and on my own cup so I don't spook her. "Why did Joey call the juniors off last year? The real reason."

She gulps down some more coffee. "Someone from Mounts Bay found out about the bet. He's Joey's dealer. Actually, he's the top of the drug dealing food chain. This guy didn't like the idea of me being a bet so he warned Joey off."

I don't like that she knows his dealers but then again Harley knows half of them from his time in the Bay so it's probably inevitable. "Why didn't Joey just find a new supplier?"

"The guy owns all of the dealers. Everyone in the state leads back to him so he told Joey that he'd never touch an ounce of anything again if he didn't back off."

Well.

There's a lead for Harley to chase up. She can't know the real kingpin, everyone knows the Jackal doesn't have friends, but whoever sells directly underneath him must know something about her... maybe even who it is that's threatening her, if it's not just the seniors and their stupid fucking bet.

I nod again and set down my cup as she tips back the last of her drink.

There's so much left to say to her now I have her alone, truly fucking alone, and yet I can't find a single fucking thing to say to her right now. Nothing.

Except then she gets up to leave.

I move without thinking about it, without thinking

about the consequences of doing fucking anything right now, because I can't help myself. My fingers curl around her wrist gently. Enough that she can pull away if she wants to, but she doesn't. Instead she freezes, her breath stopping dead in her chest like she's under some spell and, fuck me, I'm caught under it as well.

I don't want this moment to end.

I don't want her to walk out of here and to go back to avoiding each other.

I don't even know if she feels anything for me other than the mild tolerance she shows me.

Then she takes a step toward me, her heartbeat throbbing in the vein in her wrist and I pull her into me, closer and closer until I can smell my soap on her skin. I shouldn't, I really fucking shouldn't, but I cup the back of her neck until I finally just fucking look at her.

She wants me too.

There's no hiding the blown pupils, the blush across her cheeks, and her heartbeat which is still thumping in her wrist. I'm fucking trapped by the desperation in her eyes, the need and the want drenching me until, finally, she draws in a shuddering breath and I snap.

I kiss her like I've never kissed a girl before.

I kiss her like she's the only fucking drug I'll ever need pumping through my veins, like I don't fucking care that she's going to be my downfall and that doing this is the end of everything I love and covet in my life. I kiss her like it doesn't matter that I'm betraying two of the most important and vital people in my life.

I kiss her like I love her.

She kisses me back like maybe she feels every last bit of that too.

When her teeth catch my bottom lip and tug, I grunt, my dick going from half-hard to fucking *throbbing* in an instant. My hands both fall to fit over the curve of her waist, not daring to touch her anywhere else yet because the second I touch her it's fucking over. I'll be tearing these clothes off of her and fucking her into the mattress like I can keep her there forever, so I force myself to slow down, stick to safer areas.

She feels too fucking good in my arms. I forget myself, groaning and lifting her up against my chest, and enjoy the feeling of her being pressed against me for a second before I flip us both over, getting her underneath me finally, fucking *finally*.

It takes a second, her lips still desperate against mine, but then she freezes and I know it's game over.

I squeeze my eyes shut at the same time she does; I don't want to fucking face this or the aftermath when everyone else finds out. Thank God I didn't lower myself down onto her, I didn't feel her underneath me, because the feel of her lips on mine will haunt me enough.

I don't need to know what her grinding on my dick feels like.

"I can't," she croaks and I nod, my eyes still shut.

Neither of us move. I expect her to shove me off but she just lets me hover over her for a second while I get my shit together. It's not the rejection that burns me, it's the fact that I wasn't strong enough to stop myself in the first place.

Now I've tasted her... no one else will ever compare.

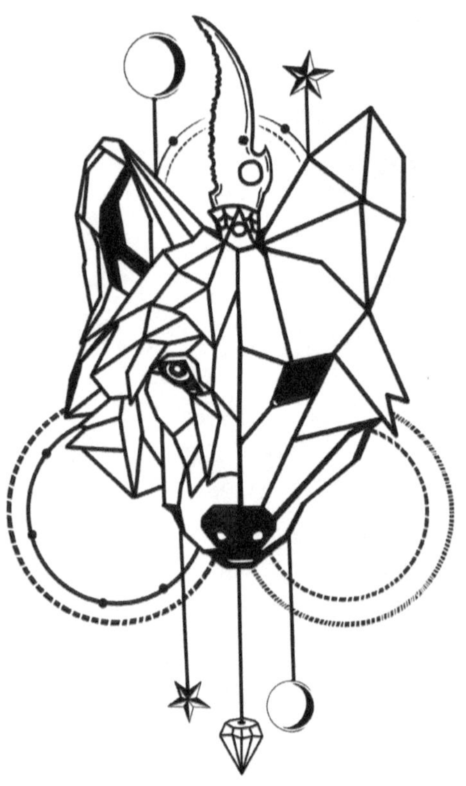

Twenty One

BLAISE

The closer we get to finals, the worse things get.

I spend half my time freaking the fuck out about trying to pass all of my classes and the other half is spent stalking Ash to make sure he really has gotten his suicidal tendencies out of his system. Waking up to find him gone wasn't such a big deal, but Harley is always the first one out of the door each morning, and I'm so fucking glad he made the call to go looking for his cousin.

Joey was going to kill him, and Ash was going to let him.

It makes me fucking cringe about all of the times I've put my friends through this bullshit, how many times I've let myself get in over my head and let the darkness in my head push me to do something fucking stupid.

I don't know how any of them forgive me for it because I feel fucking strung out following Ash around all day.

He fucking hates it too.

"Your obsession with me is getting out of hand. Don't you have secret study sessions to get to or something?"

I wince at the sneer in his tone and shrug with a smirk as we walk toward the dining hall for lunch. "There's spoons in there that can definitely count as a weapon, so I'll be babysitting your morbid ass until we're sure you can be trusted."

Avery and Harley are already in there waiting, Lips nowhere to be seen. I notice Ash trying to look discreet about checking for her, but he's about as subtle as I am these days.

We're all fucking pathetic.

I grab a couple of pizza slices, and Ash ignores all of the food in favor of an iced coffee because apparently caffeine is a three-course meal for him these days. Avery eyes him with suspicion but doesn't say a word as she slides her salmon over to him.

He sighs and then eats it, knowing better than to argue with her today.

"Why the fuck isn't she coming down to eat with us?" Harley snaps, and Avery rolls her eyes so fucking loudly I'm surprised Lips doesn't hear it from wherever she's holed up.

"She's freaking about exams and gone full Mounty scholarship girl psycho about it. I think she's sleeping less than even *you* do at the moment and there's textbooks everywhere in our room. I had to move one off of our toilet seat at 3am to pee last night."

He frowns at her and stabs at his lunch dramatically. "Shouldn't you be forcing her to eat and sleep a bit more like you do with us? Why does she get a pass?"

If looks could kill Harley would hit the fucking floor. "Do I need to remind you that Lips is my best friend and not yours? She's not a child; I don't need to babysit her."

The words 'like I do with the rest of you' hang in the air, clear as a freaking bell for us to hear. Ash still doesn't say a word, only now it's really starting to look suspicious.

Harley thinks so too. "What the fuck have you done now? This is your doing, right?"

Jesus, the table is about to be fucking flipped and Ash is going to choke him the fuck out.

Except he doesn't.

He just ignores us all, which is the biggest fucking red flag I've ever seen in my fucking life, but Harley is too set on Lips' ass to follow up on it, instead harassing Avery about her until I'm sure she's about to stab him in the throat. So I sit in silence with Ash and just eat my lunch, trying and failing to not wonder what exactly it is that Ash did to her.

I do everything I can to forget about the whole thing and I come pretty fucking close until the rumors start during the last class of the day. I'm in math with the rest of the underachievers, trying to take half decent notes for Lips to deconstruct for me later when some idiots behind me start their gossiping.

"I can't believe the Mounty finally put out and the bet is done. Fuck, two million dollars that my parents didn't know about… it might've been worth dealing with Arbour and the beating he'd have given me."

My neck nearly fucking snaps as I try to figure out who the fuck is talking about Lips because I'm going to kill them for daring. I never really notice any of the sheep around me, but I need to know who the fuck is dying.

Then their words actually filter into my goddamn brain. *Someone has won the bet.*

Fuck.

Fuck, was it Ash? Is this why she's avoiding us all now? Harley is going to fucking murder him. There's no coming back from this shit; Avery has no chance of keeping us all together now.

"The Mounty shouldn't even be eligible to win; all that fucking money and it goes to some slum kid? It's fucking bullshit."

I turn around completely, ready to rip Sebastien's fucking head off. "What the fuck kind of shit are you dribbling right now, dickhead?"

He blinks at me like he forgot I was even here in the

same class before fumbling over his words. "The bet... the scholarship freshman kid won the bet last night; he's getting the money. I wasn't... I wasn't saying shit about any of your friends, just talking about the money, man."

There's no fucking way.

"Spreading fucking rumors is talking shit, dickhead."

He gulps. "I'm not! He handed in proof; ask anyone!"

I get up and walk the fuck out.

The teacher calls out to me but I don't give a fuck, my feet just fucking propel me away from that tiny-ass room before I do something stupid like break Sebastien's fucking face just for being the bearer of bad news. It's such a bad idea, but I text Harley and Ash.

Better they both hear it from me than some other asshole.

Lips fucked Lance and he's taken proof to Darcy for the winnings.

Classes let out before I make it back up to my room, the entire school population fucking buzzing over the news that Lips finally put out and I want to fucking punch something. I get it, I'm a hypocritical asshole, because this is definitely the longest I've gone without sex since I first got my dick wet, but this just feels... wrong.

She was better than sleeping around. Fuck, that still makes me sound like a fucking asshole but no matter what insults we all threw at her, she always was just better than us. She didn't fuck around or go out of her way to get back at us for anything. Hell, there's a fucking list of guys she could've made a deal with to split the bet, but not once did she lower herself to the bullshit games that are played in the halls of Hannaford.

Until now.

And with that fucking piece of shit.

Of all the guys in this place, she picked that loser. I'm halfway up the staircase when the text from Avery comes in. At first I think it's Ash ranting about her again or Harley starting a fight but nope, Avery is calling us all in for a family meeting.

Dinner in our room. Attendance is compulsory, this means you, Ash.

I've barely made it through the text when another comes through from Harley but in our group chat that the girls aren't in.

Don't say a fucking word about the bet, I'm dealing with it.

Jesus H. Christ.

I don't know whether that means the Mounty fuck is dead or if he's going to strap a chastity belt on Lips and tattoo his name on her fucking forehead, but I get the feeling my night is only going to get worse.

Fuck. How it can get worse than imagining her rolling around in the sheets with that fucking cunt, I'm not sure.

Funny thing is that the thought of her fucking Harley isn't half as bad as this, fuck, if only it were him who'd won the stupid bet. Don't get me wrong, I'd still be jealous as all hell but I wouldn't be feeling so… fucking sick.

The thought of anyone else touching her makes me want to throw up.

I'm the only one who shows up to the boxing session down at the gym.

It's frustrating to have to hit the bags by myself, but probably for the best because I doubt any of us can be civil to each other, or anyone, today. Fuck, Ash might even admit just how much he is fucked over the Mounty at this rate.

We all are.

When I've finally hit the bag so hard and for so long that my arms feel as though they've stopped working, I call it quits and hit the showers. Even the freezing water doesn't help cool me down and, fuck, if my dick had any fucking interest outside of the Mounty, I'd be finding someone to burn some of this anger out on, but she's fucking ruined that option for me.

I grab the food Avery ordered in on the way up and walk slowly up to the girls' room, the whole time trying to convince myself that there's nothing to be so fucking pissed about. It's just sex, it's not like they're fucking married and running off together. Maybe she did need the money and now she's got a bank balance higher than any Mounty kid could dream of.

If anything, it just makes things worse.

When I get to the door, I'm right behind the girls, catching it before it closes and brushing past them both. Harley looks like a fucking serial killer waiting to happen and Ash is fucking glowing with asshole energy.

I don't want to be here.

"What's Joey done now?" Avery snaps, and then when none of us answer her, she snarls, "Well?!"

"It's not Joey. Harley's got some emotions he would like to express but he has to work through them first," says Ash, the condescension dripping. I guess we should be glad Arbour is so fucking focused on Lips otherwise Avery would be losing some furniture in the fight between the cousins.

I start setting out all of the food to stay busy. Lips thanks me, but I can't open my mouth right now without saying something, so I just give her a curt nod. Avery glares at me, then Ash, before finally settling her ire on her Harley, who is still staring at Lips with a mix of fury and writhing jealousy.

We eat in complete silence.

It's awkward as fuck and I kind of want to die. My

fingers itch for a blunt and the beer Avery is letting me drink barely touches the sides... it's not enough. Fuck, whiskey straight from the bottle wouldn't be enough right now.

Harley waits until every last one of us is done before he strikes. "I didn't peg you for a liar."

Ash laughs and throws a napkin at him. "Of course she's a liar. If you chose to believe anything she's said that's your own fucking insanity."

Jesus Christ.

I take a second to finish off my beer and then I grab Harley's unopened bottle. If I have to sit here through this then I'm going to have a buzz, goddammit.

Lips pulls herself up into a fighting pose if I ever did see one and, I'm not going to lie, I start to fucking sweat for Harley. "What is up your ass now, Arbour?"

He doesn't see it at all, too fucking butt-hurt about this entire situation. "You. You lied about being in danger, you lied about hating the other Mounty, and now you've gone and fucked him. I hope the money was worth it."

The girls share a look across the table and then Ash catches my eye.

That look tells me more than it should, but I still don't know what the fuck is going on. Is Avery cool with her fucking the Mounty? Was she in on the planning? Jesus fucking Christ.

"Uh no, I didn't. He threw himself at me and I said no," Lips says, her voice still just a little too calm.

Harley snorts at her, pushes out of his chair, and stalks over to the fridge to grab another beer. Avery stands to start cleaning up our dishes, another red flag, and snaps, "What does it matter to you if she did fuck him?"

He shrugs casually but the sneer stays fixed to his face. "You said you didn't want to fuck any guy at Hannaford but you made an exception for him."

Ash is watching Avery with narrowed eyes. There's very fucking clearly something going on and if Harley wasn't so pissed, he'd notice the cleaning, too.

"I didn't fuck him. I kind of thought you'd believed me over the gossiping bitches but clearly I was wrong," Lips says through clenched teeth.

Harley slams the beer bottle on the bench and moves to stand over her. Even though she's fucking tiny, she doesn't back down an inch, her shoulders rolling back and her jaw tight; it's fucking hot to watch but I can't enjoy it because of how fucking... *jumpy* she is.

"He handed in proof. He's been declared the winner and he gets the sweep. All two million dollars of it."

All of the color drains from her face.

All of the air gets sucked out of the room. All I can see on her face is pure panic and not the kind you get when you're caught in a lie, nope, this is the life-or-death kind.

Ash goes into high alert instantly, shifting to his feet with his fists clenched like he's going to punch his way out of whatever the fuck is going on.

I put the second beer down because, apparently, now isn't the time for a buzz.

"Right. This is bad." Avery's voice is thready and high-pitched, her own panic coming through. Harley looks like he's going to put his fucking foot even further in his fucking mouth, so I do the right fucking thing and throw myself under the bus for him.

I'm a fucking saint today.

"So some asshole Mounty guy ends up with the money, what does it matter? With the bet over with Lips won't be followed around anymore. We should have a word with him about the money. He should really split it with you."

Apparently, even that is the wrong thing to say.

"She didn't fuck him! Get your heads out of your fucking asses and believe us both. We're fucked because of that asshole's lie!" Avery screeches at me and then Lips fucking collapses to the ground without a word.

I scramble to my feet to check she's *breathing* because, fuck, maybe someone poisoned her and I'm going to fucking lose her before I ever get the chance to… fuck, I don't know what. Tell her I'm fucking obsessed with her? Or that curating the playlists for her is the best part of my day? Maybe I'll tell her every song I've been working on since I first saw her has been about her?

If I was brutally honest, I'd tell her she's the melody in my head now, the sweet notes that get me through each day, and that Ash, Harley, and Avery have been my family since grade school and yet she tempts me to fucking ruin everything with them just to keep her and that terrifies me.

She's a fucking trembling mess on the floor but at least she's *alive*.

"What are we missing here?" Ash asks, carefully, and she glances over at him with her wide eyes. There's something between them, something has definitely gone on there, but then she squeezes her eyes shut and starts mumbling in gasping French.

Is this some sort of stroke?

"I'm telling them, Lips. We need their help to fix this, that little fuck Lance needs a beating and we all know I can't throw a punch to save my life," says Avery, and Lips nods with a jerk of her head. "Okay. If word gets back to Mounts Bay that Lips has fucked Lance her life is in danger. The Jackal will kill Lance, no question, and he deserves it so *fuck him*. But there's a good chance he'll also kidnap, torture, and rape Lips."

Holy fuck.

Holy. Fuck.

"What?! Why?" snaps Ash as Harley starts cursing up a storm behind him, regret and fucking loathing rolling off of him.

"Because he's a sadistic egomaniac who thinks he owns her. He threatened Joey away from her because he doesn't like to share his toys. He's waiting her out, playing a game that he thinks he'll win, and if anyone messes with it he takes them out. *If we don't fix this he's going to rape and kill her.*"

Lips lifts one shaky hand up to her face and covers her eyes, her breath rattling in her chest, and we all just fucking stand there and watch as she pulls herself together. It's a sight to see, watching her just piece herself back together on the ground until she's whole again. We've underestimated her.

She's stronger than any of us.

When her eyes finally open, she looks us all over, radiating calm like a fucking pro.

Harley gives her a nod and turns back to the rest of us. "We need to fix this and we need to do it now. Ideas?"

Well.

That's kind of obvious, isn't it? There's only one real option that will clear her fully. "The bet says proof has to be either a photo or a video. We get our hands on it and prove it's a fake. No one wants Lance to get the money so it'll be an easy sell if we can find something."

Ash snorts derisively, his voice a twisted snarl. "How exactly would that be good proof if no one here has fucked the Mounty before? Who could vouch it's her?"

"Besides the obvious that her face would have to be in it? The photos last year," says Harley.

Fuck.

Those fucking nudes. They'd circulated around the school for *months* and dodging them was harder than it had any right to be. I wouldn't ever willingly check out revenge porn, and it fucking kills me to think of how many guys have seen them.

Jerked off over them.

Great, now I want to kill everyone just as badly as Ash and Harley do.

"We need to get the photos and pray. Lance is taking photography and advanced digital design. I'm sure he's got the fake photos damn near perfect," Lips says, her voice strong and steady even as she rubs her face with shaking hands.

Lance is a dead man walking.

I turn for the door, stalking out as I say, "Give me twenty minutes. I know who'll have them."

Twenty Two

HARLEY

Lance the Mounty is fucking dead.

Beyond dead, I'm going to torture him in the most horrific fucking ways before I kill him, because he deserves nothing less than the worst fucking death possible.

Avery shoves Lips into the shower while we wait for Morrison to come back with the photos and the second the water cuts on, Ash turns on his sister with a snarl.

"Why the fuck didn't you tell us about this? The fucking Jackal? *Have you lost your fucking mind, Avery?*"

She huffs at him and turns to walk away but he catches her arm and stops her, gently because he always treats her like glass, but firmly enough that she takes notice and rolls her eyes at him.

"At no point have I been in danger, Ash, so don't get all overprotective—"

"I'm not angry about that, I'm angry that she's been

fucking stalked and terrorized by a literal crime lord of the Bay and you didn't say a fucking word to us. What if he came here for her? What if he sent someone here for her and none of us knew? She's been in danger this entire fucking time and we've been chasing our own asses thinking it was some school bullshit when it's been the fucking Jackal this whole time. He's one of Joey's dealers for fuck's sake!"

That's awfully close to admitting just how much he wants her and Avery is too fucking smart not to spot it. "Why do you care, Ash? I thought you hated her?"

I expect him to leave, to just bail on this whole conversation because it's all just too fucking intense and he's not going to want to be exposed like that.

He doesn't.

His eyes narrow at her. "I care because if he comes up here for her, I'll kill him. If he tries fucking anything, I'll show him exactly how *Beaumont* I really am."

Holy fuck.

Avery's eyes flare and her mouth opens like she's about to pick his brain wide fucking open but then the water cuts off and Ash turns away, stalking over to the table and slouching into the seat there. He downs the rest of his beer and then groans, cradling his head in his hands.

I get the feeling.

I grab us both fresh drinks and join him at the table.

"If you're here to stake your claim on her, I already fucking know."

He sounds fucking miserable and something close to guilt curls up into my gut. "I'm not. I'm here to say we should fucking drive down to the Bay now and gut the rapist fuck before he sneaks up on us."

Ash chuckles under his breath but it's full of self-loathing. "He's the most dangerous member of the Twelve and even if we did succeed, they'd come after us. You taught me half of this shit; what are you thinking?"

I shrug and drain half the bottle in two gulps. "I'm not thinking, I'm fucking angry. Of all the girls, we pick the most fucking complicated one… and the same one. All three of us."

The bathroom door opens and Lips walks out wearing one of Morrison's shirts, an old one that she's clearly owned for fucking years and he's going to nut himself over. Ash takes one look at her and finally picks up the beer I grabbed for him, tipping it back like he wants to forget the night is even happening.

"Ease up a bit. You need your head for whatever the fuck Morrison brings back."

Avery parks Lips on the couch with a giant bowl of ice cream, constantly on a mission to get some weight on her tiny frame. I fucking love her for it too, because Lips has gone from a strikingly beautiful but starving slum kid to a fucking *stunning* Mounty girl. She'll always be a little rough around the edges but that's what comes from growing up in the Bay.

I'm the same.

It feels like home to me.

"One of us should be with both of them at all times," Ash mumbles and I shrug.

"There's no fucking way Lips is going to be cool with that; she barely tolerates eating with us."

Ash grimaces. "Well, we give her no choice then. If he's watching her closely enough to know about the bet then he could grab her at any fucking time. What classes do you have with her? Let's work it the fuck out."

Fuck.

Fuck, he's more than just a little interested in her.

Ash never, ever gives a shit about girls. They're just some fun, a way to blow off some steam, but he's never given any more thought to it than getting laid.

He's in love with her.

It's like a punch to the gut because my stake over her wasn't just that I wanted her first, it was that I wanted her for keeps. Fuck, if Morrison feels the same fucking way, I'm screwed. Totally, utterly fucking screwed.

I need another drink. "We're in all of the same classes except choir which she has with Morrison. We need to figure out what the fuck we're going to do about summer break, it's coming up and she can't go home to the Bay by herself."

He shrugs as the door opens again and Blaise walks in. "We'll get Avery to get her a room with you up on the coast. Avery can probably talk her into it for us."

Morrison startles at Lips' shirt and then ushers her and Avery to the table to join us, not so discreetly rearranging himself in his jeans. I give him a savage look which he shrugs off completely, sitting down and handing out piles of photos to each of us.

I could've died happy not seeing this shit.

They're fucking convincing, if I hadn't seen the Mounty's reaction I might even say she had to be lying because there's zero distortion or blurring. I don't want to puss out of doing this but fuck if I don't wanna break something right now staring down at them.

"Fuck, Avery, don't look at them," snaps Ash as he tries to pry them out of her hands. She rolls her eyes and turns away from him.

"I've seen nudes before, Ash. I'm not happy about being forced to look at that little fuck's dick but I'm the only person here that's seen Lips naked besides Lips herself so I'm the best person to be looking."

Can't argue with that, even if I have seen a little more of her than she'd probably want to admit right now.

Morrison's eyes flash and he purses his lips like he's

trying to seal them shut and I punch the asshole in the arm because of course he's being a fucking creep about it.

I would probably be too if it didn't involve Aves.

He smirks and shrugs. "I'm not even sorry; I can't help it."

Lips blinks at us both, still not looking at the photos in her hands. "Can't help what?"

Avery answers as she holds one of the photos so close to her face that she must be searching it pixel by pixel for inaccuracy, always the perfectionist. "He's being gross about how I've seen you naked. Boys always are." Then she grins at Blaise and swipes her tongue over her bottom lip, a sure sign she's about to stir some shit up. "I've seen her naked, dripping wet in the shower, in every piece of skimpy lace Ash picked out for her, and all sweaty and panting after a long, hard workout. Oh, I've also seen her in yoga poses that would make a monk weep."

Oh, fuck.

Fucking hell, like I need those fucking visuals right the fuck now and the worst part is that something finally pings in my brain and I remember her words.

I can't fuck a Hannaford boy.

I need to fucking know.

Ash clears his throat before I can say a word. "How exactly does this relate to what we're doing?"

Nope, I'm not waiting around for fucking answers so

I butt in, "So, about this sex ban the Jackal has you on. Is that the real reason you won't fuck a Hannaford guy?"

Lips doesn't even bother to look at me to answer, but I don't blame her. She still looks queasy and her hands are shaking just a little bit where she's holding the photos. "Yes. If there's a chance it could get back to him that I'm with someone then I can't do it. Hannaford is a pit of snakes and no one gets laid here without the entire school hearing about it. Just not worth the risk."

Fucking checkmate. I see Morrison's eyes flare and I consider knocking the asshole out but Lips still seems pretty fucking oblivious to us all so I don't want to make a scene.

If we kill the Jackal then she's free and clear to live whatever life she wants and that life is going to be with me, god-fucking-dammit.

Avery chuckles under her breath and it's a devious sound. "Besides, the majority of males at this school don't know how to make it good for girls. Why risk torture and death if you're not even going to come?"

Lips snorts with laughter at her, a sound that has no right being so endearing. "Better off doing it myself, right?"

I think *the fuck* not.

There's a hundred fucking things I could say to her right now and half of them would get me murdered by Avery...

the other half would air out Lips' secrets by pointing out that she's a virgin and has *no idea* what she's missing out on. There's so much that I would personally like to teach her about.

I want to be the one to show her *everything*.

She glances up at us as Avery cackles like a fucking witch, a blush dancing across her cheeks at the intensity of our glares. Ours, because it seems Ash and Blaise both have a helluva lot to say on this topic as well.

Thank God Avery is here to keep things from escalating.

Lips holds her hands up in a placating gesture. "Woah, settle down. I'm sure you guys are…great or whatever. You must be if Annabelle is mourning your dicks like she's missed out on the second coming of Christ."

"She's mourning the potential for a wealthy husband not their dicks," murmurs Avery, her tone scathing and acidic, before she finally yells, "*Ha!* There! Lips, we've got him."

She starts waving around a photo and I grab my own copy to try to figure out what exactly it is that calls it out as a fake. Lance has Lips—fuck, *no*, the girl—flipped over and is doing her from behind. He's leaning back and the photo has been taken with a nice close-up of his dick in her, the fleshy globes of her ass spread by his hand.

It makes zero fucking sense.

"Snap, motherfucker," Lips mutters and Avery threads

their arms together.

"Let's go end that Mounty fuck."

As amusing as it would be to watch Lips fucking destroy Darcy and Lance at midnight wearing nothing but a ratty band tee and a pair of fucking sinful booty shorts, I text the bet keeper to meet us the next day to clear things up.

No matter how hard we push, Avery refuses to tell us a fucking thing about the photo and why it's the one that proves they're fakes.

I tried asking Lips exactly once during class and decided that I like my balls where they are and maybe today isn't the best day to be questioning her.

I've seen what she can do when she's provoked.

When classes let out and we can finally go deal with this bullshit, Avery marches into the chapel ahead of the rest of us like she's about to start scalping people, Lips trailing behind her looking like she'd rather be anywhere else.

"What the fuck happened today?" Morrison murmurs to me, jerking his head in her direction, and I shrug.

"She's obviously fucking furious over this whole thing and I copped the brunt of it this morning so just leave her the fuck alone. We're here to watch their backs and, hopefully, see the Mounty fucking destroy him."

Ash's eyes gleam a little, sadistic light shining through. "The only thing better than making him bleed would be watching her bleed him out."

Blaise glances at him, still shocked he's admitting to how fucking badly he wants her but I've had time to adjust to that shit. I'm not happy about it but there's too much on our plate for me to worry about his feelings right now.

Lance needs to be dealt with.

The entire walk down to the chapel it's easy to see how widespread the rumors are about Lance winning the fucking bet and the damage done. The whispers and snide looks follow us the entire way and it's fucking hard not to do something about it. Fucking hypocrites, the lot of them. This entire school is one giant orgy every fucking night and they want to be judging Lips for the one and only time she's supposedly had sex?

The minute we're done here, I'm killing them too.

The girls both stop the second we step into the room and Lance is already there, laughing and joking with Darcy like he's some kind of big fucking deal.

I'm too busy checking out the rest of the room, so we haven't walked into some sort of ambushing fucking situation, when Blaise turns to fucking stone next to me. I glance up in time to see that fuck Lance biting his lip as he makes a big show of checking Lips out like he's thinking all about what she has going on underneath.

I ball my hands up into fists so tight my knuckles pop.

I don't want to piss Lips off any more by launching at him before she gets to have her moment but *fuck* do I want to wipe that fucking smirk right off of his slimy fucking face.

Darcy saunters over to us and smirks at Lips like a smug-ass dickhead. He deserves to fucking die for this too. His voice is fucking dripping with condescension. "You can't be pissy just because you finally caved, Mounty. You still have the moral high ground, you fucked one of your own."

To her credit, Lips is as calm as the eye of a storm. "It's a decent Photoshop, I'll give the kid that, but he's picked the wrong position."

I'm nowhere near that level of calm and when Darcy laughs, I lose my shit, and the only thing that stops me from choking the life outta him is Blaise body checking me.

I could throw him across the room to get to them but he knew that already. The move was more of a reminder to let our girl do her thing.

Fuck.

Our girl?

Jesus fucking Christ, no girl would sign up to deal with the three of us at the level we all so desperately want her, so I need to get that shit out of my head and fast.

"You're claiming it's a fake because you don't fuck doggy style? That's not good enough, babe."

It's a fucking beautiful thing, and I'm so fucking glad Blaise stopped me from ruining it.

Lips is faster than anything I've ever seen as she strikes, taking Darcy's legs out and slamming her knee into his windpipe in a single move. I couldn't recreate that shit even after all the hand-to-hand training I've done in my life and it's killing me not to know all of the moves she has up her sleeve.

Her face is completely blank, a void until he's gasping underneath her like he's choking on his voice box now she's knocked it three inches down his pathetic throat.

I fucking love this girl.

She stares down at him like death incarnate and I have to tell my dick to calm the fuck down because there's never been a hotter sight before me. Fuck, this is better than porn. After she's gotten her fill of his terror, she presses in close to him and whispers something I can't hear.

He nods his head a fraction and she climbs off him, gracefully in a skirt like it's nothing to her. Lance is staring at her in horror, finally seeing firsthand who he's fucking with and maybe regretting his life choices.

His eyes flick up to us and he gulps.

I hope he can see the death I have waiting for him staring back at him.

Avery slaps a blown-up version of Lance's fake-ass photo down onto the table in front of Darcy. He doesn't look her in the eye at all, just nods along while he tries to suck deep lungfuls of air through his damaged throat.

Lips shrugs off her jacket, handing it to Avery, and then pulls her shirt out from where it's tucked into her skirt. For one heart-stopping second, I think she's going to strip it off as well and I'm about to murder everyone in the room but then she turns on her heel to face us, lifting it only far enough to show them her lower back.

I have no fucking clue what she's showing them, other than the fact it's obviously a scar or marking.

I can't remember feeling anything when we'd made out but I'd been more focused on other parts of her at the time. I didn't realize there was going to be a pop quiz and my fat mouth ruined it for us anyway. Well... that and the fact that she's, you know, *a fucking virgin.*

Fuck.

Can't think about that either, my dick should not be rock fucking hard at this kind of situation. Avery will try to force me into therapy again if she notices the tent I'm pitching.

"What the fuck happened to you?" hisses Darcy and that calms my dick down a little. Definitely a scar then, and by the flush on her cheeks I see before she spins back around to him, it's one she's self-conscious about.

"There's your fucking proof. Are you satisfied?" she snaps back, and there's no way Darcy is going to be stupid enough not to believe her. Sure enough, he stares at her for a second and then, with a glance at the three of us glaring behind her, he nods and shoots a glare at Lance, who's backing away from us all like he can get away.

He isn't getting away from us without medical assistance.

"No hard feelings, Mounty. I'm still up for it if you want to end this thing for real," drawls Darcy and Lips turns on her heel, stomping out of the room like we're all done here.

Ash, Blaise, and I don't move a single fucking muscle.

Avery smiles at us all as she passes us, waving her phone and calling out, "I'd like a video of it. My Mounty will enjoy it once she's feeling a little more… sociable."

Darcy disappears into thin fucking air like the fucking vermin he is, but the moment Lance looks for an exit, I pounce on him, a fist to the jaw planting him on his ass like the pathetic little shit he is. I trust the others to have my back completely and I lose myself in just beating the shit out of him, brutally and with fucking glee.

It's only when he's trying to crawl away from me that I see the lace poking out of his pocket.

It could be anything, fucking anything, but my gut starts screaming at me and I don't ignore that shit. When you grow up in the Bay, you learn pretty fucking quickly not to ignore that shit.

I stoop down to grab it and sure enough, one pair of lace underwear that could belong to anyone but we all fucking know who they belong to.

Ash and Blaise start muttering to each other about why I've stopped, but I'm too fucking furious to tell them yet.

I feel fucking *wrong* even holding them, like I'm betraying her, because this is something she's been so embarrassed and frustrated about and he's been walking the fucking halls with them hanging out of his fucking pockets like a pervert.

I shove them into my pocket and then grab a fistful of his jacket, yanking him back onto his feet and shoving him to start walking.

"Are we taking him out the back to dig his own grave?" Ash drawls, and then I pull the pin on the grenade I'm holding, knowing that he's the one who's going to explode.

"Nope. We're going back to his room to find the rest of Lips' underwear. I doubt the pair in his pocket is the only set he has."

And that's how Lance finds himself pinned to the wall, gasping for air while Ash loses his fucking mind.

Filthy fucking pervert.

I come close to just throwing caution in the wind and killing Lance.

I barely know the asshole but finding the underwear on him is like the last fucking nail in the coffin. I have to remind myself, over and over again, that we're at school and this isn't the fucking Bay, and while Avery *can* make things disappear that doesn't mean that we can just kill this fuck.

As long as the Jackal believes that he's lying, Lance lives to have the shit kicked out of him by me another day. Fuck, I might even make a sport of it from now on, just schedule that shit in for every day at 7 p.m..

The moment we open the door to Lance's room all I see is Lips' face, her photos covering entire fucking walls in the tiny fucking storage cupboard of a room. My mind whites out in rage, every coherent thought just fucking leaves me, and Blaise nudges me to the side.

"Go and keep an eye on the girls. Wait, take these for Avery first. Get out of here before you give us a whole new fucking mess to clean."

Morrison shoves some of the photos into my hands and I turn to find Ash knocking Lance to the floor, kicking him in the ribs as he stalks past him to toss the rest of the room.

"How are you so fucking calm about this? You don't want him fucking buried for this?"

He shrugs and starts ripping the photos off of the wall,

starting a pile of them on the bed. "If Lips wants him dead, she'll do it herself. She knows her way around a knife, and I'm not taking his death away from her."

Lance's blackened eyes swivel over to me and I can see by the look on his face that he doesn't believe we mean actual death.

We do though, we really fucking do.

I leave Ash and Blaise to toss the rest of the room because I might just go back on my own decision not to kill the fuck if I have to see whatever else is hiding in there, and I barely remember anything about the walk over. Sure, there's still people fucking gossiping, the word having already gotten around this place about Lance lying because gossip spreads faster at Hannaford than herpes, but it rolls the fuck off of me now.

Something about knowing that Lips' aversion to Hannaford boys is about the Jackal's sick fascination and nothing to do with tastes or morals has added a little pep to my fucking step.

Avery answers the door with her phone in her hands and a distracted look on her face until she realizes I'm alone and holding the envelope of photos.

"Ash has already text me; he's found a stockpile of her underwear there. This is so much more than a little crush or hurt feelings."

I nod and look over her shoulder at where Lips is tucked

into bed with ice cream and headphones. "Have you told her yet? I'll go back over there and slit his throat right the fuck now if we have a cleanup organized."

Avery shakes her head as she steps aside to let me in. "I haven't yet, I wanted to wait it out a little. She's PMS-ing and not in the greatest of moods. I didn't want her charging down there and hacking him to pieces just because her hormones are raging out."

Huh.

Well, I guess that explains her ripping my head off this morning.

Avery giggles like a psycho at the look on my face and we both head over to break the news to our Mounty. She startles when I sit down on the edge of her bed, barely fucking perching there because she can be weird as hell about shit. I keep my entire body tense in case she shoves me off or takes a swing at me, Avery has taught me to always expect the unexpected, but she just blushes and winces a little as she sits up. I glance at Avery but she doesn't look worried so the wince isn't an injury.

"What? What's happened?" Lips croaks, her voice drenched in exhaustion.

I don't want to, but I hand the envelope over and watch as she pulls the photos out one by one, looking them over blankly. Her face gives away nothing about what's going on in her head; her shit is locked down so fucking tight.

I can't stand the silence.

"Ash and Morrison are trashing his room as we speak and looking for anything else he might have. He stays on the planner," I say and she finally looks at me, something close to sickening horror in her eyes.

I don't want to make this worse for her.

She looks over at Avery and my cousin rips the goddamn band-aid off. "Harley found your underwear on him when he beat him. He was carrying it around like some sick pervert. He said he took it as extra proof for the bet but we all know there has been dozens of pairs taken."

Three seconds.

All it takes is three seconds for Lips to go from disgusted to filled with rage, the calm and deadly kind that I'm so used to seeing her with.

I fucking love it.

I smirk at her and she gives me a nod like we've come to an agreement. "Give me two days to sort my uterus out and then I'll deal with him myself."

A chuckle bursts out of me at her words, she's such a fucking Mounty street kid sometimes, but Avery's eyes narrow at her. "I can hand all of this over to the school board and get him expelled; you don't have to be involved in this."

Lips shakes her head back, her words slow and carefully thought out. "This sort of disrespect needs to be punished, Aves."

Fuck.

They're talking about shit they haven't clued me in on again, I can fucking tell by Avery's curt nod. I hate it, I fucking loathe not knowing what the fuck is going on *especially* if the Jackal is involved, but I'm playing the long game here. If I keep showing up, being here for Lips and proving I'm not the next guy just trying to get into her pants for money or some sort of weird agenda… hopefully she'll come around.

The hardest part is that I know she wants me too.

It's written over every fucking inch of her. I'm not some arrogant fuck, I can see she wants Ash and Morrison too, but knowing I have some kind of a chance is the only thing stopping me from raging the fuck out at the secrets.

I grab the photos back off of her and shove them into one of Avery's drawers. We don't need that shit hanging around but I'm sure they'll come in handy for something.

Lips slumps back against her pillows with her eyes shut, seething and angry for so fucking long while Avery and I just stand here like idiots watching her. Right when I think I'm going to have to drag her out of bed for some whiskey and more ice cream, she slides her earphones back into her ears and pulls her covers up, falling asleep like none of this ever happened.

"I'm staying here tonight," I murmur, and Avery huffs

at me.

"Well, of course you are. Ash and Blaise will too because you're all stupid, pig-headed boys who can't get your acts together without me doing it for you."

I blink at her but she shoves a blanket into my chest and pushes me toward the pullout bed.

She's completely right because we are all that fucking hopeless.

Ash and Morrison get back in a little after midnight and pass out here too without a word. We haven't all bunked in together like this since Joey's campaign of terror last year, when Ash was in over his head and wouldn't ask for help so we had to just fucking stalk the both of them and pitch in on Avery Watch.

I go to swim training early the next morning because I need the distraction from all of the anger balled up in my chest. I meet the girls back in their room to walk down to breakfast together and I plan on fucking glueing myself to Lips' side for the rest of the day. Sharing our classes means she probably wouldn't notice except that I blatantly tell Avery over lunch that I'm sleeping on the rollout bed in their room until Lance has been dealt with. Lips chokes on her toast and almost dies.

I don't care.

I'm not letting this situation turn into another Rory.

Lance needs to fucking go.

Ash and Blaise arrive at the door not long after me and when we all leave together they walk Avery down and I follow Lips when she takes a detour to the photography room.

Fuck knows why she's suddenly so interested in photos; you'd think after seeing her stalker's work she'd hate being down here, but she looks around at everything intently.

I stand guard over her the entire time, ignoring the little sighs and huffs she lets out in my direction. She's always going to be a loner at heart, a kid who's had to do everything by, and for, herself but that doesn't mean she can't learn to lean on me a little.

She leans on Avery… not often, but she does.

"I can take care of myself," she murmurs as we slip out and head back up to the dining hall together.

I shrug. "You can, but that doesn't mean you have to. I'm not fucking risking it, Mounty, nothing you say is going to change that."

She clamps her mouth shut and doesn't say another word until we're at the table with everyone else, food spread out and Avery more focused on her phone than what the topic of the day is.

"I don't need a guard, just leave me alone to deal with this myself."

I peg her with a look across the table. "I'm not doubting

you're skilled with your knife, I'm just saying any guy at this school is twice as big as you and Lance is clearly fucking deranged."

Ash glances between the two of us and then shrugs at me. "She took down Rory. Don't baby her like we do Avery, she doesn't need it."

I want to kill him. "She had the element of surprise with Rory and he had his dick out. She's inviting Lance somewhere and I doubt she's going to get him in such a compromising position."

Lips shudders at me and pretends to gag. "I've seen more of him then I ever wanted to. If it means that much to you then you can keep watch for me but you're not coming into the classroom. I've got something very specific in mind for the little fuck."

Well... that at least sounds devious and promising.

She sets the meet up for after classes and the fucking creep agrees to meet her as if we didn't spend the night destroying his life. Lips and I bicker about her plan for the rest of the day and finally I relent, but only to stay out of the photography room itself. I take up watch in an alcove outside the room where I can still hear if the little fuck tries anything, and I make Lips swear to call out for me if she needs me.

She doesn't.

I can barely fucking believe my eyes when after six

and a half minutes—I was timing—Lance comes bolting out of the photography room like his ass is on fire. He's beyond pale, shaking, and looking like he's going to throw up. I catch the whole thing on camera, sending the clip off in the group message right as Lips steps out of the room without a single mark on her. Not a speck of dust or crease to show what the actual fuck went down in there.

I'm instantly pissed off at myself for not snooping.

I cover it with a smirk, drawling out to her, "If I asked you what you did, would you tell me?"

"Who says I even did anything? We had a chat," she says with a smile.

What a load of shit.

I snort and pull my phone back out of my pocket, turning the screen and hitting play on the video. There's no arguing with the sheer terror etched into every line of the creep. Her eyes light up as she sinks her teeth into that perfect lip of hers. Fuck, I wish it was my teeth. I miss the taste of her, the feel of her body on mine, her hips moving like they have a mind of their own.

Fuck.

Focus, Arbour.

"A chat did that?"

She nods and then tucks her arm into mine like she does with Avery. I force my body not to freeze or show any reaction but this has to fucking mean something, right? If she's comfortable enough to casually touch me, I have to be making some progress. When I'm silent for a little too long, running all of the variables through my head and sending myself just a little fucking crazy, she blushes and tries to move.

Nope.

No fucking chance of that happening, so I grab her hand and thread our fingers together. Of course she doesn't just let it go, but there's no way I'm giving in now.

"Uhm—"

"Get over it, Mounty, we're friends now, remember?"

She sighs and drags me down the hall like this is so fucking inconvenient for her, but her fingers are holding on just as tight as mine are. Even with my phone blowing up in my pocket with texts from the others, I just enjoy this little fucking moment in time where she's letting me in.

Even if it's only for a minute.

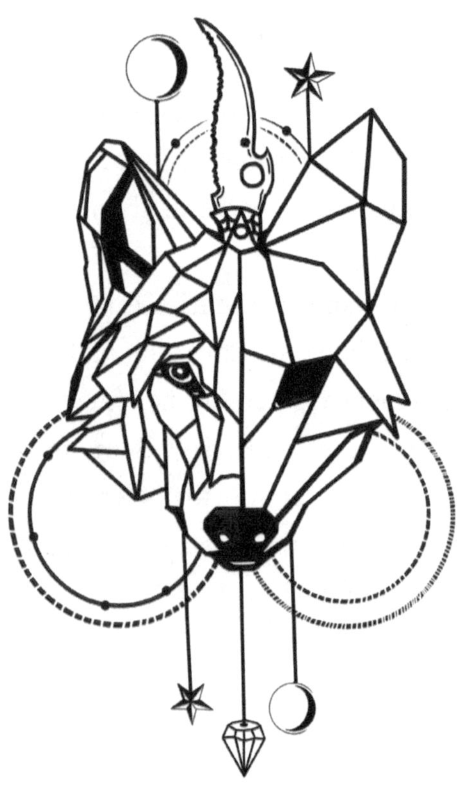

Twenty Three

ASH

Whatever the Mounty did to get Avery and I clear from Senior, it's fucking life changing.

I know it had to be her doing, that maybe she wasn't ordering a hit back in Haven but instead buying us a reprieve, because I haven't set eyes on the man since then. Not a single demand to come home and that can't be a coincidence.

The phone call I received from one of my father's men to say that we'll be staying at Hannaford for the entire break was short and cutting, but I feel like a weight has shifted off of my chest. Sure, it also means Joey is staying here and I'll have to watch out for him the entire time, but that's nothing new.

I pack a bag to take over to Avery's room and when I get there I find the Mounty giggling like a schoolgirl on her bed with earphones in.

Clearly a present from Blaise and I refuse to let myself get jealous that he can make her that happy… or that she's listening to music I might not have heard yet.

She spots me staring down at her and glares back at me, her cheeks flushed and rosy. "What time are you leaving?"

I smirk back, playing along for now. "Avery didn't tell you? Our father has been called away on business and he told us to stay here. You're stuck with all three Beaumonts this week, Mounty."

She shrugs like it's nothing, like she has had nothing to do with this and instead shoves the earphone back into her ear to shut me out.

I don't take dismissals well and certainly not from her.

I tug it back out, ignoring the glare she throws at me. "I haven't seen my father since you had your mysterious little midnight meeting in Haven. How long should I be expecting this separation to continue?"

Her face falls into that carefully blank slate she's the expert at wearing as she sits up on the bed, her eyes flicking behind me as she answers, "If I had anything to do with your father's busy schedule, I would think that after graduation you and Avery would both be free of him anyway and the… interference would no longer be necessary."

And what the fuck can I say back to that? She's told me everything and absolutely fucking *nothing*.

I want nothing more than to spend the rest of the break stalking her until I know every last one of her secrets, all of the things that she won't tell us in the shared looks with my sister, but Avery runs interference like she's spent her whole life training for this moment.

I sleep on the pullout just to be sure that Joey isn't going to show up and try to kill Avery the moment I turn my back for a second… and, honestly, I'm here to make sure that the Jackal doesn't send one of his men in to kill Lips.

Or kidnap her.

I get fucking livid just thinking about it.

When the school fills up with students again the night before classes go back, I head back to my room, feeling safer once there's more bodies in the building. Joey is easily distracted and with his stupid fucking friends around he'll just get high and fuck some brainless girl instead of worrying about us.

Harley grills me about the break, but there's nothing to tell him. Blaise fared better at home with Harley as a buffer so at least we're not back on suicide watch. There's a long list of people I'd love to see buried in cheap pine boxes, and the Morrisons are on that fucking list.

Impressive considering they're the only 'clean' people on it.

I pass out for the night, ready for the early start of

getting back to training before classes in the morning, but I'm woken by my phone at 2 a.m..

Avery is the only one who calls after midnight.

"Joey's at the bar in Haven. Ria said he's cooked, we've got to go now."

For fuck's sake.

Harley is already awake, the insomnia still wrapping him up tight. When I glance over to where he's studying on his bed, he huffs at the sight of me. "Joey? Gotta be that asshole if you're looking like that."

I nod and heave myself up. "Of course it's him, when is he not ruining my fucking life. Get Morrison up; I need to take a leak."

I pull a pair of jeans on and shove a jacket over the tank I was sleeping in while Blaise grunts and groans his way back to consciousness. Harley looks fucking wrecked, he always does on the bad nights, but he tamps down his usual asshole bitching.

At least until we lock up and head out to meet the girls.

"Why the fuck do we have to pick that asshole up?"

I shrug. "My father will be pissed if we don't."

That's more information than I usually give him and he shares a look with Blaise about it. "So what? Tell him to parent his own fucking kid. If he rages out over you trying to drag him home, are you expecting us to just let him? Because I will kill the cunt the second he raises a fucking hand to you or one of the girls."

I'm saved from answering as we get to the stairs, Avery and Lips already waiting for us there. I give Lips a nod as I tuck Avery under my arm, because I know she'll be freaking out about the potential shit-show this might turn into.

When we get to the Maserati, Lips mumbles something, probably snarky, and Avery cackles at her. I find myself feeling really fucking grateful, not only that they found each other, but that my sister told me to fuck off about being friends with her.

I've never seen her so happy and relaxed with a friend before.

I could have ruined that for her.

I tuck Avery into the front seat with Blaise and then sit in the back seat with Lips between Harley and I. She sits so stiffly, it's as though she thinks we'll kill her for touching us.

Really, I'd kill to have her touch me.

"Park around the back, Ria will let us in the service entrance. She's lost sight of him, we need to get in and out fast," Avery says, her phone now glued to her ear as she fixes up Joey's mess once again.

I don't want to know what the fuck he's been doing here all night. There's very possibly a trail of dead bodies we're about to trip over and won't that be fun to explain to everyone.

Once Blaise parks, we pile out and wait at the door for Ria. We've been here to pick him up a hundred times over the last few years and she scoffs the moment she comes out, snapping, "It really gonna take five o' you to git him outta here?"

It kills me not to roll my eyes at the old hag, but we've learnt that Blaise is the right person to smooth things over. He stalks over to her like he's done a million times and lays the charm on thick. "When have we ever turned down the chance to spend the evening with you, Ria?"

And just like that she chokes on her own tongue as she gets the fuck out of our way. The scenery never changes, we go through the stockroom, then the kitchen before making it out to the bar area. It's dark as hell out here and I have to pause for a second to let my eyes adjust.

The place is fucking packed.

It's usually busy but there are people jammed into every little nook and cranny of the place until I feel my skin crawl, my stomach roiling a little at the lack of air.

I don't let any of that show on my face.

Harley takes the lead and I push Avery between us, giving Blaise a look so he'll do the same with the Mounty. She startles and I'm sure she'll want to argue about it but I'm too focused on watching Avery to help Blaise convince her. This place is well known for girls being assaulted, too many people and too damn dark to be safe.

We should have left them in the car, safe and locked in.

We search the ground floor but Joey has never been big on alcohol. He's always wanted the harder shit so we're forced to head upstairs. The music is too fucking loud and shit and half the people up here are off their fucking heads. I tuck Avery back under my arm and see Blaise do the same with the Mounty from the corner of my eye. It's crazy enough up here that she lets him do it without a word.

Because he's the only one with his arms free, Harley takes over the search. After a few minutes without any word from him, I pull Avery over to the restrooms, our usual meetup point, to wait him out. The girls huddle together again but Lips' eyes are sharp as they take in the writhing bodies, like she could see through them all if only she looks hard enough.

We're all startled by the disability restroom door opening and Harley's head popping out.

"Mounty, I need you to look at this," he snaps out and Lips moves without question, ducking behind him as he stands like a fucking wall in the way.

"Move, Harley, we need to get him out of here," Avery says, but he shakes his head.

"Just let Lips get a look at him first. Give it two fucking minutes, Aves, don't—"

"Why the hell would she need to look at him?"

I share a look with Blaise but then Lips calls out, "Don't judge me for asking this but I am supposed to try and save him or are we waiting this out then calling it in for a cleanup?"

Save him?

Fuck.

No more playing nicely, I jab Harley in the gut to move him and shove my way into the room.

Joey's dead on the floor.

Fuck.

Wait, no, he's breathing but just barely, he looks like a fucking corpse.

Senior is going to kill me.

And Avery.

"I die if he does." I don't even mean to speak, the words just rip their way out of me, but the most painful ones stay lodged in my throat, *Avery is dead too.*

Lips instantly springs into action, not another word needed for her to transform into a field nurse and start working on saving the fucking useless asshole brother of mine. She rolls Joey to his side and shoves her fingers into his mouth to clear it out. His hacking breath starts to even out and she props his head up at a different angle until his breathing stabilizes a little more.

Blaise and I both watch her but Harley is watching me, his eyes too fucking fixated. He heard what I said and the puzzle pieces in his head are slowly moving together.

I've done everything I can to keep him from ever knowing about the guillotine hanging over my neck. He had enough worries with his own ticking time bomb family.

"I can call a doctor. What does he need to reverse this?" Avery asks as Blaise gets the door shut and locks it.

Harley finally looks away and moves to help Lips, kneeling down to help to support Joey's twitching body. Fuck.

What did he even OD on? The list of shit he takes is about as long as the list of shit that's available. I stoop down to start rummaging through his pockets and, sure e-fucking-nough there's a pile of little clear baggies. The Jackal's insignia grins back at me. I hate him even fucking more.

"There is no drug to reverse a cocaine overdose. They just treat the symptoms," Lips mumbles, loud enough that we all hear her.

"Fuck. Okay." Avery is starting to panic and Lips looks up to meet her eyes.

"He needs an ambulance and 24-hour care until he gets through. Look, it's not too bad."

Harley shoots me a look so I know for sure that she's lying and then he catches Lips' eye, swallowing roughly at what he sees there. "Is there anything we can do while we wait?"

"Recovery position and we need to make sure he doesn't choke on his own tongue. That's it about all we can do in this restroom. We should call an ambulance."

Fuck.

It's my turn to look at Avery, all of the pros and cons of that option floating silently between us.

Joey doesn't do well in ambulances or in hospitals.

The red tape that Avery will have to get through for him will be a fucking nightmare.

Senior will be fucking *livid*.

Lips clears her throat and says, "I'm not waiting for an ambulance, we need to move him now."

She gestures to Harley to go with her and so Blaise and I kneel to take our places beside Joey to keep him where he needs to be. Avery locks the door behind them and then we fucking wait, watching Joey's chest the whole goddamn time to make sure the asshole keeps breathing.

Harley hot-wires a van at Lips' request.

It's not a hard job or even dangerous, Avery has Haven's CCTV tapes wiped before she's fully seated in the fucking thing, but the fact that the Mounty knew he is a pro at this shit eats at me. Did he tell her? Are they getting closer? I'd thought he was too busy making an idiot of himself around her but maybe he is getting somewhere with her.

He's my cousin, one of the four people I trust more than anyone or anything in this world, someone I would kill and die for… and I want to fucking bleed him out for being the one she's going to pick.

It's my own fault.

But I don't care.

I'm fucking haunted by the memories of her lips on mine, of how easily she fit into my arms and the way her body molded into mine like we were made for each other.

I'm obsessed.

And I'm going to have to watch them together and pretend that it's fine, that none of this matters and that I'm not watching the only girl who's ever meant something to me, love someone who isn't me.

It puts me in a foul fucking mood. When Blaise and I get Joey to the back of the van I drop him in too hard considering we're trying to keep the asshole alive and Avery shoots me a look. I let Lips and Blaise arrange his body so he won't suffocate on his own tongue before climbing into the back and sitting on the musty old carpeted floor. I sigh and then climb in after them, trying not to think about what the vehicle has been used for because… no, thanks.

"So, we're criminals now? We just take things whenever we want them? I'm not sure I have enough black in my wardrobe for this, someone should have pre-warned me," drawls Blaise as he wipes his hands on his jeans.

"We were always a little criminal, Morrison," I scoff.

"Lips, if we can't take him to the hospital is there somewhere else we can take him?" Avery asks, and she sounds so fucking scared I want to kick Joey all over again. Fuck. Someday, *someday*, I'm going to beat the fuck out of him and it's going to feel so fucking good.

"How the fuck would she know?" I snap, too harsh but everything about tonight is fucked.

They ignore me anyway.

"Yeah. Head to the Bay. I'll give you directions once we hit the city."

Harley nods like this is all so fucking normal, and then the van falls silent. The roads are quiet until we hit the highway to Mounts Bay, the sounds of traffic coming through Harley's cracked window even this early in the goddamn morning.

I notice straight away that the Mounty is feeling every goddamn bump and turn. I keep expecting her to move or to yell at Harley to slow the fuck down, but she just sits there and takes it. It's such a fucking Mounty thing to do, something that Harley would do as well, and eventually I roll my eyes at her stubbornness. I elbow Blaise and we each grab one of her arms to drag her over to wedge her between us. I clamp a hand on her knee and Blaise winds an arm around her hips to secure her.

She clears her throat, then rasps out, "Thanks."

I shrug and Blaise nods, a little distracted like he always is when she's this close to him. I get it. I'm also having to talk my dick down.

"What, no smart-ass comment?"

She's still so goddamn sure I hate her. "No. I don't have anything left to say."

She stares up at me for a second before her eyes fall shut. She's not sleeping, her face is twitching too much for that, but she stays silent. Her hands flex in her lap like she doesn't know what to do with them, and I try to focus on Joey's rattling breath.

As we get to the city limits, Harley breaks the silence. "How much will this cost?"

Lips' eyes pop open and she shrugs, her shoulder brushing against mine. "Nothing, I'll call in a favor."

Harley snarls and rips his body around to snap at her, "*Fuck no*. You're not using up a favor for this fucking murderer. It's bad enough you spent one on me. Get a price and we'll pay it."

A favor.

There's a million different things a favor could mean in the Bay, and I'm shocked to know that she has access to any of them. Just how far into the criminal world is she?

She sighs and says, her voice sounding fucking exhausted, "Not one of those favors. The Doc owes me for some work I did for him last year. It'll be fine."

Some work for a doctor?

What the fuck would a Mounty kid be able to do for a fucking doctor? I don't like the sound of this, but Joey's breathing is still rattling away in his chest and we're running out of options.

For once I just keep my mouth shut.

I don't miss the look that Avery and the Mounty share, but neither of them say a word and the van falls silent again. I can't stop thinking about what the hell Lips could have spent her childhood doing here on the streets in the most dangerous and notorious city in the country. How the fuck did she get grades good enough to win the scholarship to Hannaford if she was running around collecting favors from fucking doctors and catching the eye of the Jackal?

Who the fuck is the Mounty when she leaves school and comes back here, back to the city she calls home?

When the van finally pulls up at the curb, even though I've been listening to all of Lips' directions and taking note of it all, I'm still fucking pissed at how shitty the neighborhood we're in is. It doesn't matter that the house is the only one that looks half decent, it's still smack-dab in the center of the fucking slums.

There's no way this doctor is legit, but I've got no fucking choice but to sit and watch as the Mounty bounces out of the car and up to the front door. It swings open straight away, but I can't see a thing of whoever is standing there.

"Fuck, are we about to lose our kidneys here?" Blaise mumbles, loud enough that the other two catch it, and Avery throws a glare over her shoulder at him.

"Obviously Lips wouldn't bring us somewhere where we'd be in danger. Use your brain before you speak; guys are such idiots!"

Blaise huffs at her and slings me a look. "You agree with me, right? Maybe the Mounty can't see how fucking… ghetto this place is because she's from here, but I'm definitely picking up the 'black market' vibes."

I shrug and watch as she finally turns and waves us over to her. "Joey deserves nothing more than to lose a fucking kidney, so as long as he walks out of here breathing, I don't give a fuck what the doctor takes."

Harley unbuckles his seatbelt and grumbles back, "Yeah, we're gonna be talking about why the fuck your life is tied to his, don't think you're slipping that in and we're gonna just run past it."

Like hell am I telling him a fucking thing.

For one he'd do something stupid, like go after Senior. For another I can't fucking stand the idea of them all knowing about the beatings I've been forced to just… accept. Take. Submit to.

Fuck.

Absolutely not.

Blaise and I heft Joey's prone body across the grass and into the house, following Lips' directions into a medical room. I blink the moment we step in because… it's an entire fucking hospital. The hallways were all tiny suburban household and this room has a fucking beat-up looking X-ray in the corner.

I drop my sociopath brother on the bed in the center of the room and then follow the Mounty out to wash our hands, because we're both covered in Joey's vomit.

Lips lets out a shaky breath and it's the first indicator that she's actually been worried about tonight, that she's been worried about whether or not I'll make it out of this if Joey dies.

It's jarring.

It's jarring because I know for sure it has nothing to do with him and everything to do with me, and I don't know what to do with that information.

She keeps her head down and leads me back into the room, only looking up once we're in there and then looking around like she's waiting for danger. I think that might be her default setting here in the Bay, but I still don't fucking like it. I hadn't even noticed how much she's relaxed since she became friends with my sister, but seeing the tension rolling through her again sets my teeth on edge.

Harley obviously feels the same way, that and he

fucking loathes Joey, because he's glaring at the doctor like he's the cause of all of this bullshit. Avery is tucked up under Blaise's arm and he's frowning at everything as he keeps an eye on her.

She's shaking like a fucking leaf.

Lips steps over to the bed and crosses her arms, taking in every inch of Joey's pathetic, twitching form as the doctor mumbles out, "Friend of yours?"

Her answer is instant. "No."

He raises an eyebrow at her, but he doesn't falter as he puts an IV line into my brother. I hope there's more than just fluid in that line; I hope there's some fucking miracle drug that will keep him breathing.

"Why bother bringing him in then? Just dig a hole."

I'd like nothing more than to reach across the table and strangle the life out of this man. The Mounty sees it too and changes topics quickly.

"He's worth saving. How's Maria and the kids?"

Of course she'd know all about his family. She's just like Avery, retains all sorts of information just in case the moment arises that it will be useful to her, but she's also… softer here in this room. She's still looking around like someone is here to kill her, but there's something about this old hack doctor that has also made her a little more human.

I don't like it… I don't like it because I want that soft

side of her. I don't want it directed to anyone outside of my family.

"She's pregnant," the doctor says with a sigh. He begins taking notes of all of Joey's vitals. He doesn't look worried or shocked, there's no urgency in him at all, so I'm assuming the asshole will live.

Lips groans, "Fuck," and he glances back up at her with a wry look.

"I've tried to get her on the stick but she insists on taking the pill then forgets to half the time. I'll be building an extension on the house by the end of the year."

"Maybe tell her to stay away from cocks for a while instead," Lips replies with a grin, and he roars with laughter at her.

Avery straightens in Blaise's arms, pulling away from him until she's mostly standing on her own two feet again. The shaken look is gone, the cold mask she shows the world back in place, and some of the icy rage in my gut dissipates.

The doctor starts to hook Joey up to his machines. "You know, if she finally has a girl I'm going to get her to name it after you. You're a good girl, we need some of that in this house."

I do *not* like him calling her a good girl.

It feels fucking creepy to me, and Harley's lip curls in the corner at the same time I take a half step toward Lips, ready to drag her the fuck out of here.

Avery glares us both down like we're unruly children.

The Mounty blanches and sputters out, "Fuck no! Don't traumatize the poor spawn. It'll be bad enough not knowing who the daddy is."

The doctor grimaces and drops his eyes away from her. "Oh, I know who the daddy is. Maria will be lucky to get to keep the baby."

"Why? Who knocked her up?"

Doc surveys the room before he speaks. "Matteo."

Pure, unadulterated panic flashes across her face.

It's the same type of panic she'd had when Harley had confronted her about Lance and the bet.

Her voice is nothing more than a croak, "Doc. Doc, do not let her tell him. Fuck, send her away."

Whoever this Matteo is, he needs to die.

"I've tried, she won't go. She's got it in her head that they're in love."

Lips reaches out and grabs his wrist, shaking it just enough to get his attention, "I'll give you the money. I'll pay to get her away, Doc."

He gives her a grim look. "I'm not stupid. I know she's going to be forced to abort the baby."

Lips looks like she's going to throw up, but she doesn't say a word. Avery glances over at me and shakes her head again, a sign to shut up and stay out of it, but I really don't like this.

After another tense minute of silence the doctor looks up and smiles at Lips again, all of the gloom gone from around him. "He'll be ready to go by midday. Stop worrying about my problems and go get some sleep, my girl."

When we arrive at the hotel, Lips and Harley leave together to ditch the stolen van. Avery doesn't seem concerned, even as she threads her arm through mine so I can lead her up to the room without tripping onto her face while she focuses on her phone.

"I have us covered, no one will ever know this happened," she murmurs to me, her eyes darting over to Blaise, but he's fucking itching for a high and isn't paying us any attention.

"And what exactly are you going to say to Harley about it? He won't let this shit go, Floss."

The lobby of the hotel is busy, and Blaise catches a lot of interested looks. It's all men in suits doing the looking so they're not at all interested in his talent, only the last name his bastard father saddled him with. He looks ready to take a swing at someone over it, so I nudge my sister just a little and then we both flank him to corral him into the elevator without bloodshed.

"Stop giving a shit about some stupid, brainless suit, Morrison," Avery mutters, throwing an icy look at a group of the men just as the doors to the elevator shut.

Blaise grunts and rubs a hand over his face. "Any second now my phone will be ringing and then—"

I cut him off, "Then what? Your dad will yell at you for not being at school? Turn your fucking phone off, let the cunt rage at your voicemail instead. All he really cares about is his image, and you're not running around naked or fucking some random Mounty in the lobby."

Avery huffs at us both and mutters under her breath, "In his dreams. On repeat, every night he's absolutely fucking a Mounty."

Dead silence.

None of us say another word the entire way up to the penthouse, Blaise and I both practically vibrating with tension and Avery oozing with smugness. It's like an itch across my skin, irritating the fuck out of me until I want to break something.

But I would never hurt my sister, and she knows it too.

She swipes us into the penthouse and opens the door up wide for us all, stalking off to one of the rooms and calling out to us, "I'll leave you two to get absolutely fucking wasted instead of dealing with your issues… typical boy bullshit."

I refuse to answer her or look Blaise's way.

The Mounty is like a ticking time bomb in our family, sitting there waiting for the clock to wind down before destroying everything. The worst part is that the more I watch her, the more I realize she has no idea just how much power she has over us right now.

She has no idea we're all circling her, stuck in her orbit, while she's busy trying to… survive? Graduate? Fuck knows what she's completely distracted by. She's so secretive that every time I think I might have some sort of clue of what her story is, something new happens and I'm back at square one.

Blaise groans, side-eyeing me a little before he stomps through the room and out to the balcony.

That's where Lips finds us an hour later.

I'm not expecting her to join us but she does, slipping out into the night air without a word. Blaise gives me a look as though I'll throw her over the balcony for interrupting us, or for existing in the first place, but I have nothing left to say to her tonight.

Not without telling her how fucking badly I want her.

She doesn't say a word. I'm not really expecting her to jump into our conversation, she's never shown any interest in sports or cars before, and she just sits and stares out at the city lights. It's the calmest I've seen her since we hit the city limits, like we're up here in a little bubble together where none of the dirty, messy, violent parts of her hometown can touch her.

At some point, Blaise gets up and walks back into the room to take a leak. He hesitates for a second before squeezing her shoulder as he moves past, his eyes on the ground as he scampers away like a fucking coward.

I'll call him out on it later.

I wait for a second to see if she runs away or has something to say but when the silence stretches out, I hold the bourbon out to her. "Drink?"

She grabs it and takes a swig straight from the bottle. I quirk an eyebrow at her, expecting some snark or fire back, but all she gives me is a tired look, one she's way too young to be so damn good at. "I need a hell of a lot more than a glass can hold right now."

"Not happy to be home?"

She scoffs at me. "Cut me some slack. I just found out Doc's grandkid is going to be brutally murdered just because she can't remember to take a damn pill."

She groans and hangs her head, misery clinging to every inch of her.

I instantly want to fix every problem she's ever had. "This Matteo will kill her instead of just getting rid of the baby?"

"He doesn't exactly value life, in any form."

Well, that's fucking bleak. I nod slowly and look back over the lights so I don't have to keep watching her, losing my goddamn mind over her. "I'll pay. Get her out and I'll pay for the costs."

There's a stunned silence for a second, one I refuse to be pissed at because of course it's a shock to her that I'd give enough of a fuck to attempt to fix this. Fuck, I'd attempt to fix it even if she weren't so fucking miserable about it. When she stares at me like she's never seen me before, I give her a sidelong look back, taking what's left of the blunt from the ashtray.

I hesitate for a second before offering it to her, but she waves me away. I should attempt to deflect her away from me for a second, knowing that "I'm not a fan of domestic violence or women being killed. Besides, you just saved Joey. I owe you."

She takes another swig of the bourbon, squeezing her eyes shut like she's in pain and I'd like nothing more than to wipe it away for her. To just reach over and take the bottle, pull her into my arms, and have her riding my dick until she can't think about any of this shit.

Her voice is nothing but a croak as she hands me back the bottle. "Thanks. I'll reach out to her."

I shrug and lift the bourbon to my lips, enjoying her eyes following the action as I drink straight from it just like she had done. Her eyes turn molten when I swipe my tongue across my lips, chasing any taste of her that I can because I'll never fucking forget how sweet she really was.

It's all I can think about.

She stands up and steps back through the door like a startled rabbit, and I know I've won something. I look back out at the city lights so I don't chase after her.

She hesitates in the doorway for a second and says, "You don't owe me. I did it for Avery and if you'd just stop hating me, I'd do it for you, too."

I can't look at her right now without her reading way too fucking much all over my face as my eyes don't waver from the lights of the city.

All I can do is nod at her and pray she knows what I'm trying to say.

Twenty Four

BLAISE

If I had any sense at all, I'd start avoiding Lips like the fucking plague, but I'm obsessed with her. Fuck, it's pathetic how desperately I want her. I'm obsessed with the shape of her lips when she smiles, the dry sound of her sarcastic laugh, and the fire that burns in her eyes when she's fucking seething with rage. I can't even get into my obsession with her hands and her legs, her ass and what little I've seen of her body thanks to her preference for oversized clothes.

The problem is that all three of us are fucked over her and no matter who she chooses, it's going to be a fucking mess.

Even though I know I should just forget about her, just move on to someone else so I don't have to face the music that she's definitely going to pick Ash or Harley over me, I can't help wanting to go looking for her when she skips dinner to study.

After we'd walked Avery back up to her room and found it empty, I'd gone back to my room with the other two like nothing was wrong, but there was no fucking way I could head to bed without knowing she'd made it back safe as well, so after I changed out of my uniform I'd taken off.

The other two side-eye me hard, but I slip away before it turns into a full blown argument… or a field trip for us all. I don't want to have to share her right now. I want my next hit of her in private to get me through my withdrawals.

I'm fucking pathetic.

I pass by two teachers on my way down and even though it's just about curfew time, they look the other way and scamper off like their asses are on fire. I smirk and there's an extra pep in my fucking step as I push my way into the library, but it evaporates the second I see Annabelle looming over my Mounty.

Fuck.

I want to tear over to them and shove her away but then I hear Lips snarl at her, her voice carrying over to me loud and clear, "Hand it over or I'll break every finger on your hand. One warning, that's all you're getting."

Well now.

That might be fun to watch, and Annabelle's eyes are wide as she stares at the single finger Lips is holding up, calm and completely prepared to break this bitch's bones.

There's quiet for a moment as Lips looks Annabelle up and down. I can't see her face from here, but I'd bet she's staring the bitch down for everything she's done to us this year. All of the shit Avery found out about her and has been biding her time to ruin her fully.

The photos she took and spread around of my father's letters.

I start toward them right as Lips holds out her hand for the iPod and Annabelle snaps back at her, "I'm not fucking giving it back to you. He doesn't even let Ash touch it! I'll be walking it back up to his room and telling him—"

I cut her off. "That you've stolen my iPod from my friend? That you're a jealous, desperate mess and instead of doing your own work you want to trap me and leech off of me? That you're hung up on Harley and hoping you'll be able to get him back into your bed once you've secured eighteen years of child support from me?"

Annabelle whirls around to face me with a pout and tears in her eyes, but I'm too fucking furious to stop the scathing tirade spilling out of me. She's always playing the fucking victim when she's the one lying and exploiting everyone around her for her own sick games. "How about you tell me all about how you manipulated your way into my room to steal my father's letters and post them for the whole fucking world to see? Or how you're still posting daily about Rory trying to rape Avery? How about you tell me and the Mounty about how you helped that sick freak Lance steal her underwear and you tried to break into her room to let him mess with her shit?"

The color drains from her face. "Blaise, I—"

"Hand Lips my iPod. I gave it to her."

Annabelle's lip is still trembling as she smacks it into Lips' hand, taking a step toward me with tears streaming down her face like she can have one last try at manipulating me.

I feel nothing.

I didn't really feel anything toward her the entire time we were hooking up last year, but there's something about girls crying that makes me feel like the biggest piece of shit. Probably because it reminds me of all of the times I've stumbled upon my mother sobbing quietly in a cupboard thanks to my fucking asshole father.

Lips huffs and moves to stalk away from us both, obviously thinking that I'm just going to let this bitch hang off of me, so I take a quick side step and sling my arm around her waist to catch her, pulling her into my side.

I turn my face into her hair and murmur, "I'm here to walk you back to your room, don't run off without me."

She startles a little, a blush creeping over her cheeks, but she doesn't pull away from me so I take it as a win. I turn us both and start toward the door, trying not to bury my face in her hair and creep the hell out of her.

It's so fucking tempting and Annabelle can see it too. "You know she spent the night with Harley while you were at Avery's recital. You blame me for loving all three of you but it's okay for her to play you all off of each other!"

Fuck her.

Lips tenses up and tries to shift away from me, but I tighten my arm around her because there's no fucking way I'm letting Annabelle ruin this. If I could go back in time and never give that bitch a moment of my time, I would in a heartbeat.

It's probably a little too honest but I can't help calling out over my shoulder, "Nice try, Summers, but we all know what's going on. Harley has not been discreet and, like you said, I don't give my music away to anyone. C'mon, Mounty. Avery will have my balls if I don't get you back soon."

She yells something back at me, but Lips and I get out the door and leave her behind. I don't want to have to let Lips go, so before she can pull away, I grab the iPod from her and hand her one of the earphones as I flick through the last playlist I'd made for her to pick out a song. When the opening bars of 'Iris' start playing, the corners of her lips turn up and I feel like I've won something, because there's nothing as good as making this girl smile.

Even if it's just a little smirk.

We walk in silence, wrapped up in each other as we listen to the song, and the moment it ends I start it again, a wild grin tugging at my lips when she ducks her head to hide her own smile. When she doesn't look back up, I glance down to see what's caught her attention and land on my carnation skulls tattoos on the tops of my bare feet.

Oh God.

I don't want to have to talk about them but if she asks me anything, I'll cave in a hot minute. "Don't ask about the tattoos, it'll only push me to drink."

We arrive at her room and she shrugs. "I'll take a stab at it and say your dad. Yellow carnations aren't exactly the norm to find on album covers so I looked them up. Disappointment and rejection. Didn't make sense to me back then but now I know what a dick your dad is, I get it."

Fuck.

Fuck, every time I speak to this girl she surprises me, and the idea that she's cared enough about me and my music to look into my cover images makes me feel like I might do something fucking embarrassing here.

Like swoon.

Or push her up against this door and eat her out until she wakes the whole fucking building with her screaming.

The last one is too tempting for me to just push aside and when she fishes around in her bag for her keys, I grab her hand, leaning down until our noses brush. She stops breathing, but I can't stop myself. I can't be the one to pull away.

My voice is rough as I say, "Stop me now, Mounty, or I'm going to kiss you. No pity, no ulterior motives, just a kiss because I can't stop myself."

Her response is instant, her lips tilting up to meet mine and what little restraints I have on myself melt away as I meet her halfway.

This is the first kiss we should have had last time.

There's no hesitance in me at all, not even at the thought of how much my friends would fucking hate me for doing this, and when she sucks my bottom lip between her teeth, all other thoughts evaporate as I grunt and slam her into the wall next to the door. I remember at the last second that the walls here are made of stone and she'll get a fucking concussion if I shove her into it, and I slip my hand behind her head to cushion it. She kisses me like she needs my lips to survive, her hands scrabbling at my shirt to drag me closer as she groans. The sounds coming out of her have me hard as fucking nails in a second and I don't want to ruin the moment by grinding on her and blowing a load in my pants, because that would be too fucking shameful.

Instead, I part her legs with my knee and instantly her hips push forward, little gasping sounds tearing out of her throat even as her lips move against mine desperately and I want to spend the rest of my fucking life dragging them out of her. I press my knee into her a little harder and if we keep going we're going to get caught grinding on each other by some fucking gossip.

It kills me, it *fucking* kills me, but I break away from her lips, my chest heaving as I try to get a hold of myself. She's not any better, her hands tightening in the fabric of my shirt a little before she finally lets go.

I don't want to break the silence and thankfully she does it for me.

She clears her throat. "I can't."

Of course she can't, I can't do this either, we're all fucked right now. No one can make a move here without burning everything we all know and have to the ground.

I nod and press my forehead against hers because pulling away right now is going to leave me fucking bleeding and I need to do some damage control. "I know. I'm being a selfish dick. Just do me a favor and don't tell Avery?"

She nods back and doesn't pull away, the two of us just standing there and breathing each other's air as we try to sift through all of the bullshit in our way.

None of us are going to survive this unscarred.

Harley calls me out the second I get back to the room.

I ignore him, because I might take a swing at him in pent up frustration and blue balls, and head to the shower to jerk off in a fit of rage.

I feel like I'm becoming Ash which is just fucking disturbing.

My headphones are wedged tight into my ears when I walk back out, the music cranked up all the way so it's obvious there's no talking to me, and I ignore the daggers Harley shoots my way as I climb into my own bed. It's too early to really sleep without getting high first but I don't want to risk the fight that'll break out if either of them ask me about where the fuck I was, so I lie there and think about that kiss, over and over again until I slowly go insane.

I do everything I can to stay the fuck away from Lips.

Avery is fucking psychic and if she sees me around the Mounty, she's going to know every last detail of what went down and ruin my life with it just to amuse herself... or because I breathe in her direction with attitude, which is the stupidest fucking thing I've heard, but it doesn't stop her from saying it to me regularly.

I think Lips is avoiding me too because it's just too easy to go days without seeing her.

It fucking kills me.

I'm going to have to spend the summer in New York with my parents just to get some space and figure out how the fuck to get through the next two years without moping and pining after this girl like a fucking pathetic asshole. No one is going to win in this situation. Not Harley if he gets her, because he'll have to deal with knowing how much Ash and I want her, not either of us having to give her up, and not Avery who's going to have to deal with the fallout.

I definitely start drinking more than I should after classes each day again.

I'm fucking itching for a beer when my phone pings during the class before lunch. It's Harley in the group message.

We're eating together at the dining hall today. Lips needs backup so be there.

Well, there goes my carefully laid plans of avoiding her, but there's no way I'm going to leave her without backup for… whatever the hell she has going on. I could just go eat in my room and blow them off, I'm sure she'll be fine with just the others, but the idea of letting her down like that has my skin crawling.

I have to accept that, until I figure out how to cut her out from where she's burrowed under my skin, this girl fucking owns me.

I meet Avery at her class because I'm the closest and I'd promised to grab her, then we head over to the dining hall together.

She's busy on her phone but I can't help but ask, "Do you know what this is about?"

She smirks at me without looking up from the screen. "Of course I do."

I huff at her and glare down a freshman who looks like he's going to jostle her to get past. The little fucker shits himself and takes off in the opposite direction. "Well, what the fuck is going on? If someone is coming after her then we need to know about it."

She raises an eyebrow at me. "And why do you need to know about it, Morrison? Anything you need to tell me?"

Fuck. I seal my lips shut and try to get my face to show her nothing. *Nothing*. I think for a second that I've managed to fool her, but then she smirks again and says, "Pathetic, the lot of you. And I won't tell you a goddamn thing, if Lips wants you to know the details then she'll tell you herself."

I grit my teeth and shake my head at her. "There's too many fucking secrets. We're going to drown in them."

Avery shrugs as I push the doors open to the dining hall, murmuring quietly so only I can hear her, "We'll talk when you idiot boys figure your shit out."

Fuck. I grimace and Avery cackles at me like my misery is so fucking amazing to her, that I can't help but sneer back at her. "Maybe you should have this little chat with your cousin, he's the one holding up the fucking line."

Then I walk to the table where the others are waiting for us. There's food already there for us that presumably

Ash grabbed, because it's all of the shit we usually eat and I can't imagine Harley grabbing me pizza. He would've been too busy making eyes at Lips but being too much of a fucking pussy to just ask her out.

There's a part of me who knows it's not that easy, but there's a larger part of me that doesn't give a fuck. I don't give a fuck that Lips is honestly the hardest, most difficult girl to approach and talk to about this shit. I don't care that if I were Harley I'd be tiptoeing the fuck around her too just so I didn't fuck shit up.

I don't care because I'm still too jealous to be reasonable.

Avery slips into the empty chair between Lips and Ash, and immediately the girls start whispering to each other. Ash eyes them off but the cold look on his face means he's just as clueless as I am about what the fuck is going on.

We all dig into our food without talking about the giant elephant in the room, though we're all sneaking glances at Lips like she's so fucking fascinating, as she ignores her own plate of food. Well. She is and we always do that, but normally we're a little more discreet about it because we don't want to piss each other off.

Knowing there's a potential threat means all bets are off.

We're nearly finished when the door flings open with such force that it bounces off the wall.

Fuck.

I don't even have to look up to know that it's Joey storming over toward us, and Harley immediately picks up a knife like he's going to slit his cousin's throat right here in the dining hall with the entire school watching.

I'm not sure even Avery could cover that mess up.

Lips doesn't look up or react at all, a sure sign that this is all following some plan she has, but Avery hisses at her, "Fuck, here he comes. He looks fucking murderous, Lips. He looks like Father does right before he backhands me, fuck."

Lips glances at her, the sharp edge in her eyes softening for just a second before she finally picks up her fork and starts in on her food. Avery follows her lead even with the slight tremble in her fingers, and Lips murmurs quietly, "Remember what I said. He's effectively neutered. Don't engage with him."

What the hell is that supposed to mean?

I glance at Harley but he's staring back at me like I'll have some answers in this mess.

Are we ever going to be in on this shit? Are we ever going to know what the fuck is going on around us or are Lips and Avery just going to set fire to our shit whenever the mood strikes them and we'll just constantly be sitting around looking like fucking dickheads?

Ash snarls at Lips, clearly just as pissed as Harley and

I are about being left in the dark about this shit, "What the fuck does that even mean?"

There's no time for Lips to reply though because Joey arrives, slamming his palms onto the table in front of her so hard everything on the table rattles.

Silence falls over the dining hall.

The freshmen sitting around us start scrambling to get their shit together and flee, not that I blame them. He really is a fucking monster, and he's proved over and over again just how little he gives a fuck about assaulting and maiming people. He's lost his shit, his eyes are manic as they dart around each of us and there's no doubt that he's in withdrawal. I've only seen him this bad once before and he almost killed two juniors in a fit of rage.

Great.

"Who the fuck do you think you are?" he spits at her, and I pick a knife up as well. I guess Harley isn't the only person going down for Joey's murder today.

Lips doesn't look worried, not for a second.

Instead, she slowly sets down her own knife and fork, crossing her arms over her chest like she has all the time in the world. She looks him up and down slowly before she speaks, her words even and calm and utterly fucking cutthroat.

"Let me tell you how this is going to go from here onwards, Joseph. You will not speak to me, your siblings, your cousin, or Morrison. You will not speak about us. You won't plot, or scheme, or belittle. You will not raise a hand. You're going to pretend we don't exist. If you come across one of us in the halls you will avert your gaze and walk the fuck away. Am I clear?"

Oh, she's about to die.

Ash tenses, ready to jump up and throw himself at Joey the second his brother flies at her and kills the little Mounty girl except...

He doesn't.

Joseph Beaumont Jr. just stands there, his chest heaving like he's about to fucking scream or puke or something, and even though his eyes are darting around the room like he's looking for an exit, he doesn't so much as flinch in her direction.

What the fuck is happening here?

"The Jackal sends his regards," Lips says in that same even tone like this is all so fucking boring to her, and then she picks her fork back up and digs back into her food.

My eyes meet Ash's but he's still sitting there, shocked but ready to act the second Joey does. Avery is like a statue, barely breathing, but after another beat she picks up her cutlery again and follows the Mounty's lead.

The whole room is silent.

Then Joey roars and turns on his heel, shoving a couple of juniors on his way out and whispers start up all around us.

"What the fuck just happened?" The words fall out of me, and Lips blinks up at me, glancing around the table at each of us like she's shocked we're showing her so much interest… as though she hasn't just achieved the impossible right here in the fucking dining hall. Avery looks smugly around at us as well, grinning at Lips like she's in love with her.

That makes four of us.

Lips pulls herself up a little straighter and then just lays out the facts. "Joey likes three things. I couldn't touch his money—that will take more time than we have. I couldn't kill him without risking Ash. That left his addiction."

I can barely believe the words coming out of her mouth. "Holy shit. You cut him off. You cut him off?!"

"There isn't a dealer in the state that will sell to him now," she says as she looks me dead in the eye like some fucking badass Mounty kid we've all been underestimating, and I fall completely over the fucking ledge in love with her.

How the fuck am I going to survive seeing her with Harley every fucking day and knowing how badly I want her?

"How the fuck does a Mounty have that much pull?" Harley says, just as incredulous as I am, and she smirks back at him.

We all watch as puzzle pieces click together in his

head."Fuck. You used a favor."

A favor.

It's as though they're speaking another language, one only the two of them and maybe Avery know, and for once I find myself ready to hulk out and flip the fucking table in a rage. Usually I leave that shit to Arbour and his pissy moods.

Lips nods at Harley slowly and when he sighs like the whole world is riding on his shoulders, she murmurs to him quietly, "I used one to save you. One to get Senior out of the way until graduation. Now I've used another to cut Joey off. I don't regret it and I'd do it again. We're all getting out of this alive, even if I have to call in every favor I have. That's why I have them."

Holy shit.

We haven't just underestimated her. We've been chasing her around thinking she needs our protection while she's been using secret connections to dig us all out of the shit we've been buried in, slowly but surely drowning in.

The look on Ash's face says everything.

Twenty Five

ASH

After the Mounty's stunt in the dining hall, I'm expecting Senior or Joey to retaliate immediately. I'm expecting a phone call or visit from Senior, a knock at the door at 3 in the morning from Joey ready to make me bleed for what Lips did, but… nothing.

Not a single word from any of them.

It goes beyond not being able to believe it, it worries me because there's no way it can be true. There's no way Lips actually managed to find something that would stop Joey from going to Senior and bringing his wrath down on us all.

But she did.

I give up all pretenses of trying to stay away from her.

I start following Blaise to their room for their study sessions and the second Harley catches wind of it, he comes along too. Avery watches us all like a hawk, like she's waiting for a fucking orgy to start on the floor, but Lips just accepts us all crashing there like it's perfectly reasonable for us all to be studying together.

I get nothing done around her.

Well, mostly because I can't concentrate with Harley glaring daggers at me and Blaise moping in my general direction because he's a spoiled brat who can't handle having to share her. The real problem here is that it finally occurs to me that Lips is utterly oblivious to us all.

She doesn't have a fucking clue of what's going on.

Harley glues himself to her side, telling Blaise and I that he's worried about Joey's retaliation but we both know exactly what his game plan is. When he insists on sitting next to her and she questions him about it, there's no way around it. She might be the smartest person in our grade, she might have all of the street smarts the Bay could ever offer her, but she has no fucking clue about how badly the three of us want her.

I shouldn't, I really fucking shouldn't, but I text Avery about it.

How exactly does Lips not see Harley panting after her?

My sister looks up at me from the other side of the table, a tray of sushi in front of her and a math book open to whatever it is that she's cramming for. No one else notices that we're texting each other, because Lips is busy explaining something to Blaise and Harley is glaring at him like he's asked her for a strip tease and not just help with geometry.

Just Harley? I was under the impression you're all panting after her pathetically. I've never helped you with your conquests before and I'm not starting now.

My eyes narrow in her direction but she just smirks at me, smug as ever until I put my phone down and get back to my own studying.

This is not going to end well.

No one give Lips any coffee, she's cut off.

The text makes absolutely no sense because coffee isn't some illicit fucking substance, but when I meet Harley at the door to the chapel he looks pissed as fuck.

"What's eating your ass?"

He huffs at me and pushes the doors open, leading the way to the front row of pews and snarling at the students there until they scamper off. I sit down and look out over the crowd but Joey is nowhere to be seen.

"Lips is a fucking wreck. You saw the text right? She's jittering around the place like she's on crack, because she's that nervous about this shit. Why the hell would they make the performance mandatory? It's choir for fuck's sake."

Lips, Blaise, and Avery finally arrive together just as

the performances are due to start. Lips is wedged between the other two, Blaise's arm slung over her shoulders as he leans in to whisper to her and Avery's arm is threaded through hers.

Lips looks like she's going to puke.

I don't like that at all.

"She's fucking terrified of doing this, don't be a dick about it," Harley snaps, and I turn to snap back at him but his eyes are still on the stage, like he's plotting out how to start a fire and get her out of having to do this.

I'm dying to hear her sing.

Avery always gets this awed look on her face whenever Blaise mentions Lips's voice, and her overall smugness tells me we're in for a show, so as much as I don't like seeing her so fucking jittery… I'm not going to lie and say I'm not looking forward to seeing what she's got in store for us.

When the choir teacher walks out and starts off on her speech about what the students will be doing, I zone out, only focusing again when Avery's name is called first and she walks confidently onstage. She sings beautifully, nothing show-stopping or flashy, but she only ever did choir to keep an eye on Blaise. The moment she's done there's a decent applause from the audience, most of the students too fucking terrified of her not to clap, and she prances off of the stage like a pro to sit with us.

The next girl is out of tune, and Harley keeps snickering under his breath at her because she's swaying and gyrating like she's the best fucking thing since sliced bread. At one point she dry humps the microphone stand and winks at Harley who stares her down like she's diseased, which, if the rumors are to be believed, is accurate.

Blaise cheats and sings a Vanth song, not exactly giving it his all but still sounding good enough to have half the female population fucking swooning. I swear you can hear them all dripping for him and the applause is full of squealing girls as he steps down from the stage.

I smirk at him when he takes his seat, nudging Harley with his elbow and picking a fight with him right off the bat. Avery leans in close to me, whispering in my ear, "Lips is better."

I don't see how that's possible so I'm assuming she's just stirring shit with me. Harley and Blaise mutter amongst themselves through the rest of the performances and Avery spends the whole time on her phone, looking through security camera footage of what exactly Joey has been up to in the last week, which is both disgusting and typical.

A lot of alcohol and girls stupid enough to fuck him because even with his reputation, the Beaumont name is a draw for them.

After an hour, Lips' name is finally called out and she

walks out onto the stage, her legs still unsteady but her face a blank, carefully controlled mask once again. She fidgets with her ears for a second and takes a deep, deep breath.

"What was that?" I murmur, and Avery sighs a little at me.

"Earplugs. She can't sing without them."

I frown, but then the song starts and she opens her mouth and nothing else exists to me anymore, nothing but the sound of her voice and, fuck me, the Mounty can sing. She sounds like nothing I've ever heard before, the hauntingly beautiful tones of her voice send shivers down my spine and if it wasn't already perfectly clear to me before... I am ruined for this girl.

I am *fucked*.

She stares out at the colored glass, tears starting up in her eyes, but she sings angelically through it all like a fucking trooper.

There's a stunned silence that falls over the chapel when the final notes of the song come to an end and then the entire room erupts. Lips obviously can't really hear it, or she's in too much of a trance after singing, because she doesn't smile or blush or acknowledge it in any way as she stumbles over to the steps. When she pulls the earplugs out, she finally cracks a weak-looking smile and chuckles at Avery's overly enthusiastic cheering.

She looks so unsteady as she wobbles over to us, her eyes darting around at each of us but I can't think of a single thing to say to her… other than how fucking badly I want her in my bed tonight.

Avery tucks her into her side and whispers to her, the blush spreading over her cheeks entirely too tempting, and I have to pry my eyes away from her.

Lips lets out a breath and settles into her seat, wedged in-between Avery and Harley, and we watch as a guy with a cello walks out onto the stage. It's only quiet for a second before Blaise and Harley start fighting, the beginning of the end.

"Move," says Blaise.

Harley spits fire back at him. "Fuck off. You've just decided to do something about it because she passed your little singing test?"

"Don't be a jealous dick and move. I need to tell her—"

"You'd have to climb over my dead fucking body, and we both know I could take you. Now shut up before you get us in the shit."

Avery is grinning like this is the most amusing shit in her life, but I'm not sure she knows how bad this really is because if Blaise has finally decided to do something… we're not going to survive this and all still stay together. This isn't about sex or reputations or any of the other bullshit it usually is. I'm not desperate to fuck the Mounty for a notch on my bedpost or just to say I've had her.

I want to keep her.

I was ready to break all of the rules and fucking obliterate Joey when he came at her the other day. I've hospitalized students all year for talking shit about her, and the thought of her going home to the Bay in a few weeks and finding some guy to hook up with there has me ready to spill blood.

I want to drive down to the Bay right now and gut the Jackal for being a threat to her.

There's no way I'd be feeling all of this shit if I didn't want to call her mine and covet her; keep her the fuck away from the Bay and all of the dangers that place holds for her.

I feel the Mounty's eyes on me, but if I look over at her right now I'll do something stupid and ruin everything, something like hauling her ass out of here and finding the closest flat surface to spread her out on.

I spend the rest of the performances trying to get a hold of myself.

The second Trevelen dismisses us, Avery sighs at Lips like she's a problem child and says, "I'm making dinner, are you coming up to eat with us or are you hitting the dining hall?"

It's a bad idea, but none of us seem to be able to pry ourselves away from Lips right now, so we all agree to go eat with Avery. Harley is glaring around at everyone and everything surrounding us and Blaise watches him like he's about to start a fight.

I focus on the girls and when Lips' leg gives way and she almost takes a dive, I'm glad I've been watching.

What the fuck has happened to her?

Avery immediately gets a hold of her elbow to support her, tucking her phone away and focusing entirely on Lips with a frown.

"You know how I tell you not to buy me shit? If a new leg is on the table, I'll take it," Lips grunts through clenched teeth, and Avery rubs her back with a little smile as they hobble out of the auditorium.

I last exactly ten steps before I step in.

It's a miracle it takes me that long because the wincing and grimaces make the killing rage fill my veins and if I find out someone did this to her, they'll be dead before dawn. I will fucking destroy them for doing this to her.

I wrap an arm around her waist, moving slow enough that she can stop me if it jars her leg in any way, and pull her into my side firmly. She tenses for a second, her own version of flailing about, but then she takes a deep breath and clutches at my waist to lean on me more fully. That tastes like victory, and Harley immediately starts to bitch me out from where he's watching us like a fucking hawk.

I don't want to deal with him, so instead I murmur, "What happened?"

"My leg just likes to remind me that violence is never the answer," she says with her usual brand of dry wit, and it strikes me again how much I *like* her. This isn't just an attraction thing, this is deeper and has taken root in me in ways that I don't think I'll ever be able to claw out.

I chuckle under my breath at her as we start walking again, and her legs still aren't steady enough. I look down at her and go through the pros and cons of just carrying her the rest of the way. Harley and Blaise will be pissed, and Lips might kick up a fuss, but the wobbling is killing me.

She blinks back at me, clearly confused. "I'll be fine, I just need to get off my feet for a few days."

Of course she'd say it's fine; there's no way I can carry her without her stabbing me or something, so I nod right as Harley pries Avery away so he can take up on the other side of the Mounty. Between the two of us we take all of the weight off of her legs until we're carrying her. Neither of us say a word and Avery stares us down one by one, like she's about to make this entire thing everyone's problem. When she opens her mouth, Blaise hauls her under his arm and pulls her to lead the way, not at all distracting her but getting her moving so the blowup that's about to happen can at the very least be away from the gossips of Hannaford.

There's already too many eyes on us all as we walk through the girls' dorm. None of them are brave enough to whisper or call attention to themselves, but there's no denying that they're all a little too interested in Lips being carried up here by the two of us.

From the corner of my eye I see Annabelle take two steps out of her room toward us, but there's no fucking way I'm dealing with her brand of bullshit today. She might be a dumb, manipulative slut but she seems to read the situation well enough that I can stop her in her tracks with a single look. It doesn't stop her from standing there and watching Harley pass with devastated eyes, eyes brimming with tears that make me feel *nothing*. He doesn't even glance her way, all of his focus and energy on Lips and, as much as I want her for myself, that's exactly where it should be.

When we arrive at the girls' room, Avery unlocks the door and we direct Lips in and set her gently down onto her bed.

It only takes a minute for everything to implode because with one sentence, Avery lights a match and flicks it onto the fire.

"What the fuck is going on here?"

One look at Lips confirms she's completely oblivious to us all, her focus entirely on the pain she's in, and I'm fuming at Avery for bringing this shit up now when there's more pressing shit to deal with.

Like killing whoever hurt the Mounty.

"Don't you look at me like that, Ash, you don't get to

decide to suddenly switch teams and be protective of her without giving me some answers. Now, I'm not going to ask you all again, tell me what the hell is going on?" Avery says, and her tone grates on me.

Harley looks her over and then shrugs. "Nothing. Nothing is going on—"

"What's going on is Harley needs to get his shit together and do something already because he's wasting everyone's goddamn time."

"What the hell does that even mean!"

But none of us take any notice of her because Blaise is staring Harley down like he's about to take a swing, and once again we're all teetering on the edge of destruction.

Harley cuts me off with a snarl, "This isn't a fucking game—"

"No one thinks it's a *game*, asshole—"

Harley loses his head and he yells, "Fuck you, Morrison! You and Ash are as bad as each other."

From the corner of my eye I see Lips' head snap in our direction, and Avery's eyes narrow as she stares each of us down. My fists are clenched at my sides, from where I'm stopping myself from taking a swing at Harley, because if he would just do something maybe we wouldn't be in this limbo space of hell right now.

If she was his then I'd have to just… get the hell over her.

Avery finally decides Harley is the best chance of getting what she wants, so with a glare she pokes him in the chest with a finger and snaps, "Calm the hell down. I'm not having you break my room because you're in a mood."

That only makes shit worse and when Blaise smirks at him he widens his stance, and there's no way in hell I'm letting him take a swing at him with Avery standing right the fuck there.

Before I can shove her behind me Avery snarls, "One of you idiots had better start explaining what the fuck is going on. *Now*. I've never seen you fight like this before!"

No one moves or says a word.

None of us want to admit what the problem is when Lips is sitting right there on the bed watching us and, like lovesick idiots, we all turn as one to look at her.

Her face immediately shuts down.

It's a bad thing too, a self-conscious tic like she thinks we're all making fun of her, but there's absolutely nothing I can say or do that won't make all of this worse, so I have to stand there and watch as she slides off of her bed and mumbles some excuse about having a shower to give us all some privacy.

When Blaise attempts to help Lips as she hobbles past us all, Harley snarls at him like a fucking asshole, because he can't handle any of us touching her now apparently, and Avery has to once again step in to stop a full-blown brawl.

I hear her murmur to Lips as they hobble past, "I need a fucking drink after this," and doesn't that sound like a fucking plan.

The second the bathroom door shuts, I stalk over to the kitchen cupboards and start searching for the bourbon, because what this situation needs is some fucking alcohol.

"Don't you dare start drinking before we get to the bottom of this, Ash!" Avery hisses lowly, and I roll my eyes at her without stopping my search.

"It's pretty simple; Harley has called dibs on the Mounty, but then he's been too chicken shit to do a thing about it. Blaise and I have respected the dibs for months, but that's not going to happen anymore."

There's silence for a second and then Avery sputters, "Dibs? You freaking idiots put 'dibs' on Lips and that's why you've been bickering like children? Did any of you assholes think about what she wanted? That maybe she isn't a toy you can covet like that?"

I finally find the bourbon and grab a glass, only because Avery will lose what little patience she has left for me if I drink it straight from the bottle. When I turn around, Blaise is already chugging back a beer and Harley is standing tall against Avery's vicious glare.

"It wasn't fucking *dibs*; Ash is just being a confrontational asshole because he's pissed about this whole… thing. I told them I was interested in her and they both backed off."

Avery squints at him like he's dense. "Oh, of course, that definitely sounds nothing like dibs to me! But never mind, let's circle back to that. Why haven't you done anything yet? You and Lips spend all day together in class, I'm sure you could've found time to say something to her… though she's not really one for dirty hookups."

He eyes her off but it's not in a defensive way, it's more like he's judging how much she knows and that piques my interest. "You did fucking hook up with her. I knew it."

"Shut your fucking mouth," Harley snarls, and there's nothing more tempting to me than his hackles rising like that.

I smirk at him. "Why don't we just end this now and go ask her?"

I get one step toward the bathroom door before Harley is in my face. "Open that fucking door while she's in the shower and I'll *gut* you."

There's no doubt in my mind that he's serious, and I'm also not at all surprised at his reaction.

Blaise's lack of defense on my behalf is a shock though.

He's never hesitated to throw himself into any fight, but this mess has him drawing back in on himself and if nothing comes from this fight tonight then he'll be back on suicide watch, because he's looking moodier than ever.

Harley throws me a glare, but Avery is far more focused

on where Blaise is throwing back his second beer, a third clutched tightly in his fist. Her eyes then flick over to the glass I'm refilling like this is all so telling.

It is telling, but I hate her perceptiveness for a second.

"Oh my freaking God. You're all in love with her. This isn't just some disgusting sex thing… you want to date her. All three of you. Well, I'll be damned."

While I don't think any of us would call this love, none of us argue with her because there's no arguing that we're all obsessed with her.

Without another word Avery starts to throw together food for us all. By the time she's plating up, the shower is still going, so Lips has either drowned or she's truly terrified of coming out and facing whatever happened out here, but honestly… nothing has happened. Nothing except Avery forcing us all to admit how fucked we are and how bad this situation is that we've found ourselves in.

Blaise refuses to eat so Avery gets him doing dishes, and then she hovers over Harley and I while we eat. I'd rather drink until I forget this night happened, but there's also something about watching Harley squirm under Avery's eye that's too amusing to miss out on.

He manages one mouthful before he starts in on her again. "So we're just going to forget this happened, right? We're going back to minding our own fucking business."

Avery huffs at him. "No, idiot. I'm going to sort this out

like I sort out everything for you lot. We're done talking about it for tonight."

He opens his mouth to argue but snaps it shut again as the bathroom door opens, Lips stepping out hesitantly. Avery grins at her as she gestures to her to come and eat, but Lips stares back at her distrustfully.

"Why are you so happy? Did Annabelle choke on a dick or something?"

Don't we all wish.

Avery cackles. "Better. So much better. We'll talk tomorrow, just eat some dinner and rest your leg for now."

"We could talk about it now," Harley grumbles into his plate, and Avery's grin shifts into a glare as her eyes flick back down to him.

"Eat your damn pasta, Arbour."

And that's the end of that.

Twenty Six

HARLEY

Avery is a meddling control freak, and she's going to ruin everything.

The only reason I didn't call her the hell out on throwing herself into this last night was the fear in Lips' eyes when she'd looked over at us all fighting over her. She's too fucking jumpy, and I seem to be the only one who gives a shit about her freaking the hell out and disappearing on us all.

Summer break is only a week away.

She could head back down to the Bay and meet some Mounty asshole who's willing to fuck with the Jackal just to have her, and I *cannot* let that happen. Not just because it's a risk for her but because I'd be charging down to the slums and killing whoever the fuck touched her.

I decide to meet with Lips before breakfast and just fucking man up, lay this shit out there, and see what she says.

The problem is that the moment I get back to my room from swim practice, Ash and Blaise are already awake, showered, and dressed to head down for food. I pause for a half second in the doorway with my bag still slung over my shoulder, and that's long enough for Morrison to smirk at me like the asshole he is.

"You honestly thought you could just scurry over there this morning without us, huh? Idiot."

I ignore him and stalk into the bathroom to change into my uniform because anything I say right now will start a war, and if we're all going over to the girls' room together then I can't be fighting with him. It'll just have the entire fucking day ruined, and Lips will probably do a runner to get away from us both, and then Ash can swoop in and save the day like a fucking asshole.

I hate everyone right now.

None of us speak a word the entire walk over. It's the most uncomfortable I've ever been around my own family, and I fucking hate it. I hate the way my skin is crawling and my gut is churning and the threads of fear that are pulling me in every direction, because this entire fucking situation is a no-win.

Someone is going to lose their shit today.

Avery opens the door to us all with a haughty look and then immediately ducks into the bathroom where the shower is already running, the sounds of the lock turning like a gunshot through the room.

Ash moves to the kitchen like he's going for the bourbon but then remembers it's seven in the morning and even a Beaumont shouldn't show up to class half cut, so instead we all just stand around, twitching and fidgeting like crackheads.

Our attention snaps back to the bathroom when the door cracks open an inch, Avery's head poking out of the tiny crack with another haughty look.

"We'll meet you guys down at the dining hall."

I shake my head. "We're here to walk you guys down; we'll wait."

Her eyes narrow at me. "No, we're fine."

Ash shrugs at her. "We're already here, we might as well wait for you both just in case Joey tries something."

Avery huffs at him and snaps, "Ash, I have cramps and I need a minute to get myself together and I'd rather not have you lot out there listening to me change out tampons."

Blaise startles like a fucking idiot, like he's forced himself to forget that Avery is in fact female and gets periods. "Fuck, saying you need a minute is more than enough information."

Ash and I both roll our eyes at him and Avery smiles at him with that fake, poisonous sweetness she's perfected. "Well, if you listened to me the first time I wouldn't have to supply you with the details."

Blaise and Ash both start toward the door, but I'm not leaving so fucking easily. "I need to talk to Lips."

"No, Lips is still getting dressed."

I roll my eyes back at her. "What, she's just going to stand around watching you switch out tampons? For fuck's sake, Floss, let her out of there!"

"We're girls, she isn't worried about my period, she has her own to deal with. Bye!" She's a little too fucking gleeful as she snaps the door shut, and I have no choice but to follow the other two down to the dining hall.

"You have until midnight tonight. That's it. Not a second longer."

I roll my eyes at Morrison's bullshit as we move along the food line, staring down a couple of the seniors glancing back at us like we're so fucking fascinating.

"I don't need until midnight—"

"I'm not giving him until midnight. Like Avery said, dibs is bullshit. If Avery hasn't already, we'll all tell her and she can decide." Ash cuts in and fills a plate up with piles of eggs and bacon. I do the same without another word because… well, there's nothing left to say.

It's up to Lips now.

We take our seats right as Avery's text comes through.

We're headed down now. Lips is still feeling shit, don't be inconsiderate assholes and pant all over her while she's not okay.

Ash's jaw tightens as he reads it and then murmurs, "Whoever broke her leg, they're on the planner. I don't give a fuck who she chooses; I'm killing whoever hurt her like that."

Only if he gets to them first.

When the girls arrive, Avery has to coax Lips into taking food, another sign she's not okay, and I have to force myself to keep my mouth shut. Morrison watches her like she's a miracle walking among us, all of his attempts at hiding his obsession gone now, and even Ash stares at her in his own twisted version of wonder. I wait until the last second before I look up at her, only because I'm sure I'm staring at her just as obsessively, and Avery shuts us all down pretty fucking quickly.

The second they reach the table, she slams their tray down with more force than necessary as they both take their seats and snaps, "Don't start. Lips can't eat when she's stressed."

Lips cringes and nudges her plate away from herself a little, and Morrison, the asshole extraordinaire, drawls, "If Harley is bothering you—"

Avery cuts Blaise off, hissing, "I said, *don't start*," as I elbow him in the gut to shut him the fuck up. Ash just watches it all play out without a word, letting us all dig our own graves.

"I'm never going to eat again. Goodbye boobs, it was nice having you," Lips mutters, and Avery cackles at her dramatics.

"That will shut them up! The boobs are in danger."

Fuck that.

I snort and shove her plate of French toast back in front of her. "Save the boobs, Mounty."

Her cheeks flush as she picks up her fork, digging in as we all laugh, the tension finally ebbing away a little. She focuses entirely on her food, eating slowly but meticulously, and we all get back to our own food. I barely taste a thing.

"So! Plans for summer break?" Avery says in her most fake sunshine tone, like it isn't completely obvious she's deflecting, but we all play along and groan.

"I'm getting dragged to New York by my father to see what's new with the Kora branch there. I'm looking forward to exactly none of it and I'm pissed off I won't be touring," says Blaise, and he pours Lips another glass of juice. She mumbles a quiet thank you to him, the flush on her cheeks still going strong.

I don't want to talk about my plans because they're completely centered on finding as much time as possible to spend with Lips, whether we're dating or not, because

I'm not leaving her in the Bay alone. I rub a hand over the back of my head as I say, "Two weeks on the coast to see my mom. Then Mounts Bay."

Ash and Blaise give me a look, but I don't give a fuck who knows that I'm going to be watching her back. They're both probably going to try the same shit.

"We'll be going to Amsterdam to celebrate Joey's graduation. He chose the city and Father agreed because he'll want to spend some time in the red light district I imagine. Hopefully he catches something terminal. Or at the very least something that makes his dick rot and fall off. Lips?" says Ash.

Fuck, we can only hope Senior and Joey both fall into some poisonous pussy and croak there.

Lips obviously agrees as she snorts and pushes her empty plate aside, wiping her mouth with a napkin. She glances at me from the corner of her eye and there's that blush again.

The problem is she's reacting to all of us and I have no idea what that means for us.

"I have a couple of jobs lined up. Oh, and some Club events to go to. I have some…plans in the pipeline that I'm working on. Lots of groundwork and carefully thought out moves," she says mildly, like she's not opening up a whole new can of worms for us all to worry about. Avery watches her with interest but she doesn't ask any questions, which means she knows all of the details and I'll be grilling her extensively later.

When Lips doesn't continue, or give us any information that might help us figure her plans the hell out, and Avery just taps away on her phone. Ash finally clears his throat and asks, carefully, "You're going back to the Jackal, then?"

She tenses a little and then glances around the dining hall. There's no one near us, barely any students came down to eat here this morning and I'm glad when she says, "No, I'm not going back to him. Do you guys know what the Club is? Who the Twelve are?"

Finally, we might get *something* from her.

Morrison frowns a little and asks, "They're like gang leaders, right?"

She winces and I want to kill him for whatever he's made her feel, but she continues anyway. "Not quite. Some are, the Jackal included. He deals drugs, runs firearms, dabbles in extortion when the payoff is high enough. But really, each member of the Twelve have their own set of skills and they build on that."

I already knew that after a childhood living down there and my time in juvie. Half the kids there already had the animal tattoos of whoever they'd sold themselves to, and there's no denying who owns the city.

Whatever she has to do with the Twelve… it's going

to complicate things, because getting her away from the Jackal is going to be hard enough without her having involvement with one of the other members.

Fuck.

"I was thirteen when the Hawk died and a spot opened up in the Twelve. They ran the Game, which should really have it's name changed to 'brutal torture sessions'. The Jackal sponsored me. I went up against thirty men and I won."

The words might be in English but she might as well be speaking fucking Swahili for all the sense it makes to me, and it takes a second before I can even reply, my words sputtering out at the same time as Ash and Morrison's.

"You won?"

"Thirty men?"

"What the fuck?!"

Avery scoffs at us and looks up from her phone with a smug look. "All hail the Wolf of Mounts Bay."

What.

The.

Fuck?!

My vision whites out a little because that's not fucking possible. That's not even a little bit possible, right? The greatest assassin in the history of the Bay, the silent and deadly Wolf who has never missed a target.

Lips Anderson.

The Mounty.

The motherfucking Wolf of Mounts Bay.

"The Wolf?!" I sputter and I can't even feel bad for the way she blanches, because I'm too busy looking for evidence. There's not that much I know for sure about the Wolf, nothing except the burn scars she has to have thanks to one of my cousins. When I duck down and look under the table at her legs, Avery kicks me in the shin sharply, but I completely ignore her. "We're wearing skirts, idiot!"

When I sit back up, Lips is blushing like crazy, and I say, "You took out one of my distant cousins in the Game. His dad was fucking livid and went after you with a blowtorch."

Lips stares at me for a second and then, with zero remorse, she says, "Yeah. Sorry about that."

And just like that, I believe her.

I've fallen head first into an obsession with the Wolf of Mounts Bay.

There's nothing left for me to do than just tip my head back and roar with laughter because what the fuck is happening right now? This is not how today was supposed to be going, and I don't think I can be mad about it. "I can't believe we were all worried about Joey killing you. If only he knew everything you've done. Why didn't you just sneak into his room and slit his throat while he slept?"

Her eyes are suddenly anywhere but on me, her cheeks

pale as she chews on her bottom lip.

Morrison elbows me and growls, "Shut up, asshole, you're freaking her out."

Fuck.

Fuck, I've let my own complete fucking meltdown freak her out.

She takes a deep breath before looking back up at us, her eyes flitting over each of us like she's expecting one of us to pull out a knife and I want to fucking scream because I did that to her.

I made her afraid of our reactions.

"I'm at Hannaford to get as far away from that life as I can. I wasn't a willing participant. I had two choices: play the Game or die at the Jackal's hands. Everything I've done has been to keep myself alive," she says quietly but firmly, with that same strength that's been in her from day one.

"I didn't mean—" I say, but Avery cuts me off.

"Lips, you should head to class. I'll meet you there, I need to have a chat with the guys."

She nods and stoops down immediately to grab her bag, hobbling out of the dining hall as fast as her damaged leg will carry her.

Morrison shifts like he's going to go after her, and Avery snaps, "Stay right the hell there, Morrison, so we can talk this out."

He doesn't even spare her a glance. "She needs help, I'm not just going to leave her—"

"What are you going to do, throw her over your shoulder? She's armed at all times; that's the quickest and stupidest way to get stabbed."

Shit.

Shit, I have to adjust myself discreetly under the table, because there's nothing quite like hearing the girl you want is both armed and prepared to kill. I grew up in the Bay, so that shit is a big turn on.

I'm fucking doomed.

Morrison huffs, crossing his arms like a petulant child, but Avery just leans back in her seat until she has our full attention. Ash looks completely cut off, nothing but the cold, blank trademark Beaumont mask on his face.

I definitely don't have my shit locked down that well.

"I spoke to Lips about choosing one of you."

My stomach drops and I have to swallow around the lump in my throat. Morrison starts fucking twitching in his seat, and I want to snap his hands off.

"She didn't want to choose. Apparently she's just as obsessed with the three of you. Personally, I think you'll all only really work if you're with the same girl. I've said it a million times, but you're all painfully codependent."

There's a beat of silence, because that is absolutely *not* what any of us were expecting.

Morrison and Ash share a look but my brain isn't making the same leap theirs clearly are. "What the fuck are we going to do, share her?"

Avery rolls her eyes. "Like you haven't shared before."

My teeth clench together. "I'm not talking about some piece of ass that doesn't matter to us. I'm talking about someone who is family; there's too much at stake to be playing games."

Avery leans forward in her seat. "Look around, Arbour. You're not the only person who's obsessed with her, you're just the only one too blind to see how far all three of you have fallen."

She looks around at each of us again and then stands, her phone in her hand. "I have some calls to make. I'll wait over by the door for you, Ash."

He doesn't say a word, just watches her with that same protective intensity he always does.

I can't help but start the fight with him. I can't risk Lips with his games. "I'm fucking serious, Ash, if you hurt her—"

His eyes snap to mine as he leans forward in his seat, his tone scathing as he says, "From where I'm sitting, you're the only one who hurt her today and if you do it again, I'll beat the shit out of you without hesitating. You want to know how serious I am about her? I'll tear this family apart for her if I have to… it's the only one I've ever had, but it's not a real family without her. I've spent fucking months fighting it, but this is just the way it is."

Morrison nods and adds, "She's ours. She has been from the second she walked through those doors. So either get on board or leave, because if she's decided she wants us to share then that's what's happening."

I blow out a breath and glance over at the doors again, almost convinced someone is going to come running through them to ruin this for us all because… fuck I want this. I want it so fucking badly. "I'm not arguing, I don't give a fuck about sharing her, I'm just saying I don't want to go into this thinking we're all in and you're just thinking it's casual."

Morrison gets up and slings his bag over his shoulder. "No one thinks this is casual, dickhead. Anyway, we're late to class. Get your shit and get moving, because she's out there on her own right now and I don't give a fuck if she's the Wolf, someone needs to watch her back while Joey is out there in withdrawals."

Twenty Seven

BLAISE

I don't even make it to my first class for the day before Avery texts the group message.

Lips isn't going to class, her leg is bad. I'll go sit with her after my exams.

I smirk and immediately change directions, because I'm the only one who's finished all of my exams and can skip classes without Avery having to run damage control.

Don't worry, I'll go watch out for her.

I shove my phone in my pocket so I don't have to see the bickering and bullshit from the others about me getting to be the one to be with her. Fuck, I don't know if they'll be assholes about it now we've sorted shit out but I'm too goddamn excited about having her to myself for a while to give a fuck.

Even if she is in pain and all we do is sit around together, I'm so fucking pathetic for her that I don't give a fuck.

I stop by my room first to change out of my uniform into an old Vanth shirt and some sweatpants, shit I'll be comfortable sleeping over in the girls' room in, because I'm not leaving Lips again until the summer break starts or Avery kills me. Whichever one happens first.

My bet is on my grisly death, because Avery's cleaning standards are fucking ridiculous.

When I get to the girls' room, I knock but there's no answer. That freaks me the fuck out, and I have to coordinate a key pickup from Avery to get in there. Avery is also freaked about Lips not answering her messages, so she meets me at the staircase with a frown.

"Message me the second you get in there. She messaged and said she was taking pain meds and passing out so she should be fine and if I didn't have Ms. Kierstone I'd just come with you—"

"Avery, relax, she'll just be asleep and I'll study or something while I keep an eye on her. I'll text you, just calm down."

She nods and takes a breath before she stalks back down to class, her phone in her hands as she texts Ash her exact whereabouts at all times. Next year will be different. Without Joey, Hannaford is going to be a piece of fucking cake and having two peaceful years with Lips here and no daily death threats sounds fucking amazing.

When I get the door open I hear Lips mumbling to

herself which calms some of my worry down, but the moment I get a look at her, I don't know if I should laugh or call Avery to get a nurse sent up because Lips is… so ridiculously high. She's lying on her bed in one of her oversized men's shirts and her thrashing around has pushed it up over her hips to reveal the tiniest pair of shorts I've ever seen. I'm instantly hard, and I have to take a second to remember she's clearly drugged to her eyeballs and off-limits, because she's stroking the fucking bed and talking to herself.

"Only Avery has keys. Avery bought me these sheets. She's so nice. I think about telling her that."

Fucking hell. I try not to startle her as I answer, "You're not thinking anything, you're speaking. How fucking high are you?"

Her eyes pop open but they stay fixed to the ceiling. "That's not Avery's voice."

Fuck, this is too much for me to handle right now. She's too… sweet, too freaking innocent like this which is beyond weird. "No shit. She's still got exams so I came up to check that you're okay. She told me to force the pills down your throat but it looks like you've got that under control."

Her eyes squeeze shut but that mouth of hers just keeps running. "Nope. I cannot have Blaise in this room while I'm off my tits. Bad idea. I can't have him around until I'm back… on my tits. Or whatever the opposite of this is."

My dick is definitely mistaking this as dirty talk, and I need to shut it down fast.

Nothing will do that like talking to Avery's condescending ass, so I need to get Lips tucked into bed to give her a call. "Stop saying tits. Look, I can't leave you here like this. Fuck knows what you could end up doing to yourself. Stop stroking the sheets, it's… kinda hot and I'm feeling like a perv watching you. Just get in the bed."

She lies there like a plank of wood, and I have no choice but to gently maneuver her between the sheets. "In, Lips. Get in bed. Fucking hell, here."

She shivers and then seals her mouth shut, slapping a hand over it like she knows just how deep she can dig herself into trouble right now, and I can't help but huff out a laugh at her as I tuck her in like a child.

Then I climb up onto the bed with her, sitting on the sheets because sliding between them would be more torture than I want to endure right now. Once I'm comfortable I get my phone out and give Avery a call. She'll be on her way to her next class by now and I'd rather have a three minute conversation than spend three hours messaging her reassurances.

"Have you ever seen Lips high before? It's adorable."

Avery huffs down the line at me. "Cut your shit, Morrison, is she okay?"

"She's fine but I'm not leaving her."

I can hear Ash talking in the background but not what he's saying, and then Avery says, "Where is she right now? If she's that… high then you need to have eyes on her because she might hurt her leg more if you don't."

"She's in bed." I glance over but Lips is still just lying there, her hand tight over her mouth as she watches me. Her phone buzzes on the nightstand, but she ignores it.

"Okay. Okay, fine, I'll get you out of your classes today, and we can figure tomorrow out if she's still in pain."

I couldn't give less of a fuck about what I'm supposed to be doing right now. "I've finished my exams, I'll email the rest of my classes for the day and tell them I have a migraine or whatever."

Avery hums under her breath, and I hear Ash murmur a goodbye to her as he drops her off to her class and heads off to his own. She waits a second like she's making sure he can't hear her and then murmurs, "Are you sure she's okay? If she's too loopy I should come up and check her out."

I glance over again, but she's still just watching me. "I swear to you, she's fine, she's just off her tits. Her words, not mine."

She chuckles. "Of course she is. Fine. I'll be up as soon as I'm done with exams."

"Okay, bye."

I chuck my phone onto Lips' nightstand with hers and then move down the bed until my head is on her pillow, turning to face her. Fuck, I might have to be here for hours just watching her sleep and ramble on and flail about, but there's nowhere else I'd rather be. She turns her head to face me, and we're so close that the back of her hand brushes against my lips from where it's still clamped tightly over her mouth. She's fucking cute, and I can't help but smile as she snatches her hand away like it's on fire.

There's a frown on her face, and her eyes are still a little glazed.

"What's wrong, little Nightingale?" I murmur, brushing her hair away from her face.

Her eyes roam over my face and they finally focus a little. "This is going to go very badly and then you're never going to speak to me again. After all my work this year to get you guys to trust me and now I've fucked it. My voice is still all weird and floaty. Floaty is a strange word."

"Right, it is a strange word but let's stay on topic." I don't want her freaking the hell out and talking herself out of this before we've even given it a go.

She startles a little. "Shit, I'm saying stuff without realizing it again."

"Yes, you are. You haven't fucked anything. Harley wasn't pissed this morning, he was impressed. Then he was awkward and embarrassed because he upset you."

Her eyes glaze over again, and I know I'm fighting a losing battle here. I just need to keep her calm and busy so she doesn't do anything stupid.

"I think I've lost the filing cabinet. I think the office is closed for maintenance. I hope they repaint."

Her phone buzzes on the nightstand again, but we both ignore it. "Fuck, we need to get you stoned. I need to see you on THC."

"Nope. Whiskey or nothing. Vodka in emergencies. Possibly tequila but sometimes I get mouthy and fight…-y on tequila."

The Wolf of Mounts Bay gets 'fight-y' on tequila. That's some vital information to remember if I've ever heard it before. "Duly noted. Your phone keeps buzzing. Want me to get it?"

She nods and I grab it from the nightstand, handing it over to her, which I realize quickly is not going to get us anywhere, because she stares at it like she's never seen it before in her life.

Then her eyes keep focusing on my chest, and I have to take charge again so the situation doesn't spiral out of control. "Here. It's from Matteo, who's that? He says he can't wait to see you tomorrow. He calls you Starbright, what the hell does that mean?"

I don't like the sound of the guy just from the message itself, but the look of panic on her face has me ready to call Ash and Arbour so we can go find him and fucking kill him.

She flails and struggles for a second before I realize she's trying to sit up, so I immediately help to prop her up until we're both leaning against the headboard.

As soon as she's steady she grabs my biceps and attempts to give me a shake. "Don't ever tell anyone. That's the Jackal. He's bad. You can't tell anyone his name. He wants me to go to see him but I'm going to put him off. I don't like him and I definitely don't want to fuck him."

Fuck.

That's the worst possible option to be messaging her in such a fucking flirty and familiar way. I know she's said a million times that she hasn't fucked him, but I can't help but wonder if she's hooked up with him at all. Clearly he's crazy for her.

I nod and run a hand up and down her spine in a soothing stroke. She takes another deep breath and says, "Most importantly, don't ever tell anyone my middle name is Starbright."

Oh fuck.

Oh fuck, I cannot laugh right now, because I get the feeling she'll either stab me or kick me in the nuts and throw me out of the room. Fuck, her mom must have really been a piece of work because Eclipse *Starbright* Anderson? Fuck me, Lips is lucky she survived middle school with a name like that.

Blaise Morrison, son of Blaine Morrison, doesn't sound so bad now.

When I've got my shit locked down tight, I meet her eyes and say with complete seriousness, "I will take your secret to the grave, Mounty."

Her eyes grow soft again and she looks back out at the room. When her eyes hit the bathroom door she blurts out, "I need to pee, but I can't move, but I don't want to pee myself."

Fuck, keeping a straight face is almost impossible, but I don't want to piss her off or get stabbed for laughing at her while she's this… vulnerable. "It's okay, Mounty. I'll help you over to the bathroom."

I hoist her up into my arms and laugh at the way she kind of flails about before she gets comfortable, her arms looping around my neck. Her mouth starts running about how much ice cream Avery has been feeding her, and I have to shut that shit down fast. She weighs practically nothing, and I'm all for the extra roundness her ass has these days.

"Calm down, there's no way I'm dropping you. I'll get you on the toilet."

The gasp out of her is hilarious. "You are not watching me pee, Morrison. Nope. That's—nope."

I scoff at her, gently lowering her to the floor in the

bathroom. There's nothing for her to hold onto, but she frowns at me when I try to help her out.

"I can shut my eyes if you're that worried, Star."

The nickname slips out but she doesn't notice it yet.

She pouts. "There's absolutely no fucking way, Morrison."

I leave her to it, laughing at her talking to herself and then when I hear the flush and the scuffing sounds of her hobbling around again, I step back in.

"Oh. He's still here."

I chuckle and brace her hips as she washes her hands. "I'm not going anywhere, Star. You're stuck with me now."

Her leg starts to wobble again, and I lift her up a little to get her weight off of it.

"What the hell does that even mean? I've ruined everything."

This again. I could fucking kill Arbour for how he reacted this morning, the dick. I try not to sound pissed though, I don't think she could take it with the way her mouth is running right now. "You haven't, Star. Look, we all agreed to share you. That means you're not getting away from us that easy. Whatever it takes, we're keeping you."

I see her brain melt a little more, and I swing her back up into my arms, walking back over to the bed and sitting down with her in my lap. She hums happily under her breath, wriggling and rocking her hips until I grab them to steady her.

The dopey, loved-up grin on her face is adorable. Fuck, I never thought I'd be calling the Mounty adorable but here we are. She starts stroking my chest, and I'm struggling not to get hard at the grinding she's absently doing on my dick.

I'm not a total asshole; I'm not going to fuck her while she's high like this, but fuck is she tempting.

I try to distract myself by recording her and sending it to Harley, a little payback for his fuck up this morning, but she's too fucking hot. The rocking has me as hard as stone underneath that ass of hers.

"If both of his hands are on my hips then that hand must belong to me."

I try not to burst out laughing at her. "Yes, that's your hand."

Her eyes widen, and I see the hazy sort of panic take over her. Fuck, after everything we've said to her for the last two years no wonder she's freaked out about touching me.

Fuck, I want her touching me.

I lean forward to whisper against her lips, "You can touch me wherever you want, little Star."

I swear I see her brain break.

I'm about to just say fuck it and spread her out on the

sheets, strip her naked, and taste every fucking inch of her skin when the door flings open and Harley storms into the room. Great.

He's pissed the fuck off for something different.

"Morrison, if I find out you've laid a single fucking finger on her while she's been high, I'll gut you."

Avery arrives back to the room five minutes after Harley, takes one look at Lips, and then coaxes her back into bed to attempt to sleep off some of the painkillers. Even as high as she is Lips listens to her best friend, lying down obediently and slipping into unconsciousness within seconds.

Harley stomps into the bathroom to take a shower, mostly to clear his head because the asshole really did think I was up here coercing our girl into something while she was off her face on painkillers.

I'm going to take a swing at him later for it, but right now I just want to be close to her, so I settle back down on my side of her bed and fuck around with some lyrics on my phone again. I've never written such… hopeful songs before. They're still dark and moody, I don't think I'll ever write uplifting shit, but there's a silver lining in my latest work that wasn't there before.

Lips has given me that.

All of the time we've spent together where she's given

so much of herself to me without asking for anything in return. The patience and kindness and dry wit, all of it has finally given me something to look forward to.

I've never really had that before.

When Harley gets out of the shower, Avery takes her turn, threatening us both as she leaves us alone with Lips. It's stupid and childish of her because she should know us both better than that, but Harley takes it on the chin and moves Lips gently into the middle of the bed, stretching out next to her on top of the covers so we're both flanking her.

Something about the pressure of the blankets on her body sets off a nightmare.

She starts thrashing around like she's being murdered. Harley and I both jump up and pull the covers off of her, hoping that alone will stop her from spiraling, but if anything it only gets worse. We both try speaking to her and waking her up, but the pills are too strong and she just keeps thrashing around.

It takes until Avery comes back out and murmurs to her, stroking her hair away from her face again and rubbing her back, before she calms down. Harley makes a comment about the shorts she's wearing as he settles back down on the bed, and Avery snarls threats at him again.

I turn the TV on and try to ignore them both.

The longer Lips sleeps, the more she gravitates into our

bodies. It starts with her legs being thrown over Harley's, then her head rolls into my lap, and slowly she shifts into us both like she's just as drawn to us as we all are to her.

It settles into my chest just how *right* this all is.

After an hour of playing with her hair, she finally wakes up. It's a slow process and watching her eyes slowly blink open I can almost see her realize that she's draped over us both. I see the tiny moment of calm and peace before the panic sets in.

The problem is her ass is too fucking perfect, and I don't blame Harley for the groan he lets out when she grinds it on him. "For the love of God, Mounty, don't move like that. Avery has already threatened to castrate me twice tonight."

Instantly she's gasping and struggling to sit up, her eyes darting around at us and then she's scooting away from us both like she's afraid we're about to ruin her for sleeping on us.

I'm angry at myself for our freshman year all over again.

"What the—"

Avery cuts in from the kitchen and saves the day once again. "Chill. You were thrashing about in your sleep and it took all three of us to settle you back down."

Lips takes a breath, her eyes not meeting ours as she wriggles back to sit between us against the headboard. I huff out a laugh at her and a blush spreads over her cheeks.

I didn't realize how much I missed her reactions until I see it. "You must be feeling better, there's color on your cheeks again."

The flush deepens and she clears her throat. "Thank you for checking on me. And letting me word vomit for hours on end. Please leave me to die of shame with what little dignity I have left."

Harley scoffs and pulls out his phone, bringing up the video I'd sent him and hands it over to her. I refuse to feel bad about it because she's fucking perfect sitting there, grinning like all is right in her world.

She elbows me and I shrug. "Hey, they asked me why I called you adorable. I figured a video was better than any explanation I could come up with."

"I am never taking those pills again. I'll white knuckle it through the pain next time," she declares, and we all roar with laughter at her dramatics.

It all feels so fucking normal, like this is how it should've always been.

There's a knock at the door and Avery opens it to find Ash back from track, still dressed in his uniform with his gym bag slung over his shoulder like he couldn't wait to be up here with the rest of us.

"Mr. Embley is a demon. I'm not doing track next year, fuck him and his shitty attitude," he snaps as he strides in. Avery scrunches her nose up at him and shoves him toward the bathroom.

"Go shower, you're not sleeping here covered in sweat."

Lips sits there quietly for a second before she makes this little gasping noise, scrambling onto her hands and knees again and sliding straight off the bed. I have to immediately cross my legs because her shorts are so fucking tiny her ass peeks out of the bottom, and there's only so much teasing a guy can take.

Harley groans and grabs a pillow, shoving it in his lap and side-eyeing me as Lips drags Avery into the closet.

"Did you do something that we should be worried about?" he murmurs, and I scoff at him.

"Nope, I fixed your little fuck up this morning. You're welcome."

He takes his boner covering pillow and throws it at my head like an asshole. "Don't start that shit. I'll fix it myself when we don't have an audience. Did you… tell her about our conversation?"

I shrug. "Yeah but you saw how fucking high she was, fuck knows how much actually went in. We'll just have to talk once Avery isn't breathing down our necks."

He grunts and turns back to the TV.

When Ash steps out of the shower in his pajamas, he pauses at the closet and frowns at the sight of the girls both huddled in there. "Why are the two of you whispering in the closet?"

There's a shrill squeak that had to come out of Avery, because I can't imagine Lips making that sort of sound. Not without my dick involved and, yup, there goes my dick again.

I really, *really* need to end this celibacy before Avery cuts my fucking dick off.

I can't hear Avery's reply, only her tone, but Ash's scoff as he answers her echoes through the room loud and clear. "With the two of you that could be anything from pairing the correct shoes with an outfit to plotting the murder of a filthy rich senator for your own gain."

Avery steps forward and pats him on the chest. "Lips is freaking out about where everyone is sleeping. The drugs have scrambled her brain and she's woken up in her ideal fantasy orgy."

Fuck.

Oh holy fuck, I hadn't even thought of the orgies we could be having with her the second we can get her away from Avery's watchful eyes. Junior year is going to be the best year yet.

Ash bursts out in a raucous laugh at his sister, calling out to Lips as she scurries into the bathroom, "You'll have to pause those dirty thoughts, Mounty, Avery has already threatened our dicks if we so much as kiss your cheek in front of her."

When the bathroom door flicks locked behind her, Avery pushes Ash toward the TV and says in her fake sweet tone, "I'd love nothing more than to castrate the lot of you, please remember that."

HARLEY

I've woken up at 5 a.m. every morning since I came to Hannaford.

The moment I arrived, I joined the swim team and started training harder and longer than any other kid here. My insomnia helped with that because it's easy to be on time when you never went to sleep in the first place, but for the first time since my grandfather killed my dad, I fall asleep without prescription drugs or alcohol and I sleep the entire night without waking up until my usual 5 a.m. for training.

It's a fucking miracle.

What's even better is the fact that Lips is there right beside me, still tangled up in Ash's arms but her face is tilted up to mine as though even in her sleep her lips are seeking mine.

I'd give anything to taste her.

I'd even risk waking Avery and getting murdered, but it feels wrong to just kiss her awake when we still haven't actually spoken about what the hell we're doing here. It feels predatory, and after everything I've learned about the men who've stalked her, I'm not about to do that shit.

Instead, I cup her cheeks gently and stroke at her lips with my thumb. She wakes up slowly, her eyes fluttering open in the darkness of the room as she looks at me. She doesn't startle or freak out, just stares at me as her breath stutters out in a little gasp.

I brush my fingers over her cheek, not wanting to let her go yet or break this quiet moment because this little moment is just for us.

Fuck, I want to kiss her though and before I have the chance to attempt to silently communicate that to her she's nodding her head at me, her eyes dropping down to my lips, and I have to force down the groan creeping up my throat.

I smirk at her then I press a finger to my own lips to tell her to stay silent. She nods, the smallest motion so Ash doesn't wake up from where he's wrapped around her. I appreciate that because I need this moment. I need something just for the two of us right now, even if it's just a good morning kiss before my swim practice, because the last few months have been too fucking much.

I carefully shift forward to cup her face in my hands

and then finally I kiss her.

I start out slowly, no matter how badly I want to just fucking devour her. I force myself to stick with slowly nibbling at her lips and gentle sweeps of my tongue on hers to taste her, but the second she pushes back against me I lose myself in her. I can't get close enough—no matter how much I press against her. Her body is fucking trembling into the kiss like she's about to fall apart in my arms, and there's nothing I want to do more right now than make her come. Fuck, I need to hear her gasps and groans as she comes all over my hands and against my mouth and fuck, fuck, I have to force my hips not to rock up into her right now. Her hands clutch at my wrists as my thumbs stroke her cheeks reverently, the kiss turning desperate as I forget where we are and why it's a really fucking bad idea to be grinding on her right now.

Then my asshole cousin ruins the moment.

"Avery is going to fucking murder you," whispers Ash, and Lips startles away from my lips.

Fuck.

Even in the dark I can see her face flush scarlet, and she squirms with very obvious shame. I lean forward and breathe, "Shh…" onto her lips as I kiss her again, trying desperately to distract her and reassure her that everything is fine.

We agreed to share her.

There's nothing wrong with what we're doing.

She wriggles against me for a second but then suddenly she stills in my arms, and Ash pulls her back into his body a little more firmly as he kisses his way along her neck. I might've wanted a moment just for us but this is probably exactly what she needs, a quiet and secret moment with both of us to test how sure we are about this situation, and I know we're passing with flying colors when she groans quietly into the kiss. Ash tugs her shirt collar away from her neck to find more skin and mumbles, "I'm blaming you if she catches us."

I only pulls away from Lips long enough to whisper back, "Fucking worth it," and then I'm sucking her bottom lip into my mouth and dragging my hands down her throat possessively, a thrill of pure lust spiking in my blood when she squirms in our arms again. Ash grunts and grabs her hip to stop her from grinding on him, and I have to take a second to breathe so I don't blow in my shorts like some inexperienced, horny teenage boy.

I catch sight of the alarm clock on Avery's nightstand. "Fuck. I'm going to be late for training. I was supposed to be at the pool ten minutes ago."

I can't tear my eyes away from her lips and when she licks them I groan.

"That sound had better be an oh-I-hate-waking-up sort of sound and not a my-dick-is-so-hard kind of sound,

Harley Éibhear Arbour," Avery snaps.

Well, fuck if that isn't like a bucket of ice over my head.

I sigh and roll out of the bed to the sounds of Avery screeching as she throws a pillow at me. Like I give a fuck. I head to the bathroom laughing. "I can't help having morning wood, Aves. Better get used to it because me and my blue balls will be here all week."

I take the quickest shower I possibly can, mostly just trying to lose my erection, because Coach will not be impressed by it, and then I get dressed and head out of the bathroom.

Avery is in the kitchen scowling and I kiss her cheek with a grin, accepting her cussing me out viciously because she hands me one of her reusable takeaway cups full of perfectly brewed coffee to take down to the pool. I duck back to the bed and kiss Lips chastely on the cheek, with a wink, and then I'm out the door.

I could definitely get used to this.

Coach raises his eyebrows at me when I get to the pool, because it's the first time in two years that I'm the last one down there for practice. I don't say a word to him and he doesn't push it. I'm not explaining myself to anyone in this hellhole.

I swim until my entire body is screaming, until my muscles feel like jelly and my lungs are on fire. It's only when every last bit of energy and tension has been worked out of me that I finally crawl out of the pool and head to the showers.

The other students all listen to the Coach and do actual training, but I established a long time ago that I'm here to work myself into the ground and that system gets results.

I text the group message to say I'm on my way back up to eat with everyone, and then I enjoy the quiet walk to the dining hall on legs that are barely holding me up. I'm so used to feeling this way that they're steady, the tight control I have over myself doing wonders to mask that shit, and the other students are so fucking terrified of me that they steer clear, so I don't have to worry about being bumped or jostled.

When I get to the dining hall everyone is already there and someone has already grabbed me breakfast so I can just take a seat.

"How are the blue balls?" Avery says sweetly, and Lips groans, burying her face in her hands like she's still mortified about this morning. I don't want Avery making her feel like shit about this though so I put a firm stop to it the only way you can.

I give her a haughty, disinterested look and drawl, "I'll worry about my own balls thanks, Floss."

Lips nudges her French toast to the side and grabs an apple instead like she's not planning on actually eating this morning. Ash's eyes narrow at her as he pushes the plate back in front of her and, surprisingly, she just sighs and tucks back into it without a fight.

I share a look with him.

"Well, my balls aren't blue. Harley will just have to learn to jerk off a bit more often," Morrison drawls, and Ash snorts at him.

Avery's response is swift and frosty. "Not in my shower he won't. Keep those activities in your room."

Morrison grins and hands Lips his iPod, watching her carefully as she nods in thanks and taps at it. It's such a small thing, but I would've lost my shit over their closeness two days ago, now though? Now I'm glad Ash is making her eat and Blaise is distracting her from Avery's pissy mood. Now I'm glad we're all still family and no one is going to go off the fucking rails.

When Lips pulls a face at whatever is on the iPod, Morrison laughs and says to Avery, "It's fine, we'll just tempt Lips into our room for the rest of the week."

Lips blanches, freaking the fuck out, and I kick the asshole in the shin so hard his chair scrapes back. He grunts and cusses me out so loudly that the students around us take notice, but *fuck him* and his idiot mouth.

"Are you fucking dense? We're surrounded, there's an

ongoing bet, and Lips is still being watched," hisses Ash, while Avery laughs so no one around us can hear him.

Morrison finally figures out what the fuck he's done and cringes, glancing over at Lips apologetically while the rest of us are in damage control, because suddenly I can see just how close the other students are around us and all of the eyes that are pointed our way.

I fucking hate this place.

"Don't bother. Lips has no interest in fucking a guy from Hannaford, she's said it a million times. Find someone who's actually up for it," I say, laying it on thick, but the students around us eat that shit up and start whispering among themselves.

Lips shoots me a thankful look and Avery takes over, babbling about her dance recital we're all going to on Monday that she'll no doubt be the only shining star of. It takes Lips another ten minutes to get back to eating, but eventually she tucks back in. Every time it looks as though she's about to stop eating, Ash stares her down until the entire plate is empty.

None of us are in a rush to split up and head to class, so we stay put even as the entire dining hall starts to empty out. Now that we're done with exams I don't want to go to class at all but Lips has to thanks to her day off yesterday, and I'll go to watch out for her.

She looks around the room, a little too tense for my

liking, and then clears her throat. "I feel like we should be talking about the dangers of doing this. I mean, we can't even sit here and have a conversation without my… baggage coming into it."

Fuck.

Here it is, here's her attempt at giving us all a 'get out of jail free' card; I should've known it was coming.

Avery takes one look around the table and decides she wants nothing to do with this conversation so she clears her throat, kisses Lips on the cheek, and then walks off with her phone to give us all some privacy.

I wasn't expecting it from her, but fuck I am glad to have it.

I cross my arms over my chest. "We're not in this for the bet and until you get the Jackal situation under control we'll just be more… discreet about what's going on. Our only other option is to wait until he's not a problem anymore and I don't want to do that. "

Ash hums under his breath as he watches Avery across the room, ready as always to charge over there and kill anyone who dares to speak to his twin. "Is there a plan to get him to back off? Do we have any idea of how long it will take?"

Lips shrugs nonchalantly as she pushes her plate away from herself. "There is a plan but it's not underway yet. It hasn't been my focus. I've been working on more pressing issues."

More pressing than being stalked by the Jackal?

Highly fucking doubtful.

Ash is the one who says, "I think it's now the most pressing issue."

Her cheeks flush. "I understand that it's important but there's still other things that need to be dealt with. Joey, Senior, the O'Cronin family, all of them are important to take care of as well."

Fuck my family and their manipulative bullshit getting in the way.

I shake my head, but Morrison answers for us all. "No, top priority is now dealing with the Jackal. Your life is the one at stake and the other situations are…survivable."

She nods and blinks like she's worried she'll cry, and once again I want to charge down to Mounts Bay and kill anyone who's ever made her feel like a worthless little Mounty girl.

Myself and my family included.

I spend the entire week in Lips' bed.

I've never slept so well in my life, and it terrifies me. I find myself panicked at the idea of leaving her behind to head up the coast to see my mom for more than just the obvious reasons, because after living on so little for so long, I don't want to give this up.

The week passes us by too quickly.

On Friday, Avery demands that we clean out all of our shit from her room while she heads out for her end-of-year ballet party. There's boxes fucking everywhere because she has a fucking ridiculous amount of shit.

I have never seen her wear a scarf, why does she have dozens of boxes of them stashed in her closet? It's just fucking stupid.

Lips sits on her bed and radiates stressed-out energy the entire time we search for and pack our shit away. It's nothing overwhelming or obvious, but I've spent too long watching her to miss it.

I start folding shirts that Avery left in a pile on her bed for me and shoving them in a bag to stay close to her. "Where are you staying in Mounts Bay? Like I said, I'm taking two weeks to visit Ma and then I'm staying in the Bay. I can get a hotel or stay with you, your choice."

She glances around at each of us slowly like she's reading the room. Avery is throwing things into her dance bag so she can head out, and Ash is digging through her closet to help her with her packing, pulling down the big and heavy items so she doesn't hurt herself later doing it. Morrison is raiding the fridge for beer, because he's barely left a thing here thanks to Avery's constant nitpicking at his messy ways.

Lips takes a breath and says, "Look, Avery's informed me that there's going to be… wooing."

She says it like the word tastes wrong in her mouth and, as a fellow Mounty kid, I understand why. "What the actual fuck is wooing?"

Morrison roars with laughter at us both, the type that makes him throw his head back and clutch his stomach. Lips eyes him appreciatively, something she does just a little more openly to us all now, and he hands me a beer as he stalks over to the bed and lounges on it.

Ash sounds smug as he calls out, "Avery is secretly eighty years old and thinks that wooing is the current terminology for—"

"For what, Ash?" Avery cuts in sweetly. He pauses for a second because we all know what game Avery is playing with us all now and then he smiles at her, his eyes still that same icy cold. "For starting something important."

Lips clearly has no idea how to process or function with that sort of information so she turns and tugs on the front of Morrison's old band tee. "I really don't care what we're calling it. I'm taking this shirt. I'm also taking that black one of Ash's and Harley's gray sweatshirt. I'll give them back after the break."

We all should've seen it coming, she only wears oversized men's shirts when she's not in uniform, but the fact that she's picked out the exact shit she wants shocks me for a second.

She really is just as obsessed as we are.

Morrison blinks at her, just as stunned as I am, and then strips off his shirt and hands it over to her. I try not to laugh at her, but I can practically see her brain melting at the sight of him.

Fuck. We're going to have some fun with her, just as soon as the summer break is over and we're back here together again.

"Thank you," she squeaks, and he winks at her before rooting around in his bag to pull on another one.

Avery gives her a look as she comes out of the closet, packed and ready to head down to her party, then she grins. "How long have you wanted that Vanth shirt?"

Lips shrugs, all fake nonchalance. "Oh, you know, all my life. I'm totally lying, he'll have to pry this from my cold, dead hands. I know at least eight Mounty girls that would gut me for it so I'm going to wear it to the next party I have to go to."

I laugh with Avery, fishing out the sweatshirt she wants and tugging it over her head. She takes a deep, gulping lungful like she's trying to breathe me in, keep me buried inside her chest while we're separated. I want to press her back into her bed and mark her up, make sure there's no doubt in any Mounty's mind of who she belongs to.

I can't and it kills me.

Avery waves at us all and then heads out for her party. Ash stalks back over from the closet with an armful of his clothes.

"You're taking our shit so you can smell us while we're gone? That's horribly sappy, Mounty," he drawls as he hands over the black shirt she wants and then gets back to packing his shit.

"I'm weird. I wear guys' shirts and sweaters with booty shorts and skirts. I listen to the same three albums on repeat. I like French toast, coffee, and cherry anything. I don't function on my birthday or Christmas. I can kill a grown man eight different ways with nothing but my bare hands. I'm never going to be normal."

It's a challenge, a test like she's still not sure how serious we're taking this, and Ash rises to the bait perfectly.

He grabs her chin and stares down at her, the blank mask that's permanently on his face gone and he's staring down at her with that same need to brand her, own her, that I'm feeling.

"If you're trying to warn us off it's not going to work. We've never agreed to anything as quickly as when we agreed to share you. I'm not planning on wooing you, I'm planning on doing whatever I need to do to get to keep you."

She swallows, and he licks his lips subconsciously, like he's just barely holding himself on a tight leash.

"I want us to keep you. I don't want you all to myself, I want to share you with my best friends and I want you to love every fucking second of it."

She blinks and then nods, completely transfixed as he eases up from her a little with a smirk.

"I won't get out of bed before the coffee machine is on. I hate blues music and listen to Vanth as religiously as you do. I run track because it makes me feel like I'm dying and sometimes I need to feel like that. I miss my mom and I hate my father. My brother is trying to kill me and my father is taking bets on how long it'll take him to succeed. Finding Joey standing over Avery's lifeless body broke something in me that I don't think I'll ever be able to fix. I'm a bigger monster than you because I don't give a fuck who you've killed or why you did it. In fact, from here out I'm helping you bury the bodies."

I glance over at Morrison, and he's just as shocked as I am at this honesty. Fuck, that's the most he's ever said to me about Joey and his fucked-up father. He's never once talked about that close call we had with Avery before freshman year started.

This is huge.

Naturally, Lips doesn't pry. She's the expert at knowing what wounds shouldn't be poked at. "I cannot believe you're a Vanth super fan and you've given me all that shit about it. You're a real piece of work, Beaumont."

Morrison sniggers at her like it's some big fucking secret they've been keeping; *everyone* knows Ash is Vanth obsessed.

Then Ash smirks at her. "I told Blaise he should get you to sing on his next album. I'll listen to that on repeat, too."

She freezes and for a second I think they've hit a nerve, but then she has this hopeful look on her face. Morrison grins at her. "I'll write you a song, Mounty. While you and Arbour are shacked up and loving every second of the break, I'll mope around New York with my parents and write you love songs."

I throw an empty hanger at him for being a jealous asshole, and Lips hands him the iPod. "I'll video chat you guys. Harley can stay with me and if you guys can get away to the Bay you can stay, too."

I can't fucking wait.

Twenty Nine

ASH

Leaving Lips to return to the Bay while the rest of us are forced to return home to our fucked-up families is my new version of hell.

What if she gets hurt?

What is she going to do in the Bay as the Wolf while we're miles and miles away in luxurious, but deadly, houses?

I can't stand the thought of it, and Avery is very quickly pissed off with my nagging about finding a way back to the Bay as quickly as possible.

Obviously I'm working on it but it takes time.

I know she's doing everything in her power to get us to the Bay, but it doesn't help the crawling feeling from rippling under my skin until I want to dig it out.

I'm not going to make it through the break without Lips.

The day we're all leaving Hannaford, Blaise and I arrive at the girls' room together because Harley is a sneaky shit and left without us.

Avery opens the door for us with an eye roll, motioning us in only for us to find Lips lying under her bed with only her booty-shorts-covered ass sticking out.

She's mumbling and grunting under there, but nothing can distract me from that ass of hers.

"Avery is going to kill us all. We should take bets on who dies first," Blaise mutters, and I nod with a grimace.

"My money is on Harley; he's too fucking obvious and if he takes her keys again, she'll snap his dick off. She said so herself."

"What are you two muttering about?" Harley snaps, and Blaise points at Lips and says, "Great view."

Avery elbows him sharply in the ribs and he grunts, "What? I'm allowed to appreciate my girl's ass, especially in those shorts. What are you doing, Mounty?"

"Construction work," she teases, and then Avery ducks down to have a look at what she's doing, impatient as always.

"That's where you hid that!"

Fuck, the possibilities are endless. "Hid what?"

"Her stash," says Harley, and he's so smug I want to break his teeth.

Before I get the chance to pick a fight with him, Lips

wriggles back out and drags a safe with her. Avery does her gimme hands at it, and Lips lets out one of her dry chuckles. "I'm not sure I can trust you with these, Beaumont."

Avery bites her lips and stares at the metal box with the type of lusty eyes no brother wants to see. "I solemnly swear I'm up to no good."

Lips scoffs, "Nerd," and opens the safe, pulling out a velvet box and handing it to Avery.

To my absolute horror, Avery *moans* as she cracks the lid, and I immediately want to forget this day is happening. Everyone gets a laugh at my expense but seriously, what the fuck could be in there and getting that reaction out of her? "Sex toys? You can't fit a pair of Louboutins in a box that small and I can't think of anything else that gets Floss that excited."

"Better. So much better. Diamonds!" Avery squeals and then she starts pawing through them, the tinkling sound is definitely the sound of multiple rocks knocking together.

I'm so fucking confused right now.

Harley's eyebrows shoot up and damn near disappear into his hairline as he looks over Avery's shoulder at the stash. "How many of them do you have?"

Lips shrugs like this is nothing. "I'm good at what I do and I'm stockpiling so we can get clear of our shit after graduation."

Avery rolls one of the diamonds in her fingers,

practically panting, and Harley clears his throat at her so she quits her shit. "Put them back, Floss. Make Morrison buy you one for your birthday."

Blaise is just as fucking dumbfounded as I am at what's happening here to snap out a comeback, but Avery pouts as she carefully packs the diamonds back into the safe. "I don't want boring old diamonds. I want priceless, blood-soaked, favor diamonds."

I decide I'm done waiting. "Someone needs to start explaining what the hell is going on."

Avery pouts as she watches Lips bury the safe in her duffle bag and cover it with her clothes so it's obscured and nestled nicely, but she answers me, "The Twelve trade each other favors in times of need. Diamonds are used as a physical representation of the favors and Lips has dozens of them. Dozens!"

That explains exactly fucking *nothing*. Millions of dollars worth of diamonds just hiding under her bed for… what exactly? "Why? Why not use them and become rich? Why come to school here and put up with us?"

Lips shrugs, looking entirely uncomfortable with this line of inquiry. "I nearly died for most of those. I've only ever used two favors and that was for situations that were life threatening. I won't use them for less than that."

She says it like it's not the fucking worst thing I've ever heard in my life. She's going back there to the Bay to work over the summer break, what if a job does finally kill her? Fuck.

Fuck.

Lips steps over to her bed to check her phone, and Avery starts directing us all to help haul her boxes around. I remind her again that she needs to pack less shit next year because there's no way she needs this much stuff.

I have my back to everyone, pulling boxes of kitchenware out of cupboards for Avery when there's a crashing sound and Harley and Avery both start talking at once.

"Lips, what—"

"Fuck, babe—"

I spin around and dash back over to them at the same time as Blaise, one of Avery's boxes of shoes still in his hands from where he was moving crap for her.

Lips' face is as white as paper as she sinks down onto her bed, the panic etched into every line of her body, and I'm about to lose my shit when finally she speaks.

"The Jackal is here. He's picking us up."

It doesn't matter that she runs us through the protocol fifty times before we walk down the staircase to meet the Jackal, I fucking hate this plan.

Avery catches my hand in hers and gives it a squeeze

as we stalk down the hall like prisoners to the executioner block. "We have to trust her. She knows what she's doing."

I get that, but I also hate it.

I hate it even more when we find Joey waiting for us at the bottom of the stairs, the junkie in him obviously so in tune with his dealer that he felt the Jackal's presence in the building. His gaze bounces over each of us until he lands back on Lips.

I want to rip his throat out with my bare hands just for looking at her.

"How the fuck do you know the Jackal? He's here for you."

Lips just arches an eyebrow and steps around him like he's *nothing,* and I fucking adore her for it. There's nothing a Beaumont hates more than such a dismissal, and Joey's lip curls at her. Harley follows Lips, one step behind her exactly how she told him to, and when Joey moves like he's going to stalk after us, I step up into his space, leaning in to hiss at him, "Do you want to fucking die?"

I can see the insanity in his eyes, the madness that was always there and that the drugs have always magnified, but he obviously wants to see how this will play out as badly as I do, so he turns away from me in his own version of Lips' dismissal.

Like I give a fuck.

Avery steps up to my side and tucks her arm in mine,

looking cold and disinterested at the scene before us, because if Senior has taught us anything it's how to hide your weak points and triggers away.

I stand there and take a good look at the monster stalking my girl. The Jackal is tall, broad, and well-presented in a suit. Dark brown hair, eyes the same color, and that natural shade of olive skin. There's nothing exceptional about him, nothing in his DNA that says he's a monster on sight and honestly he'd look like any businessman my father would meet with except for the thick black lines of his tattoos running across his cheeks. They mark him as something else entirely.

"There you are."

My hackles raise instantly at the possession in his voice. Harley does well not to stiffen or react to it, and it must be killing him.

He's brought that asshole from the docks with him and Harley's uncle, Diarmuid. They're both standing on either side of the Jackal and grinning at Lips like they're eager to take her home to the Bay. I add them to my kill list.

Diarmuid grins and sweeps Lips into a bone-crushing hug. She laughs at him but I can tell it's fake, patting his back until he lets her go. The moment he drops her back onto her feet, he steps around her to hug Harley. Fuck, he must be biting his fucking tongue off at that.

The other asshole steps forward and takes Lips' bag with

a smile, and then the pissing game really begins when he locks eyes with Harley and swoops down to kiss her cheek.

"I'm going to kill him. I'm going to hunt him down in the Bay and slit his fucking throat. Mark my words."

Avery huffs, but Blaise meets my eyes over her head and nods, as serious about dealing with the asshole as I am.

There's a small pause, like everyone is holding their goddamn breath, and then the Jackal says in that same possessive tone, "Where's my hug, little Starbright?"

What the fuck kind of nickname is that?

She steps forward into his arms. He presses himself into her fully, chest to thigh, and Avery's nails dig into my arm as a reminder, because *fuck* am I about to break every last one of Lips' rules and go beat the fucking life out of that cunt.

Lips pulls away from him and allows him to tuck her under his arm, though even from here I can see how stiff she is. She's repulsed by him and not only can he see it, he's fucking feeding off of it. It's like watching every last one of Senior's interactions with unwilling women and the rage building up in me is fucking insane.

The Jackal flicks out a hand to get Harley and his men to follow them, and then they stalk out of the door.

I hate it more than I've hated anything in my life, and my mind is made up before they're even in the car.

I'm going to kill the Jackal

SIGN UP FOR MY NEWSLETTER TO HEAR ABOUT UPCOMING RELEASES

ALSO BY J BREE

The Bonds That Tie Series

Broken Bonds
Savage Bonds
Blood Bonds
Forced Bonds
Tragic Bonds
Unbroken Bonds

The Mortal Fates Series

Novellas
The Scepter
The Sword
The Helm

The Trilogy
The Crown of Oaths and Curses
The Throne of Blood and Honor

The Mounts Bay Saga

The Butcher Duet
The Butcher of the Bay: Part I
The Butcher of the Bay: Part II

Hannaford Prep
Just Drop Out: Hannaford Prep Year One
Make Your Move: Hannaford Prep Year Two
Play the Game: Hannaford Prep Year Three
To the End: Hannaford Prep Year Four
Make My Move: Alternate POV of Year Two

The Queen Crow Trilogy
All Hail
The Ruthless
Queen Crow

The Unseen MC
Angel Unseen

ABOUT J BREE

J Bree is a dreamer, writer, mother, and cat-wrangler. The order of priorities changes daily.

She lives on the coast of Western Australia in a city where it rains too much. She spends her days dreaming about all of her book boyfriends, listening to her partner moan about how the lawns are looking, and being a snack bitch to her three kids.

Visit her website at http://www.jbreeauthor.com to sign up for the newsletter or find her on social media through the links below.

9 781923 072107